To our beautiful wives, Stacey and Melynda, two of the most wonderful women to bless this Earth.

PROLOGUE

I f you are reading this! Then you have been fortunate enough to find "THE JOURNALS OF THE ALMOST UNDEAD". An attempt to become the first and maybe only person to record a history, documenting the recent rebirth of a new species, our species. A first person account, written by a novice documentarian who was given a second chance at life, 30 years after the apocalypse. Who's only goal (AT FIRST!) was to make sure, that someone, anyone, would have known we existed at all. A brave (but clumsy in every way) reborn, post-apocalyptic, wiry, wonderful half-human, half-undead species. Whether here by mere circumstance, or some strange twist of destiny, we are grateful to be here at all! Back from the undead, living every day as if it were our last. Only now, as I sit here writing on the eve of what could be my last entry in these journals. I finally have the ability to appreciate how amazing a life can be. What a cosmic gift it all has been, experiencing so much life in such a short time!

In short, if this is really the last time I get to write in these "journals", I want everyone to know I am sorry. Sorry for all the pain my undead condition once caused. Through

JOURNALS OF THE ALMOST UNDEAD

The story of an unlikely hero...
***

PATRICK C. KEHOE
JOSEPH WEINGARTNER

Written By: Patrick C. Kehoe and Joseph Weingartner
Illustrated By: by Patrick C. Kehoe

my sacrifice I hope to atone in some way for what I once was, while giving back to those I care about today. That my life was lived well, saving those who were counting on me with every last breath of my being. You see, a wise compassionate woman with real power, speaking through a man who deserves respect once told me:

"A hero is not born specifically for some great moment in time, they are forged from great moments in time."

I hope you understand that I never wanted the power that I now possess...

JOURNAL ENTRY# UNO

NOT QUITE UNDEAD, NOT QUITE HUMAN, BUT A ZUMIE!

I'm not sure when I regained the ability to think clearly once again, but I can. The part of me that felt human is back, and I sure ain't mad at it. Somehow the air is breathable again, and I can hear a voice in my head that is finally my own. I feel almost 100% percent alive, even though part of me is still undead. No real memories or echoes of my human days, but still a few left of when I was just a mindless flesh eating robot. Yeah, we get to remember being undead, and trust me it is not a plus. It's like being reborn with a new lease on life while carrying the baggage of the old one on your back. Now I still have a "GINORMOUS" appetite, but not for the brainz of the living. Food of any kind will satisfy the average Zumie. Cooked or raw it doesn't matter. We have small furnaces for stomachs that can burn up anything we consume. It is a great benefit to eat whatever tastes good, whenever we are hungry! Don't get me wrong brainz still rule: cattle, horses, pigs, and sheep will do just fine. Except now we cook them in stews or whatever make our tummies talk back.

Even though I have a lot to learn, the world around me makes sense, and everyday feels new and full of things to discover. I know there are others like me who seem to get the scope of how awakened we really are. It is sad, no, unfortunate for our community that there are still those who have not yet grasped the possibilities that having choices has given us! So, they echo their old human lives to give them some purpose in the new consciousness that we seem to have been given. Let me explain! We are not quite undead anymore, and we are not all human! We possess qualities of both species, we have become something new. So I have taken the liberty of naming us ZUMIES!! Some of us are smart, and some of us are cool. Some of us not so smart, and some of us not so cool at all. Just like any other race or species we have those who are great examples for our kind, and those we claim, even though we wish we didn't have to. Despite our differences, getting along has come easy, and we have each other's backs if things were to get rough. Only time will tell how long we can stand each other, and how long it takes for others to become fully aware like me. I guess that me is a smart? Wow!!! Wait I... I mean that I am smart, but still learning and evolving myself. Yet, I can still say with confidence that I am intelligent. Smarts come with experience, I hope, and I plan on having lots of experiences in the future.

It seems that Zumies have retained skills or talents from our human days. (At least we think we have anyway...) My skills seem to lean towards reading, writing, arithmetic, and engineering. In fact, not to toot my own horn, but the awaking of the valley, was due largely in part to me and the council. I read all the manuals that got the valley going, but that's for another entry. What I do now, and what I love, is telling stories with pictures and words. See I apparently have something called, a photographic memory. Recording things in my mind, as if the memories were a photo or a picture show inside my head. I can rewind and fast forward with ease, remembering every word, and smallest detail down to the letter. I can also heal extremely fast! The stamina lasts for days, with agility that seems to be in check as well, but more about that later! In all of this self-discovery, I figured out this one important revelation. That writing, and drawing was more than just a hobby, it gave me a purpose. To document as many different Zumie experiences as I could, using my gifts to guide me as I told the stories of me and my people. Our own footprint on the world. I hope my decision to do this is the right one. I mean, you've got to start somewhere! Not to mention that it is fun! I truly enjoy how having purpose makes me feel. Like I matter. Maybe it's a little selfish, but no one is perfect. All I can hope for is that whomever reads this and sees these drawings, appreciates the love and realness my words are trying to get across.

Unfortunately, not all of us are coordinated or equipped with talents or skills. So, even though they are self-aware and alive again, intelligence may not have awakened with them. Now these individuals aren't dangerous on purpose, but if you are not paying attention... They can turn something simple into a whole new kind of trouble!! Mechanical skills and basic functionality are there, but common sense and reasoning? Not so good. Sometimes they blow things up, or break your favorite limb, but otherwise they are cool. We let them go about their ways, however ridiculous it may seem at the time. When they get into trouble its either funny, or really annoying. Let's not even mention that their appetites for food of any kind can really make some question if we are part human at all... mmmmmm that reminds me, all this writing has made me hungry... macaroni and really stinky cheese mmmmmm!

JOURNAL ENTRY# DOS

*NOT JUST ECHOS OF OLD LIVES, BUT
DECISIONS MAKING THE DIFFERENCE IN
EVERYDAY LIVING...
WHILE DEALING WITH THE CLOSE COUSINS
SURROUNDING US...*

The Zumies that remember how to read and function in an intelligent manner made a choice. (Ooohhhh... there is that word again, choice, what a difference choices make!!!) They decided to bring the valley back to life, just like our people came back from the dead, so shall the city. Zumies of a higher caliber took on responsibilities, so that things like running water, power, and natural gas were something we could depend on.

This sparked all kinds of new, yet old familiar aspects of our past lives. Instead of them being echoes of our old lives, we made them ours, and enjoyed making them part of our daily endeavors. Cooking, cleaning, and all sorts of regular jobs were being appointed to those who seemed to lean in those directions. Wherever there was a soul with some talents and nothing to do, they would be given a uniform and some directions and away they would go. Little by little the town became a buzzing beehive, full of life and vigor. Sights and smells that totally made everything a whole degree better in our little wannabe city. REALLY!!! Opening up small business, places like restaurants, the Zoo, TV station, and many other cool human like things. Except it was our way! The "Zumie" way! Movies, sports, music, and so much more was all possible now. More than just aware, but a living part of the world that we all inhabit. Yeah that's right, our own little slice of progress, untouched by the dead world around us. Occupying buildings and streets until the whole valley was as alive as we felt we had become.

A small city like community near the coast emerged! In a large valley hidden by a wall of mountains to keep us from being discovered unless we wanted to be. I've had several conversations with the other curious souls in my city and they all seem to agree. HUMANS ARE STILL HERE! They just do not want to be found, and to be perfectly honest... we aren't looking for them either! In most cases, if you would ask one of the inquisitive types, they would speculate that Z-Bots, (Z-Bots are what we call the real undead, because they resemble robots who can only do one thing. Eat whatever bleeds!) after a while were easy to handle. Insinuating that clever humans, should have found ways to deal with the undead effectively. After gaining control of the undead, the real threat would have been other humans! Fighting over resources like food, water, and fuel would have driven some people to hide and find new ways to conceal their everyday activities. Occasionally a not so lucky human is found dead among the organic camouflage that is a sea of undead hiding our valley from the rest of the world. We have nothing against the humans, but exposing ourselves to them could mean our end. I'm not afraid like the others are, although I understand their worries, and I try to stay neutral when they are expressing them. As far as I have heard there has been no real contact with any humans, and the majority of my people want to keep it that way. Using the de-evolved versions of ourselves, the Zumie population has managed to block any remaining entrances or exits from the outside world. Who knows how long the wall of undead will work for this valley, but for now it will do.

Now, Z-Bots aren't the only defense our valley possesses, but the two groups of Zumies that protect the city are not the most experienced in their field. The first group call themselves the Z.B.I. (Zumie Bureau of Investigations). A bunch of Zumies in black suits that fly around the valley in small helicopters whenever there is a problem that isn't military needy. That's correct, we have a group of militant minded Zumies who train, and use weapons with the promise of glory... honor even! Their sole purpose and belief, is in protecting the new home of our people with their lives. Intense, but very commendable if you ask me. They are honorable and loyal to a fault.

Zotal Zombination

It's my honor to have drawn their likeness so others can see how their way of living started. This way others will be inspired to do the same. Not to sound like a wuss, but I hope they never need to use the skills they have acquired. Something tells me though, like a strange voice in my head, echoing over and over... Their bravery will be tested some day!!

JOURNAL ENTRY# TRES

ZUMIES AT PLAY!!
I MEAN WE CARE, BUT NOT REALLY, REALLY!!

The past few days have been pretty eventful. I've witnessed Zumies at play all over the Valley. I have made sure to draw some of the characters who made an impression on me while I was out and about. The impression a sound mind might perceive if they were to come upon our community, without a proper education of our kind. Well let me be honest. There are many clicks of Zumies who gather after their tasks or responsibilities had been fulfilled for the day. This has been our way. To just have some fun. It's how our whole society runs itself. Work, or a talent, gains you access to all the things that we love to do as living beings. Cooking, building, bartending, being an electrician, a doctor, or whatever you can do to contribute to our little world. The council interviews each Zumie individually, and based on the answers given in the interview, the individual is bestowed a grade and transported to the employment center. From there, the individuals are given a choice of available tasks based on the grade given. Based on the complexity and the difficulty levels of their jobs or tasks, different levels of off time are awarded. Off time can last from as little as one week to as much as one month at a time. Also factored in is the positive effect on the community and everyday life of the people. The combined reward of a Zumie's contribution to the community is food, clothing, and a free pass into all of the things a Zumie's heart could desire. The messed up part! The grade the council gives the individual is what determines the availability of those things a Zumie's heart could desire and the amount of time it will take before you are done with the employment process at all. This has created a human-like pecking order of sorts. Me? I have an A rating. I rarely show my level to jump the lines, but if I wished I get first dibs on anything, except in front of an A+... (And to my knowledge, only the members of the council have an A+ grade in the city!) The cool thing about our people, none of us, except a rare few jump the line. We respect each other for the most part. My grade is due in part to skills with writing and reading. I have been given the responsibility of reading the manuals that got the city running again. Quietly reporting to the council, and helping the crews turn the city back on. It took a few months of finding the right Zumies to fill the positions that would get the small coastal city back on its feet. My talents also include mechanical skills and over all handy ingenuity. I used it all to bring the community to life. Staying just long enough 'til they could read and manage the cities resources themselves. For me that meant that I had fulfilled my responsibility to the city, and now I get to live out my days enjoying all that the valley had to offer. Now, deeming myself the official historian of my people is how I pass the time or fill the void where purpose used to be. This week I hung out with the Superfans, Sports Nuts, and the Workout Fanatics. There is more out there but these are the clicks I ran into this week.

THE SUPERFANS:

MT. ZuMiMore

These wonderful Zumies are in love with the human's gift for entertaining themselves in the form of movies, T.V., music, and more! They love it so much that they attempt to reenact the very things they see on all those discs that seem to have all this cool stuff recorded on them. Humans for the most part seem to be really, really attractive. Not always, but most of the time the actors and actresses of humanity all have these stunning features that are hard not to notice. This love for the beauty of the human race, has inspired the Superfans to put on makeup and outfits, and pretend to be pretty and cool. Let me tell you that when Zumies do something worth doing, they go all the way! The spelling and some of the specifics get lost in translation, but the spirit of whomever they are impersonating is usually spot on! It's amazing how close they actually get to becoming their new heroes of the silver screen and T.V.

THE KiNG LiVEs, again!

The UNDEAD Stallion

ZAMBO

...WAZZOMBBAAA...

...WAZZOMBBAAA...&!

First Bite PART I   WAZZOMBBAAA!

THE SPORTS NUTS!!!!

See for this group of characters being athletic and talented in their old human lives has translated well in the new Zumie life. This doesn't mean they are super smart, but they are not total dumb-asses either. This means that not every rule is remembered for every sport. So, paying attention is necessary if you want to know what is going on. Since humans left us a brewery smack dab in the middle of Zumie Valley, we quickly learned how to brew beer, and drank what they had left behind as well. That is why fun, exaggeration, and not being real serious is very common in our everyday life. This also has affected sports. I mean we care, but not really, really. In case I haven't been totally forthcoming with this little bit of information: ZUMIES ARE HARD TO KILL! We can regenerate tissue to a certain extent, and man we can do it fast. Injuries don't last long, and when things get real bad a Zumie can take on a donor body part from one of the Z-Bots that are walking around! When our blood mixes with the undead blood, ours takes over and turns the dead limb into a bonafide working thriving body part. In short, we are frickin' awesome, and we have only been around for a cool year or so, in the scope of the human calendar before the apocalypse destroyed the human's world.

In short, Football, Basketball, Baseball, Golf and other sports are still in existence. We found the rule books, and have watched countless movies and highlight reels. Zumies feel confident that our versions of these sports are... close enough? Just not at such a serious level as the humans once did. More like it is extremely fun watching these guys give it their all trying to emulate the human athletes that made it look so easy. They may run down the field in the wrong direction, or rip off someone's arm trying to tackle them. Maybe throw a ball at a batter or two. Unfortunately it is usually the one in the warm up circle waiting to bat next. A leg instead of a baseball bat, an eye for a golf ball, man we do it all. A ball thrown into the stands, while the Zumpire is calling you safe even though you are at home base waiting to hear ball one. Like I said, we feel confident that we are sort of close, but at the end of the day it's all for fun.

ZEFEREE

GET YOUR HEAD IN THE GAME !

Keep yo I on the Brain

Winner eatz da lozer.

WORKOUT FANATICS!!!

The Zumies that I call Workout Fanatics, that's right you heard me, WORKOUT! They spend a lot of time in gyms and these gatherings of people riding bikes that do not take you anywhere, called spin classes. One spin video led to a movement, and now some of our population are obsessed. Since we heal so fast, working out is very effective for our ever-evolving species. From what I understand weightlifting, cardio, and aerobics are ways to tear down the body a little bit so it can rebuild itself back even stronger each time the workout is done. For humans it took some time for this process to be effective, but it absolutely was. For us it takes no time at all. Our muscle tone and stamina are tremendous, so don't be jealous if you're not a Zumie. These workout undead-heads are real believers. They really think that if they keep doing these classes, or routines, that they will look and feel awesome forever! Maybe they will, but I'm not that much of a fanatic to stick to their regiments, and routines!

They spin class their butts off. These guys love to spin their wheels. It seems to be a real hit with the fit crowd. They can do it forever, I swear they don't realize that they aren't moving! A few of the "GIHUGIC" Zumies weightlift like madmen, and man do they look yoked. Protein shakes that taste goooooood, early mornin' wakeups, and lots of showing off. Not my scene, but I respect that they are serious about not squandering our second chance at life. They definitely will last the longest, if we even die at all?

JOURNAL ENTRY# QUATRO

WHEN PLAYTIME IS OVER, ZUMIES GET TO WORKING!!!

This past week was different. I decided to observe and record my people doing the things that make the reward of playtime possible. Our race may make a lot of mistakes, but we work days at a time without sleeping, or needing rest... just food!

BLOWED UP !

It seems to be that for most Zumies who didn't have it together mentally in the beginning, taking care of the working city was now their responsibility. The everyday upkeep and maintenance that was required to keep everything running was on those who couldn't contribute when things got started. Let me explain! While I and about 40 or 60 other sound minded "Zumz" turned the city around and cleared the way for our new, but old home to emerge, the others were still figuring it out. Dancing about in the euphoria of the new state they were in, they slowly came to life and realized that they were part of something bigger. Fulfilling tasks, and contributing to the cause of turning the town and the small city-like community by the ocean back on. It has become a working living thing, and for all its flaws, it runs like a well-oiled machine. Now don't get me wrong. My people aren't exactly the most intelligent beings in the universe, but they are more like young minds in big bodies. This ultimately affected how and when tasks were passed out. Some of the population got jobs they could handle and some just did not. Long story short, I had to draw these people to really show how amazing, relentless, hopeful, and daring their souls could be.

ZOPSICLe

M.D. Mostly dead?

.....20 Min or Death!

Biter Education

Teaching classes on reading, writing, arithmetic, and other mental tools or fixing the broken aftermath from a weekend of fun left behind that most of the valley can't wait to repeat. One of the Zumz was dressed like a doctor, but I don't recommend seeing him unless you're really, really desperate! His office was nice, but it smelled like death in there.

While passing by the new airport for the valley, I was able to witness the first flights of our emergency escape planes. Hopefully we will never need them. They were old passenger planes we fixed back up in case another apocalyptic event were to occur, or if for some reason humans were to find us and force us to leave. A lot of the planes landed, however, I wouldn't say they landed safely.

ZuMiE World AiRwayS
Come die with us, really!!

We probably should not be flying anyway! It would most likely give us away, and make the paranoid ones worst nightmares come true.

On the way back from the airport I stopped at one of the coolest places in our humble valley... "Z-MART"... Even in the new world the marketplace is still the center of all the towns buzzing activity that most of us love. Everything for the growing appetite of an exploding society. I'm not exactly sure when this place happened, but damn am I glad it did! Need a new hand, or some canned cow's brainz to eat? Z-MART has it. Human music, Zumie local sounds, old TV shows, movies, and other human forms of audio-visual entertainment. Cloth to make clothes, clothes already made, tools, toys, and all the human relics you could ever want.

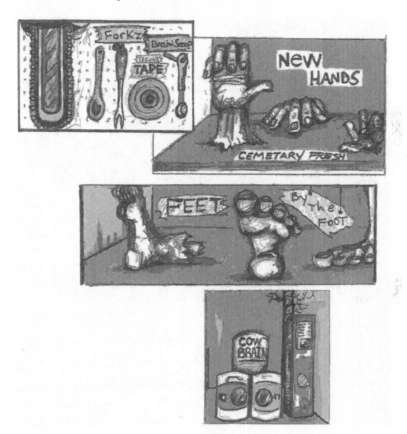

Its inspiration comes from the human side of our species that still loves to shop, and all the work you put in gets you a free pass at the many items the mega-mart has to offer. Even after an apocalypse we still crave a little variety on a day to day basis. Being a huge milestone in our progress as a living community, we are very proud of our Z-MART, and it's somewhere that we all look forward to visiting. CASHIERS, SHOPPING CARTS, and BODYPARTS!!! I know, sad, isn't it?

CHECKED out

I know that it was mentioned that we Zumies don't have to sleep much, but I did, and the next morning I thought why not the ZOO? I could have a little fun checking out the animals that are being taken care of there, and see some of the different tasks they perform there as well. Two for one, get some work done, and have loads of fun, the Zumie way! With my curiosity peaking, I drank my rare pleasure called coffee. Wow, coffee is the bomb-bay! It tastes real good, and gives you a noticeable boost as you drink it. I read how much humans loved it, and here in the days after human existence, the coffee is hard to come by. Since I am an original Zumie, who helps the council from time to time, I get to have the COFFEE! I put down my Undead O's, and headed off to my destination. Never had I been there before so my expectations were off the charts. I've heard some complaints from the Zoo staff, but besides that it was supposed to be pretty damn cool. Let me tell you! I was pleasantly surprised, it was worth the smell!

Well there I was, after a nice ride from my friendly neighborhood Goober driver! Just standing in front of "THE ZOO" was a pretty awesome representation of our accomplishments!! I mean, hello!! A rescue-habitat-ZOO, in the middle of an apocalyptic world? Freakin' Amaze-balls! All of a sudden a voice whispered softly. From where I wasn't sure...

THE VOICE: I can hear you...

It came to me as I began walking through the first set of doors. That voice was in my head. Was it mine or someone else's? Just then it happened again...

THE VOICE (in a regal tone): Relax young man, I will reveal myself when the time is right... enjoy your tour.

ME (in my mind, freaking out just a tad): OK... that was freaky?

I can't explain why, but I really wasn't scared, just curious. Freaking out inside because somewhere in this Zoo, was something or someone extraordinary. It could be said that it was pure instinct, but it was inside of my mind. I felt it! Something more than a mere moment of instinctual reactivity, I knew that this being meant me no harm. If I were to meet whoever it might be, a stroll through the Zumie Animal Rescue-Zoo was what it was going to take. At first it really did seem like the animals were the ones in charge. It smelled (IF I HAV'NT MENTIONED IT YET) a little bad, and it was bubbling with a shit ton of activity. I see where this place got its name from "ZOO"! You could feel the contagious crowd mentality vibe, infecting the minds of the capacity crowd lumbering through the newly opened facility. I tried to scoot along with the rest of the Zumies who also came to see the sights, even though standing room only was the status quo!

Finally, I made it past the lobby, making my way to the first attraction in the huge park that you could easily get lost in. The Spiders... oh wait I mean Arachnids. Things seemed contained, but I'm glad the super thick plexiglass was in effect. The thicker the layer between me and the giant spiders, the better off I was. The bigger of the arachnids looked pissed off, and his handler was... well let's just say he was in no shape to handle anything at that moment.

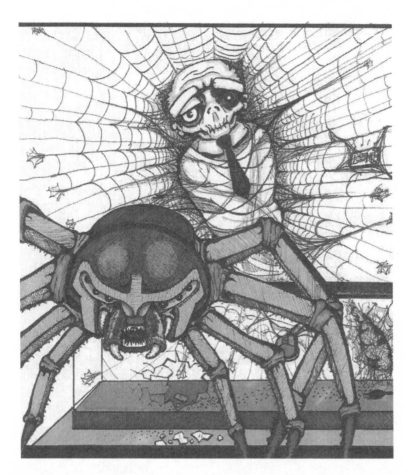

I could have sworn that I heard the big one telling off the poor guy. Hopefully his task is one that doesn't require too much more of his time. He could sure use a cold one and a back rub. In fact, if he spends too much more time in that habitat, I don't think he is going to last much longer. I did not want to test the strength of the safety glass any longer so I moved on.

To my surprise the giant ANACONDAS were next on the tour, and man did they seem playful. Playful, and really freakin' hungry, or... loving? Naw... hungry 4sure. See, the caretaker was in no mood to play, but the giant snakes had a different take on it all together.

These ginormous garden snakes were squeezing this poor caretaker so hard he couldn't breathe anymore. Definitely not the task or job I would wish on anyone. Wonder who this guy pissed off? OOOH... maybe he lost a wager, or bet? That would make more sense than anything else if you asked me. This poor guy probably gets double passes at Z-MART so he can replace his body parts at the end of the week, or the day, or by the hour. Still the giant Anacondas were quite impressive for cold blooded animals. After the Anacondas came the cute little bunnies, or should I say the very scary little hungry fluffy nightmare bunnies. Not good candidates for the petting zoo if you ask me.

Another job or task I'm glad would never be mine! Poor nightmare bunny caretaker, he looked like he wanted some help, but unfortunately for him, the Insects were coming up, and I was jazzed to finally be so close to the bugs that survived the apocalypse.

Besides my sides were starting to hurt from laughing my arss off at the bunny-man trying to survive his assigned habitat. It wasn't long before I was bored and started to wander around the park. While walking around the grounds of the zoo, I observed many small mundane tasks that Zumies were doing to earn their keep, and I wondered, "Is this all we are meant for? There must be some reason for all this life happening around me." Just then I heard the little regal voice again:

> *THE REGAL VOICE: Come see me in the insect habitat and I can shed some light on your very good questions.*

> *ME: How can you here my thoughts? More important how can I hear yours? Not to mention, who are you?*

> *THE REGAL VOICE: Because young man it's not me that can just hear thoughts, it is you that makes this possible. I heard you the moment the Goober cab pulled up. Now, would you please meet me inside the insect habitat?*

He said it with patience in his tone. It's scary, I kind of knew that I was different, but I just wasn't sure how different I really was.

So, I made my way to the "INSECT" habitat with caution. Even though I felt that there was no danger, still being a little careful never hurt anyone. Even an apocalypse can't kill these guys. Maybe we could learn a thing or two from these incredible survivors. Some of these insects look unusual and cool. Little glass habitat after little glass habitat housing these special guys. Kind of sad they survived the end of human civilization, only to end up in a cage of sorts. I understand why people want to see all these different species while we can, but part of me wants to free them. Then, as I got near the end of the tour there was a really big lab room before you headed out of insect world. A sign read "Lab Techs Only", and mind you I still hadn't met the voice yet, but something told me that this was the way. I cautiously looked around for security and headed into the doorway, slowly pushing open the slightly cracked security door. Coincidence? I think not. As I made my way into the lab, thinking that I was alone, an old but loud voice almost made me shard my cargo pants!

> *OLD MAN SCIENTIST LOOKING DUDE: Hello, young man? You look smarter than the average Zumie. What is on your mind?*
>
> *ME: Oh nothin' much. Just enjoying the stimulus around me. Quite fascinating, the new world we live in.*
>
> *OLD MAN ZUMIE: Yes, nothing like a second chance to make things right!*
>
> *ME: Make things, right? What do you mean old man?*
>
> *OLD MAN SCIENTIST: Well, when we were Z-Bots there were things that I did that I am not so proud of. People whose lives I took while in my endless nightmare. I can remember the countless futures that I had stolen to satisfy THE HUNGER. Do you have such memories that haunt you as well?*
>
> *ME (with a heavy feeling in my chest): Yes. I've never really talked about it, but I have them too.*

Now I said that aloud, but as soon as his lips spoke the words I couldn't stop the flood of memories that force their way into your dreams while you sleep! Because being undead was like one long nightmare, and as terrifying as it sounds, there was no waking up from it. All you could hear was the voice of hunger. An extreme, unrelenting voice that would never be satisfied. It was as if you were walking in the dark, to some unknown destination you would never get to. Reaching for any sign of direction, or clarity. Only to find more hunger and extreme confusion. A stain in my mind, and whenever the memories that I can never unsee rear up, it makes me feel the pain and unforgiving guilt those memories represent in my past. This guilt drives me to achieve in its name, and hopefully atone for the things I did in the past; whether it was my fault or not.

OLD MAN: Well this new life is a chance to make things right. See even though these intelligent insects are mad at me right now, when I release them they will be able to create a whole new world of intelligent life. Even though they think they are ready, I know that another month or two of experimentation and nothing will stop them. Giving them this gift of sorts is my way of giving back to the world. A meager attempt at paying back the fates, in return for this second chance at life. They use telepathic powers to communicate. The possibilities are endless for them, if my calculations are correct.

ME: Wow they look a little pissed off, but if you say so!

OLD MAN: Well I will not keep you any longer. Look around as long as you like, but please do not touch anything. Who knows maybe we will communicate like these insects someday!

ME: Naw... Zumies like talking smack too much, so I don't think so, but nice thought.

He laughed quietly as he left the lab. Man, this was some kind of flying insect warrior race. Very cool! When the old man put the magnifying glass in front of the habitat, you could see them talking with the telepathic gift. The crazy thing is, the whole time the Old man was confessing his soul, the REGAL VOICE was telling me all about how awful this old man was.

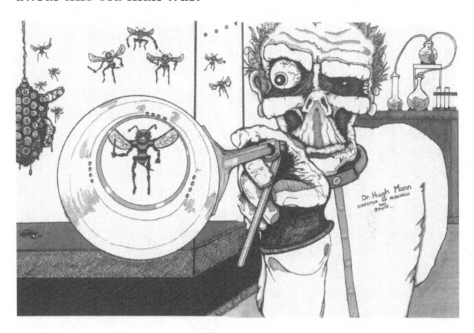

Poking and prodding them with needles, and injecting his blood into their little fragile bodies. They became aware soon after the injections, and have been trying to escape ever since. Wow, injecting our blood into another species! (No wonder the Zoo was being overrun by the animals.) I had no choice in my mind, I took a torch from the beaker that was being heated up for whatever reason and opened up one of the breathing holes so they could escape when the time was right.

VOICE OF THE LEADER OF THE BUGMEN: Thank you young Zack. We will meet again someday and then you will understand that you are special. You are meant for more than this little city can offer you. Only when you realize your gift, will you truly understand the path you must take. Like we were trapped in this small habitat, so you are trapped. Limited by the society you helped to build. When you break away from this safe valley, then and only then will you reach your true potential. You must listen to your heart, it will not let you down. Until we meet again, I wish you success... our lives could depend on it. FAREWELL YOUNG ZACK!!!!

I waved to the wise insect and made my way out of the Zoo like a ninja! Didn't want any trouble from security, and after what the warrior insects told me, this Zoo is not exactly my favorite place after all. Lately, I've been thinking that I don't seem to fit in anymore. What a difference a few days can make. My view of everything is in question now. How could this little bug seem to know so much about me? I feel something growing in my mind: curiosity, intuition, too much beer? Who knows, but for now a rest to ease my mind. Hope it was just indigestion... Yeah! That's what it was, a bad can of chicken brainz!

JOURNAL ENTRY# CINCO

WHAT A GREAT WAY TO SPEND A SATURDAY
THE SIGHTS, THE SOUNDS, THE PEOPLE,
FOOD, OH AND DID I MENTION?
WE CAN ROCK!!!

After having an eye-opening experience at the Zoo, my mental batteries needed a recharge of good old Zumie fun. Since fulfilling my tasks and responsibilities to the city ten times over, most days do not begin or end with the feeling of satisfaction the way this one did! Most days are filled with sketching the characters around me, while taking mental notes for the journals. When the time comes to write, I find a good spot and begin to unload my memories onto the pages. Usually I wait 4 to 7 days at a time before my memories are unloaded. BUT, this day had so much going on, I had no choice but to work on it right away!

Woke up today like it was any other date on a human calendar, ate my bowl of FROSTED BRAIN FLAKES, which are undoubtedly delicious. Then, proceeded to spend a few hours drawing some pictures of the Posers. These two Zumies who swear they are artistic models, posing in the little park before the Zoo. I happened to see them the day before while riding in the Goober cab. They really impressed me with their confidence.

As I was sketching in my favorite chair, a buzzing sound was coming from my phone. Yup, we have a small local broadband communication system. Like Wi-Fi in the days of the humans. It was meant for emergencies of a mass scale, like:

BLACKOUTS...
EXTREME WEATHER CONDITIONS...............
WAR OF SOME KIND...
APOCOLYPSE..CHECK!
HAVN'T PAYED BILL IN 20 YEARS OR SO......CHECK!

We all have phones, and Zumies love to send each other pictures, and text 'til they need to go get knew digits (or fingers).

ZELFEE

There is always some attention starved Zumie who couldn't wait to shock the valley. Only one guy was in a league of his own. We call him Paulie, the hamtag... wait slashtag king! Traveling from one disaster sight to another, just so he could leave his funny slashtag with the disaster in the background as a muse for his brand of comedy. His obsession is so far gone, that he puts a phone on a camera stand to take a picture of him taking a picture for his post... narcissist much? He has a small following, somewhere around fifty or sixty faithful followers. At least there is that many Zumies who can read and write in the valley. I'm sure that more have learned the ways of the cell phone alphabet, they just don't care to respond to Paulie the King's sense of humor.

#Someone Ate Fresh

After checking out Paul's slashtag and pic of the week, I got dressed and headed out to the park. The "BIG PARK" is always cool to me. It is where the Zumies are at their happiest, and most harmonious. Spirits and greenleaf shared without hesitation. No greed or territorial instincts in their hearts. Food is shared, and stories of clumsy, but courageous endeavors of human-like behavior, that leave you laughing from your belly, are told with vigor. It has always been this place that made me feel like life was being lived for a change, and not just survived. The cleaning, the planning, the teaching, tirelessly, as if the cities rebirth was driven by an actual voice in my head. Telling me that my sole existence, and the only thing that mattered was giving our new species a chance. Now that it has been realized, I find peace in watching my people enjoy the small world that a handful of others, and myself brought to life. Let me take you on a Saturday trip with me.

A Saturday is any day that you have no tasks to do, and the day is dedicated to fun, and fun only. With an official burst of anticipation and adrenaline, my feet got me started through the Big Park. Right away I saw some Zumies gathered playing our beloved DISC GOLF!

Humans did not give this sport any props, but we love it! Anyone can play, because all skill levels are welcome, and it help us keep the Z-BOT hoards under control. It's pretty damn impressive seeing these once uncoordinated flesh eating machines rippin' discs across the golf course like they were born to do it. With enough velocity to take limbs off the Z-Bots like they were made of paper Mache! This one Zumie was cut in half by accident while trying to get his disc out of a tree! As he crawled across the ground to get out of harm's way, the other golfers laughed and call him a bottom feeder.

Not real nice, but funny. I'm sure Z-MART will help him find the parts he needs, but man that had to SUCK! Moving on through the park, you could see The Superfans dressing up and showing off their ability to virtually become the human celebrities that they love. Some of them were impersonating actors, others were living as if they were the characters themselves in the stories humans tell about their adventures. Whether the stories were true or fiction it never mattered to the Superfans. It could be a story about little miners who lived for their leaders, and loved it!

Maybe a TV show about lifeguards! Strangely, even though they run really, really, slow they still somehow get to the people in the nick of time!

ZuMbay - Watch

Just before utter disaster or life loss happens... weird man, just weird. I also need to mention that these Superfans change it up all the time. This way it doesn't get mundane and boring. Like tasks they do, they also get to live out the fantasies they dream about as well. What a strange but fascinating bunch, it always is a pleasure to see them living out their dreams.

My stomach rumbled with hunger, so I wandered out of the Big Park towards my favorite place to eat in the whole Valley. The Chateau De BlaBla, Le Bla! No really!! Named by Chef Boy R. Death himself.

Chef Boy R. DEATH

Zordurves, Zumittizer?

uuhhh.....
Need more
brainzz...

No matter it has the best Zordurves, or Zumittizers that would shock and delight you. A cuisine to satisfy the undead side of our race. Kind of like sushi in the human culture I imagine. Remember we can digest almost anything, and when you combine that with a chef that makes everything taste better? Well you get a restaurant like The Chateau De something, something, or other, to satisfy the dark hunger we no longer are controlled by. The service, the food, and man, his beer on tap was to undie for. Took some awesome BLACKEYE PIE to go, and was in the mood to press my luck in our local casino. THE Z-BAR CASINO, with its tasty beverages, gambling, and intoxicating atmosphere was a place I have heard Zumies talking about, but never frequented myself. I figured it was time to press my luck. Luckily for me it was within walking distance, so I headed on downtown for some more fun. I made my way down there and heard some music faintly in the distance. Ahh, something to investigate when I'm done winning some hands at the tables, I thought to myself. Made my way to the Z-Bar, and when I got to the front door I noticed that the door man looked straight ahead and didn't utter a word. I then grabbed a huge frozen drink and commenced with the gambling. Played some DEADMANS HAND!

A game that resembles traditional Blackjack and poker combined, but if you get 2 Aces along with 2 eights you receive an actual hand of a dead man. I have nothing for that! No, really. No response that makes sense, it's the king of messy moments if you ask me. Even the principle of it is kind of sick, but someone always needs a hand, so

I just take the chips and give the hand to someone who could use it. I cashed in my "Win a Car" credits (Cars are fun but dangerous in the hands of Zumies, so to keep the city safe cars are only driven in the outer areas of the valley so casualties stay at a minimum.

Not to mention the property damage prevented) towards winning a coastal car. The casino lets you have a car for a month if you win enough car credits to exchange for a ride. I have almost enough for a truck! Hope I get one, you can explore the edges of the safe zone, and I'm itchin' to see if there is more? Especially after my encounter with The Swarm, the wise Warrior insects that I set free from the Zoo labs. My curiosity has really set off a hunger for pushing limits. What is wrong with me? Two weeks ago, and I would have never even payed attention to something like the Swarm.

I headed to the bar to drink my curiosity away, and I couldn't help but notice eyes spying my every move. I noticed an extremely attractive Zummette staring me down at the end of the bar, so I asked the bartender who she was.

BARTENDER: Ahh, that's The MADAME. She owns this joint.

ME: She is very attractive, could she be single?

BARTENDER: Well she is single, but I wouldn't mess with her if I were you young Zumie. Big, hot tempered Vixen on wheels is what she is. Don't get me wrong, great boss, just don't cross her she is definitely as smart as she is pretty!

ME: What do you mean, why?

BARTENDER: See the last owner of Z-BAR was her boyfriend. He cheated on her with a waitress. Then two days later his car and 9 others were destroyed, in movie fashion. The whole lot of automobiles owned by him and his entourage was blown to Kingdom come! Not even their bones to bury.

ME: Got it! Stay away from jealous hottie. Yup! Advice well received, thank you... later man.

I looked around and she had gone... what a relief. The story had an immediate effect on me... I was scared of this woman. That was my cue to leave, so I grabbed my pie and walked towards the door. When I got outside, a Zumie was down on one knee and looked a little out of sorts. Without hesitation, I helped him up and gave him my perfect Blackeye Pie and he said:

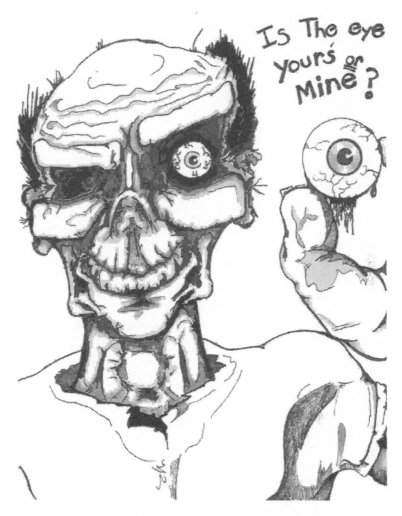

DOWN AND OUT ZUMIE: You will do something great in your life. You were meant for more, someday all will be clear, and your path will reveal itself to you.

ME: Uhh, ok! Your welcome, man? Take it easy!

After another proclamation foretelling my future, I started making my way home, back to my little house outside of the little city we have created. I often wondered how humans survived after their homes were taken by the undead plague. Unfortunately for me, it doesn't take much to break my concentration. Food, noises, and smells can draw me off track sometimes. Sound happened to be the culprit this time around, due to the fact that our people seem to love the language of music. This language is amazing and exciting to us Zumies. It is the glorious sound of MUSIC that draws us together whenever it speaks to us, and man, does it speak to the Zumie! Even when I was a Z-Bot, loud noises and loud music was fascinating, mesmerizing the undead population. Smart humans would use it to distract us so they could avoid dealing with our crazy butts. We Zumies do that very same thing to keep them in certain areas for that layer of protection that I have told you about. To this day, it still works like a charm. So, when I started to hear music and the sounds of a party, I went to explore with extreme enthusiasm! Music makes me feel like whoAAAhhhYYYehhh! Love it, got to have it, MUSIC!!

Karaoke, DJ's, or live bands, we love it all. It speaks to us on a spiritual level. Taking us to a cosmic place, where we all just hear the beats as one mind. It rocks! As I'm walking it gets louder and louder, the songs of the undead are awesome. DJ's are Gods of the music party world, and the dancers live for the beats that get created when the scene gets heavy and the party is jamming! The dancers become a wonderful extension of the music's influence as their bodies become instruments of the beats themselves.

BUT FOR ME! No matter the choice of musical tastes! LIVE MUSIC IS THE END ALL BE ALL EXPERIENCE FOR ME! To see it happening right in front of you is the best. It takes real commitment, talent, timing, and a real understanding of the musical arrangement to successfully captivate the audience that fuels your passion. As if you were pouring your heart out for everyone to see, whether it rocked, or was an epic fail. You must respect the pure bravery it takes to perform in front of your peers, I do!

Now what I'm so badly trying to get at is, the Music was live at the party I was about to enter. Over the hill, on the corner of a street, in a housing complex a band was rocking out, and yes! They were freaking amazeballs! The entire corner was full of people mesmerized by the sound of these rockers. The first band was "UNDEATH METAL" and their sound made the crowd dance around like Native American warriors getting ready for battle!

UNDEADTH 🤘
METAL

They called it "MOSHING" lots of fun if you asked me! The next band called themselves "GUTZ & ROSES" their songs were pretty damn good. Singing about taking this new life, with more seriousness, but not too seriously. Jammin' out to human tunes, and then some of their own original stuff as well...

It is amazing how the notes almost seem to be tangible, like I can touch them if I close my eyes long enough. Just swayin' back and forth with the rhythm itself, while the lyrics connect me to it all...

This is the time we all can relate!

A second chance at life feels great.

I am gratefuuuul! To the fates, who made this come to baaeeeee!

But a life of servitude is not for maaaeeee.

What the heeeeeell! Are we here foooooor.

I can't take this anymoooooor........ What the hell, is it fooor!

This is the time, we all can relate!

That a second chance, it really feels great!

The questions on my mind, and I've come to find.

That caring about to much keeps me confined.

That caring about to much keeps me confiiiii-iiiii-ined, confined!

Confiiiiiiinnned, CONFINNED!!!!!

HEAVY MANNNN, HEAVY! I stayed for the final set and began to say goodbye to the band members before heading home. Stumbling home after a long, wonderful, fulfilling day, I came upon the realization that life was good here in the Valley. WHAT A DAY! I remembered thinking as I put the key in the lock, and opened the entrance to my safe-haven. As this thought entered my mind so did one more, but how? What else is out there? Why do I feel this pull to see and aspire for more than the extremely comfortable rut I am in? What is this voice in my head, pushing me ever so slightly? The mention of any happiness, and my mind starts to ache for something more, but what? I sat down, and in a moment of routine muscle memory, I began sketching the memories in my mind. Right then the decision was made to get this memorable day out of my twisted skull. This way I have the room in my head for the next hopeful days to come.

Without these journals, I feel as though I would lose my mind. The memories of my undead past, combined with the loss of purpose in my life, would take me to this place eventually. Even though I have the journals, I do not think this is enough. I feel something more coming, but what it is I am not sure of. Dare I say I long for it? I need it! Whatever it might be.

JOURNAL ENTRY# SEIS

LOOKING FOR SOMETHING MORE!!
GETTING BRAVE?

Since I had conquered my little city and all it had to offer, I figured it was time that I look for more. In response to my inner voice pushing me to do more, I ventured out into some lesser developed woodland areas of the valley. Had to start somewhere. Being adventurous is a little scary, but that's the whole point. No risk no reward, I guess. For some reason the mountains were calling my name. Following my instincts and not really thinking about the consequences of being alone in the outskirts of the valley, I made my way up the mountain pass that protects the valley from the world out there. I brought a knife to protect myself from the Z-Bots that frequent the area, but little did I know of the real dangers of the mountain's hidden caves. With my sketch pad and some guts, I pushed further up the dark mountain.

After hiking for a few hours, I came upon the river that brings us all our fresh water! This fountain of liquid life runs a path through the mountains, and moves with enough velocity, it spins the generators that bring us electricity. Not to sound too proud, but that was me! I even tweaked the connections and relay terminals to boost the output. Amazing we have come so far! Yet, we still haven't ventured much farther than I have gone today as a people. The population is content and unaware that we are actually an endangered species of sorts. Since humans are just a fairy tale, like Santa Claws, and the Feaster Bunny! (Crazy stories that smarter Zumies tell the not so smart to keep them under control.) You know, if you are naughty, Santa Claws will come and shred your sheets while you sleep. Anyway, I was about to venture up the mountain further, when out of nowhere there he was... THE ZUMSQUATCH!...

I thought he wasn't real, but I stand corrected. Extremely hairy, big, and he was buff, too! You know muscles n stuff! He didn't even know I was there, so I attempted moving towards some cover. BUT! Since I was sucking at that time, a stick or twig of some sort snapped under my foot, and the startled 'Squach turned in a panic! When he turned, I could tell something was wrong. His arm was missing, and his eyes had a look of desperation and concern. The strange thing was... I could have sworn he spoke:

ZUMSQUATCH: Go back! Danger, EVIL REAL! RUUUNNN!!!

The strange thing is... well, his lips never moved, but... I know what I heard! I know it! Maybe he was thinking it, but before I could react, he ran away. He ran down the river's edge, looked back, and then vanished into the trees. Gone, but not forgotten. It had to be in his mind, just like the Insect Warrior's. Wow, now I really feel lost... I thought to myself as the sun was passing over me, "man the daylight flew by." Got a good mental picture of him staring right at me, and as I scanned through my memory I could tell losing that arm was recent, a fresh painful wound! Wish he could have let me tend to it, but I could tell he was more scared than he was in pain. Maybe the Evil he was describing did that to him? All the more reason to use my ninja like skills, and stay hidden as I explore the mountain side. Now when I say "ninja" don't get all excited! I know I am not a frickin' ninja. It's just that I am unusually quick, have kick ass muscle memory, and agility. With a side of, I'm a skinny bastard! Which makes it easy for me to hide, and or disappear if necessary.

As I used my stealthy skills to slither up the hill, I came upon a tattered path. Barely visible to the naked eye, yet I seemed to notice it. I heard some grunting, and heavy footsteps in the distance. Could it be? The Evil?... Had to find out... you know? Any more curious, and I would be dead if this was a human horror film. Quietly like a sniper, I crawled through the bushes and there it was! My hands slowly made an opening through the bushes to reveal a cave! Littered with bones, piled up as if they were picked clean a long time ago!

How long had it been here? What could it be? Without further delay, there it was!... A beast that resembled the werewolves of human folklore, but different. Even though the werewolf is supposed to be immune and immortal to the human condition, it appears the virus that turned the human race into undead dead-heads also affected this beast! It makes me wonder if he was also affected by the same event that awoke us. Could it be? Did I see a... WEREZUMIE! That's right! I said it, or uh, wrote it! A half wolf, half Zumie, and ugly as could be. I didn't dare get too close, or I would have given myself away. He did not look friendly, and he was impressive in stature and swagger. Even though it looked savage, there was a definite intelligence behind his eyes. Just couldn't put my finger on it yet. Since the pile of bones looked like it was from all different species I figured pickiness wasn't its forte when it came to food. Didn't want to end up a part of that pile, so I took a mental picture and slowly crept away. Every little noise gave me chills... could it hear me?... Could it smell me?... How would I stay alive?... I thought all these things to myself as once again... SNAP went the stick underneath my dumb-ass foot! It turned to locate the sound, and man it was me that wolf-boy was looking for. I did what any self-respecting Zumie would do in that situation. I ran my ass off! Ducking, dodging, diving, and never did I look back! I stumbled like the broke down, wannabe ninja that I was, and fell down the mountainside! Finally coming to a stop, after I tumbled out of control to an area I did not intend to end up in. All that worrying and the escape happened without me even knowing if the beast turned back. If he even gave chase after my boney butt! Not very impressed with myself, especially since I have no clue as to how I got down the mountainside unscathed.

My less than impressive journey down the mountain led me to a second path I had never seen before. I dusted the embarrassment from my shoulders, looked back one time, and with not a soul around, I heard a voice:

THE VOICE (quietly, as if whomever it was knew I would hear): Not yet young one, not yet...

It was then that I realized these voices in my head thing, whatever it happened to be, was not going away anytime soon. In fact, it was only getting worse, or better depending on how you might look at it.

I shook it off. It was getting late, and home was sounding like a great idea right about then. My answer was to follow the path, hoping a solution would show itself as I made my way down an unfamiliar side of the mountain. It wasn't long before a windmill on a small house started to appear at the end of the hill. AHH HELL!!! BAAAMMMMM, POW!!!! There he was standing right in front of me. He was GINORMOUS and had scars everywhere.

Kind of like every part of him was from some other body. It was sick, but fascinating at the same time. Again... things you can't unsee!!! His name was Frankenstern, Frankensteam, or something along those lines. The way he spoke was mumbly so it was hard to understand him.

> FRANKENFOOTER (struggling to speak): Maah... maa... nam... es...

As he was telling me his name, I think that's what he was doing, an angry mob of Zumies from the housing at the base of these hills were not happy. Armed with pitch forks and fire, they came marching up the path after this huge Zumie. Maybe they were the people he took the parts to fix his body from? Who knows, I didn't stay long enough to find out. I left the scene because it was getting dark, and this was not my fight. Besides, I'm sure Frank and his guests had plenty to talk about, and I would just be in the way. Using my ninja skills once again, I slipped out of the situation without a trace. Man, I'm getting good at this sneaky stuff. Barring the fact that I tumbled down a hill, after giving my position away to a hungry, scary looking beast that probably wanted to eat me. Otherwise, getting better at the sneaky stuff 4sure!!

Just as I was getting cocky, the full moon betrayed me and I was spotted. This time it was some Zumies in sports cars, riding on the outskirts of the city where the long windy roads are plentiful. My better that average eyesight could see their headlights in the distance. Vibrating ever so slightly to the feel of the road while their finely tuned, precisioned automobiles raced towards my position. The music streaming from the stereos became louder as the headlights grew brighter, and larger. I waited patiently to see what kind of characters would emerge from these impressive autos. It felt like forever, but they pulled up and called me over to their wheels. Strangely, I knew what they were going to ask, and these were no ordinary Zumies. If you haven't gathered, the apocalypse affected every species this planet had to offer. No discrimination when it came to the selectiveness of the virus. I assessed my new acquaintances within the first few seconds of their persistent and blunt method of asking me if I saw anything strange, and I replied honestly, quickly...

ME: Sure did. Their den was hidden in the mountainside, but somehow, I found it. A beast of large stature, with a garden of bones at the entrance of its cave.

All of a sudden, the engines shut off and the Zumies got out of their shiny automobiles. The handsome one smiled and revealed some healthy vampiric fangs that made it clear, this was no ordinary group of Zumies! I had a hunch, so I expressed my gut feeling:

ME: Wow you guys are Zampires. Only come out at night, and feed on the blood of the undead Z-Bots to stay alive.

ZAMP LEADER: Ding, ding, ding! CORRECT LITTLE SMART MAN! Don't be afraid, we only eat Z-Bots, you're safe. Besides we just ate, I promise... hehehe.

He laughed as if I was luckier than this guy was gonna let on...

ME: I need to be going, so is there anything else I can help you with?

ZAMPIRE: If you look over your shoulder you can see two WereZumz tracking you... and I wouldn't doubt if we didn't show when we did. Well, let's just say that they are the only things in the valley that are stronger than us. But we can manage to keep them from venturing down the mountain. In short little-man, that is what we do to pay for our way into the valley. Not to mention, we get to keep these nice cars. Fair trade for us... so just be careful... we are not the ones to be afraid of... Good day young explorer.

The majestic, proud few got back in their cars, and started them back up.

ZAMPIRE (leaning out of his window): And remember, just because you were lucky once, doesn't mean you will be as lucky next time. Usually a Zumie gets that close to the wolves... and they become a rack of ribs to pick their teeth with... You get me explorer?

His stare lets me know that I am lucky to have survived him and his crew as well. How I knew I can't tell you, but I just knew.

Perhaps I was braver than I thought, because for some reason I wasn't scared like I should have been. The old me would have run to the Z.B.I. and cried like a kid with no cookies in his lunchbox, but the new Zack was not afraid. Now that is it, something is different! Exploring, putting myself in harm's way without hesitation, and confronting monsters! Am I possessed or something? Reading minds and feeling like a ninja. WHAAAAT IS GOING OOOOOONNNNN!!! I know this is wrong, but I need some greenleaf and soda pop! For-reals!

Why me?... Am I changing?... Can't tell anyone... They would never understand, no way in hell, or heaven for that matter! I'm the one writing this down, and I don't want to believe it. Pushiiiiittt... POP goes the pop top of my cola! GULP... GULP... GULP... AAAAHHHHHH... MMmmmmm, better than goooood. I guess today luck was on my side. Maybe it was just fortunate timing, or some kind of fate, leading me to this... Not quite sure what I am becoming. Just hoping I can handle whatever is coming.

JOURNAL ENTRY# SIETE

MEMORIES THEN FEELINGS, OR IS IT, FEELINGS THEN MEMORIES?

Well, had a moment of clarity today. Kind of deep, and full of those things called feelings. I have been warned not to mess with feelings, because they are almost always attached to a memory. NO, wait! I am not to mess with memories, because they almost always come with feelings. Either way, here I am once again remembering a person who was pleading for me not to bite them. Screaming as I came for them with only one thing in mind. Must eeeaaat! Must eeaaat! Soooo hungry, huuunngry! Recalling when I once was a Z-BOT from hell still plagues me. The screams, the blood, the memories of my victims, prevents me from enjoying the world I helped construct. When I was all the way undead, the screams of the innocent were just faint background noise that could never stop the noise of unrelenting hunger that filled my head and seemed to eat away at my insides. But now... the voices of those same people who satisfied my insatiable lust for flesh, even if it was just momentarily, are haunting me when I am alone. Well... let's say my memories feel like a huge weight inside my chest, stopping me from exhaling in the late hours of the night. There are other Zumies who are dealing with these same haunting visions. Some use the greenleaf and alcohol to suppress the memories. Others stay busy doing things they love, while keeping the pain of their deep dark pasts to themselves. The saddest of us deny having ghosts in their pasts at all, pretending the pain doesn't exist. These Zumies scare me to the core, because this mindset is what brought about the apocalypse in the first place. If we are not careful, we too could bring about a similar cataclysmic event to end our people. I can't let this happen... not again, no way would I ever want to harm another innocent person! NEVER AGAIN!

For what it is worth, the Zumie population will always agree on one thing. That we are grateful, and in love with the gift of being aware, alive again. Since knowing the other side for so long, we appreciate the almost immortal life we have been given, attempting to make every day mean something. I remember my life as the undead, and it was a nightmare. All you could hear was the cry of your own body and mind as it fed on your insides torturing your broken sanity. The only thing that could stop it was the body and mind of the living. The forbidden fruit of the flesh was the only antidote to the pain of being undead. When the voice was not as loud, you walked. Walking, and walking, and walking... to some unknown destination you would never get to. Reaching for any sign of direction or purpose. Only to find more hunger, and inflict more pain. An endless cycle drowning out the soul, trapped behind the eyes of madness, and immortality.

Since having these emotions, experiencing voices in my head, and having these thoughts of unrest. I have come to one conclusion, that maybe there is something different about me. My little evolution had seemed to be normal, the simple rebirth of what was once a gifted human. I always knew that I was a little different, but I never thought it was to this extent. My mind is having trouble accepting the truth that is apparently all around me. Until now, I still felt a part of my community. As of late, it has been hard not to notice I'm moving passed the people who I once stood beside. Even when we are together and having fun, I still don't feel connected to them in the same way anymore. This means keeping an open mind is key while I write these journals. Someday, when I look back at all of this, it will hopefully make more sense than it does now. The sweet challenges of the unknown, and the nervous excitement that is driving me to explore my boundaries is exhilarating and frightening. Coupled with a newfound sense of responsibility, compassion, curiosity, and most of all guilt (if I haven't mentioned it yet.) Probably best to keep it secret just for now, 'til I can figure out myself what this means. Freaking out my shallow, paranoid people, who love to visit "DA-NILE"... (a beautiful river somewhere in Egypt)... is not something I would like to experience right now. Especially since I have no clue what I am to begin with. How could I even explain... No frickin' way man! I am freaking out just writing about it. It's bad enough that I have one blue eye, and what looks like an undead eye. But if you look closer, the pupil is white and the eye itself is a green-blue. I never knew what this meant, and it is the main reason why I was not accepted into the council of elder Zumies in the first place. All the other Zumies have one normal eye and the one undead eye. You know, a dark decayed eye socket, with a withered white grey lifeless eyeball inside. NOT ME!! As luck would have it! It was this slight difference the council feared. If it wasn't for my skillset, they might have exiled me all together. Hence the fear of telling people the truth is truly justified, if you ask me. As far as these things called feelings are concerned... I FREAKING HATE THEEEEEEM! GUILT, REGRET!! And this looming shadow of my past discretions hangs over me like an angry shadow. Will I ever shake these things I've done? Maybe I'm not supposed too? Maybe that's what paying your dues means. If that's the case, I owe big time, and the pain of the past will remind me to do good in the future.

There must be a reason this second chance at living was given to my kind... and to me? With all that I have seen and experienced; hearing voices, ninja like skills, along with this new sense of adventure, I barely recognize my own thoughts of late. I mean not to sound dramatic but, HELLO! But, this could be the only way I can redeem my soul. If I stay here in the safety of my valley, nothing is what I will accomplish. Besides, the longer I stay here, what are the chances of my secret staying a secret? If just one Zumie finds out, the whole community would know within minutes. Which means I would have to leave anyway, for fear of retaliation from my own kind. If I really am one of them to begin with, who knows anymore? My only chance, well? The humans, that's it! There has to be some left out there somewhere. Wow, heavy man... It's a huge risk, but what if I could pull it off and walk between the two worlds? It could mean peace and prosperity for everyone. Not to mention, that together we could bring about the end of the apocalypse and begin a new era on Earth, I'll call it A.T.A. (After The Apocalypse). If we could somehow find the humans, and help them regain some of their world back, we could atone. Atone for the twisted past that haunts so many of us each day. Any Zumie who was willing to help would receive relief from the pain we feel from the sheer guilt of our memories.

The humans controlled earth for a very, very long time. It must be awful, and degrading being reduced to rumor. Most Zumies have declared the human race all but extinct. Just a few small tribes left and some loners living in hiding, somewhere! Mountain fortresses and Island sanctuaries are the lore of those who believe humans still exist. Now if you were to ask the Z.B.I. it would go something like this:

Z.B.I. AGENT: Oh, well humans are almost extinct, and can only be found in small camps or tribes. If you encounter a humanoid, please stay hidden and contact us A.S.A.P. Then get home until we handle the situation. The secrecy of our way of life is imperative to our survival. So, if that is all...

ME: So don't talk to them or anything?...

Z.B.I. AGENT: NO, NEVER CONVERSE WITH THE HUMANOIDS, THEY WILL SHOOT YOU ON SIGHT! Is this clear sir?

ME: Uh, k! I'm cool man, thanx!

Z.B.I. AGENT: Thank you for calling, have a nice day!

Unfortunately, the truth is somewhat tainted. The citizens of the valley are fed whatever is decided by the council, and the militant group. It is their version of what happened as truth, and nothing else. This is why finding out information about human possibilities is difficult, and that's being kind if you ask me. My only solution is to be like a private eye and hit the bricks. Like the detectives on the TV shows, I asked questions about humans 'til I was even more blue in the face than normal. Until one day, when I found a Zumie woman, who couldn't wait to tell me about this one girl who was face to face with the humans and lived! She pointed me in the right direction, and off I went. Hitting the bricks let me process some of the events and choices responsible for the questions that appeared to be pulling me to the answers I was hoping to track down. When I arrived at the home of this girl, she was already outside with her man. Slowly, with a calm demeanor, I approached the handsome twosome. I asked the couple if they had contact with, or had seen any humans recently. They were quick to answer... YES 4SURE!! Before I could get out another question, the boyfriend reached into a hole in his girl's head and pulled out a tiny chunk of her brain. I was shocked until I remembered... duh we were Zumies! It will grow back in a few hours, not a big deal if you think about it. "The Dude" extended his hand, and said with enthusiasm:

THE DUDE: Dude! Just eat this little chunk-a-doodle of her brainz, and you can see what she saw. No questions need to be asked. Besides the experience is unreal!

ME: But when we were Z-Bots I never experienced memories?!

THE DUDE: I know man, don't expect me to explain it. It's just a cool perk to being a Zumie, so use it broham! Or don't! It's no sweat either way (he looked at his hand, dripping with his lovers' brain matter)... It's just that, well it would be a huge waste. I've already pulled the memory out. Might as well see it. I have! It was awesome, and scary, for real Bro!

ME: Ok man! I will try it! What do I have to lose, right?

Reluctantly, I agreed with the Dude, and took the brainz from his slightly bloodied hands. When he gave me the brainz, the look on my face gave me away. It was then, I saw the look of confusion, and disgust on Dudes face. I guess he thought I should have been more enthusiastic about the whole experience, and I seem to be forgetting that I still am a Zumie. Anyway, getting back to the brainz. I quickly put the brainz in my mouth and swallowed the little brain bits as fast as possible. I looked at Dude, and in a crackly voice said:

ME: MMMMMMM tasty! She must live pretty clean or something.

DUDE: For sure man. Just hold on and sit down in my righteous lawn chair. The process takes about 30 seconds or so, and then you zone out of your mind. You are then transported to that moment of the memory itself. Seeing everything like you were there behind her actual sockets.

ME: Not feeling annnnyyyyyththth......aaaannn...

SHAZZAAAAM! There I was all of a sudden in someone else's memory. It felt like I just breezed into the scene. I got a quick second or two to adjust, and away we went. It was like watching one of those really bad human movies. You know the ones where the camera man moves around way too much to make things seem more real. Sucky, sucky, no one likes that crap! You'd think the apocalypse could have at least destroyed something that sucky mc-fail-ertson, but noooooooooo. And the worst part, the plot is probably good, and the acting is cool, but then you realize that in a few minutes you're gonna puke, and miss the good part of the movie anyway! (AND THAT'S ALWAYS AWSOME!) So anyway, I was in this girl's memories... creepy. The two of them were near the outer limits, trying to get to the shoreline near a small cove that leads to the open sea. The outer limits are littered with about 4 of these cove like places. Here is where the memory got interesting! While heading to the shore, they were surprised by a handful of humans. I could almost hear the one with the gun. He was holding it in the girl's face and said:

> HUMAN SURVIVOR: She almost looks scared. Could it be? Naaah, a livin' dead-head don't feel a damn thing. Let alone look scared out of her mind!

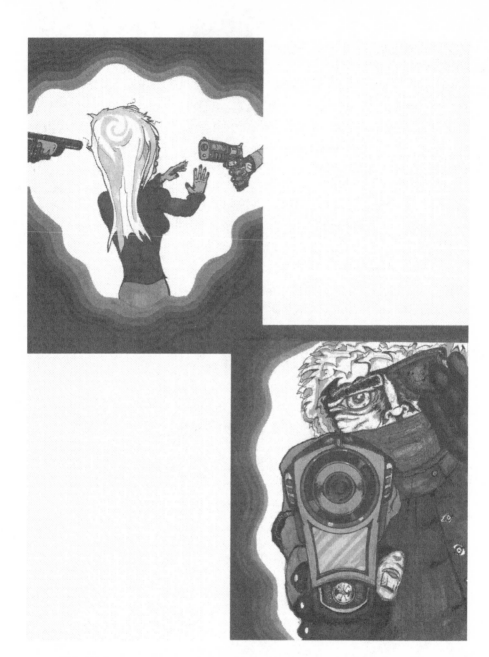

HUMAN #2: Never seen a lick of caring either way from a biter. Just death and desperation.

HUMAN #3: But this one has not a drop of blood on her, and her clothes are clean? Look at her face!... Is that... MAKEUP? CAN IT BE?

HUMAN SURVIVOR: I'm not gonna waste a bullet on her. She is different, but I'm not hanging around to wait for her friends... LET'S MOVE OUT... NOW!

I was amazed at what had transpired right in front of my eyes! I mean her eyes! He could have killed her, but instead they noticed the clues that separate us from the other undead. According to the Z.B.I. they should have shot her on sight. The Dude was hidden and froze to avoid being noticed, but she was at the mercy of several humans, and they didn't even harm a hair on her head. In fact, the hole in her head was from her falling down the stairs after they got back...

SHAZZZAAM! Just like entering the memory, coming out was just as quick. No pain, just a moment to adjust, and I was back. Back in my body, and full of hope. I thanked the couple, then started to walk and think at the same time. I really thought seeing humans would answer all the questions I dared never ask, and unfortunately for me, it did! Could mankind and Zumiekind exist together? I now know it's possible. Not easy, but possible. They could have killed her, but they didn't. Why didn't they?

Memories come first, then feelings. If you were still wondering! Then they feed off of each other. Until you realize, the only way to appease the pain this causes is to face them. After that, it is up to you to go forward, or to let them haunt you. Just in case... you were still wondering.

JOURNAL ENTRY# OCHO

THE BIG BADA-BANG THEORY!!
NO REALLY!

Whooopsi, I kind of forgot to explain how we became... well, Zumies. MY BAD! The truth is we we're not 100% sure how it happened. More like 75% sure. You know how it is. Some things have to be filled in with logic. Like all intelligent life we had to find the history of what got us here, and the rest we filled in. See, when the other Zumies who were intelligent finished shaping the fabric and rules of our little world, a few of the more adventurous council members wanted to know how the miracle of our awakening came about. So, when the time was right, we investigated by finding the details describing and pointing towards the reasons why we were here. Even though I wasn't their favorite at that time, I agreed to go along with the small group of Zumies who wanted to see how we came to be.

Because my skill set happened to be reading comprehension of human books, and figuring out how things work inside and out, it was up to me to find clues that might lead us to the answers we were looking for. NEWGEN Research and Manufacturing Facility. It was a few miles outside of the city at the entrance of our valley, and the place where the first Zumies started guiding others to the city after they awakened. This is where I told the council to concentrate their efforts in piecing together our history. It was hard to convince them at first, they always treated me with a tone of disdain since I was smarter than they were. I was the dirty little secret that was behind their success.

Never did I want credit anyway, but a few notes of respect would have gone a long way. After explaining, the recommendation of going to Newgen was accepted. This is where so many Zumies were first found lost and confused with the new life's-blood flowing inside them. It was the only logical conclusion as far as I was concerned. Edmond the Wise looked me over (He is the leader of the council, and well known throughout the valley as the last word on almost every matter) with a bit of skepticism in his stare. He waved his hand around, and pointed to the broken structure that was once Newgen Laboratories!

When we got there, it was unbearably creepy, and overrun by the undead. So, we did what we always do. Played some classic rock-n-roll and watched the Z-Bots sway their way to the source of the music, then zone out. As the group kept the undead occupied, I went inside the facility to attempt to put the pieces together. It was very clear that a fire, and/or an explosion took place. Inside the labs were coffee cups that still stood in the same place for decades after the fact. Skeleton like figures covered in dust and time. Old flat screens and equipment that was once used for, well lab stuff I guess. As I made my way through the lab facilities I noticed a bunch of undead and human remains crowding a set of double doors. It looked as if a last stand of some sort transpired and the doors remained closed. Being the clever man that I am, I looked for the ventilation shafts and climbed inside. Popped on my flashlight, and made my way to the room behind the door with stacked remains keeping anyone from getting in or out. Like a ninja! I jumped down to find a single lab coat covered skeleton slumped over a laptop and some notepads. I picked his head up off the notebooks, and proceeded to pick them up. This was obviously important stuff, so I read what looked like the last pages of the science man's lab journals.

Doctor Avery C. Jamison
Experimental cure

Journal entry# ocho, cinco...85... (Someday I must learn Spanish!)

> Trials are coming along well, and we are hopeful. The infection has made its way even to us, leaving our city in peril! The people we love that are depending on us, I cannot fail them! The antivirus I have engineered will save the world, and my family. It must work,

or... well... it is over for the human race. The soulless ones are on their way here. Not much time! Must get back to work...

Journal entry# ocho, seis

The antivirus still does not want to mutate in the blood stream. What to do? Maybe injection is wrong, but the bite causes the infection to spread through the blood stream, not scratches. Must keep trying... cannot give up!!!

Journal entry# ocho, siete

Put the antivirus into an inhaler to see if a mist of some kind could be absorbed through the lungs. Cross your fingers, PLEASE WORK!!

Journal entry# ocho uh ocho

NOTHING WORKS! It seems hopeless, and now they are pounding on the doors and windows. Their moans and screams of agony are unbearable. It is getting hard to press on, my sanity is being tested. Now the people I once worked, lived with, and loved on a daily basis want to eat me alive! My food supply is minimal, maybe a few weeks at best. Will I last that long? It won't be long now, those doors won't hold forever.

Journal entry# ocho nueve

I have done it! The antivirus will work... I just need more time to figure out how to administer it effectively. The inhaler worked but the dose was too small and the virus took the body back over again. I HAVE MADE ENOUGH TO CURE EVERYONE, I JUST NEED MORE TIME...... THERE IS NO TIME!... TIME!... TIME!... MORE TIME!......

Journal entry# Ocho...... it doesn't matter!

They're here. Security, what's left of them, held off the mass of undead as long as they could. I'm locked in this room. It is where I will undoubtedly die. This facility has the makings of the cure. We were so close. But, I failed mankind... please FORGIVE US!... Me... They are close now, the dead ones that still walk the earth. They have taken the world from us, or did we give it to them. I hope someone survived our undoing... I hope humanity somehow... help us someone, we lost our way...... we lost our way...

As I read these entries it kind of painted a mental picture of what went down in this valley during the last days of human civilization. How regretful and sad these people were. I admire that they fought to their last man. The chemical plant had to have all that antidote stored in those tanks that BADA-BLEW-UP years after the human race was scattered to the wind. When the tanks blew up, maybe in a lightning storm, or some kind of fire, the antivirus must have evaporated into the atmosphere. The clouds would have filled with the vapors until, RAIN!... The rain would have dosed the whole valley and kept dosing us 'til the undead virus couldn't take the mind back over. What the undead virus left behind was a body that can't die, with an awakened mind to control these incredibly resilient bodies. NEWGEN'S antivirus never made it to the people who gave their lives to dare dream of such a cure. Instead the lives of these people they loved, shattered in tragic fashion. Only to haphazardly bring us back to life years later, and give all of us a fresh start on this forsaken planet.

I found some containers for my evidence, and brought out as much stuff to explain my findings as I could. Knowing that the others would want to see for themselves, my hope was that what I had was enough to convince them what I had discovered was real. I told them my findings, and waited for a response...

EDMOND THE WISE (The first that was awakened): That is good young Zack. You are special and will always be taken care of by the people of this valley.

He looked at the others and said with a stern voice:

EDMOND: THIS WILL BE CALLED THE BIG BADA-BANG. IT IS THE MOMENT THAT THE GEARS OF CHANGE BEGAN TO TURN. THIS IS WHERE WE BEGAN, THIS IS HOW WE BEGAN... THESE JOURNALS WILL BE LOCKED AWAY FOR SAFE KEEPING. FOR IT IS OUR LEGACY TO LIVE! IN HONOR OF THOSE WHO AWAKENED US!...

And that was that. The ledgers of the human scientist were hidden even from me. Little did they know I could remember anything I want, like it had just happened, and that day I will never forget as long as I live. According to what I found, my intelligent conclusion is... the damage on the outside of the buildings reminded me of lightning strikes.

I've seen markings like these near the shoreline, on the rocks where lighting had struck before. These strikes could have caused the massive storage tanks to explode! Along with the nitrogen tanks that were attached to each structure, the ones housing precious antiviral ingredients.

When this happened, the storm that caused the labs to explode, then became the delivery system that the brave scientist could never have counted on. All of these ingredients, and the already cultured tanks filled with viable antivirus just vaporized into air and became the cure itself. Then the storm clouds absorbed the cure into their fluffy goodness and rained all over us.

Washing over us like a shower on a hot day! Waking us from our miserable prison of death and pain. To free us, and remake the human/undead into something that was unplanned and original. A beautiful sloppy accident that I am extremely grateful for.

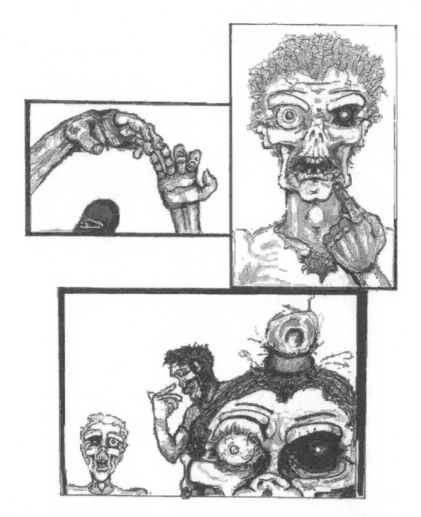

I mean, it is the very reason I am back and able to write these journals in the first place! Since fulfilling my obligation to the people and the city, I think often about that scientist, who worked to cure his people 'til the very end. How he was so painfully close to the cure, and how awful it must have been to know his tireless pursuit would bear no fruit. It had to leave him guilt-ridden, and broken. It made me feel like it was up to me, to make sure it doesn't happen to us... not to my Zumies. I could be that guy! I could feel his pain! While writing these passages the realness of it all smacked me in the face. I'm here, not only to take care of my people, but to do the honorable thing by that human scientist. That scientist who risked it all, even against unfathomable odds, until he had no time or hope left. He had talents none of the other humans possessed, so instead of running and surviving the apocalypse, he fought to stop it. Most would have fled, but he pressed on, and this inspired me. For me, this was the moment the seed was planted. I must find a purpose. I will honor my people, and this man, somehow, someway. Like I said, I admired the humie! My gifts are for a reason, they have to be...

JOURNAL ENTRY# NUEVE

SO, I WILL KEEP IT TO MYSELF!
IT'S BETTER FOR EVERYONE THIS WAY.

It's been a few days, and writing about the memories that I have kept to myself for some time are starting to invade my every thought. I know I'm different, but how different? (Not sure myself.) See the Zumie world is a very unpredictable place. Every day has a new experience to gain, a new fact to discover, a new bone to break, and so on. Sometimes when you live this way, you're taken aback on how small your world happens to be. Until you realize that it is just a tiny thumbtack, on the map of a bigger, scarier world. You are hopelessly being drawn to without relent, even though it terrifies you as much as it calls to you. There is no warning, or sign it will never give you a heads up. All of a sudden some event, a person's words, or a single thought can change the way you see the world forever. For me that event was seeing the memories of that cutie whose hapless boyfriend let me eat a small chunk of her brain! It confirmed that the Zumies who were told every human was dangerous, and I know who they are, well, they basically suck. The journal of the scientist combined with the memory I saw proves it, and I must tell no one.

That's not all! In attempt to explain why I'm hearing thoughts, along with the slipping in and out of the undead's heads... yes, while walking around the outskirts of the outer limits, I ran into a few undead and it just happened. Without warning, I slipped into one of their heads and could see myself through its eyes. Freaked me out, and this is the first time I am admitting it even took place! In light of these would be anomalies frequenting my daily routine, I finally went to a cove on the outskirts of the safe zone, to make an effort in understanding it myself. In a place where no one could see me, or interrupt me. What I found was, recently the few undead that had come into contact with me... how do I explain? OK! At first it was just an accident, but now! A single Z-Bot, when I concentrate! I can see through its eyes somehow! It took some getting used to, but taking that day to experiment with my... mmmmmm, gifts? Was the day I discovered, how different I was becoming for real. As if it wasn't bad enough, the whole Zumie population already thought I was a few beers short of a case. What will they think of me now? OH, and to make matters even more complicated, if I really, really concentrate I can sort of tell them what to do! They really have no objections. It's weird having control over the broken-down body of an undead. (I prefer to call it the suggestion method.) It's a form of mental control but in a less intrusive manor! A huge perk to this suggestive method of mind control, and that happens to be why I like it. This method allows me to still be conscious of my own body, even though I am directing their physical actions. Not only giving me a crew to lead, but it also leaves me less vulnerable, and takes the same amount of concentration. The most I have attempted was 5, and that was just comedy. Whatever I suggested they all did at the same time, it looked like a dance crew with no rhythm or talent. Like I said, bad! Not confident enough to go after controlling, or suggesting commands to any more number wise at that time or juncture.

Because to every upside, there is a downside, or side effect, and danger filled consequences to having such gifts. For my dumb ass, it came in the form of a brainstem crushing headache, while leaving me drained of energy if I did it for too long. Granted I practiced and experimented all day, so I should have been tired, but man! I feel like a train ran over me... like someone had left me out in the desert with an anchor hanging from my neck. Remember that we recover fast, and since this took a nap to recover from, it may have sparked some concern of sorts. It only took a nap of about 9 hours (OK IT KICKED MY ASS!!!!) for me to fully recover. Hard to admit it even in the journal, but it took me down a notch. The next day I felt amazing, like the notch was never there. A total recovery. It allowed me to practice some more, and dream about using this talent for good. But, can I tell anyone? There is so much to consider. For now until I can figure out a way to say what I am, keeping this secret is the smart choice to avoid any panic or conflict with my people. There are times when I worry about the paranoid militants of our species; the Z.B.I. for instance. If they found out that I can sort of do these things, it could possibly mean the end of my so called freedom. Using me as a means of control for the undead population of the valley, or maybe a weapon. I know it would not be peaceful, and because of my firsthand knowledge of the origins of Zumiekind, I would be a risk to the whole bag of manure the council has spread over the people. A healthy serving of a lie! Well let me just say this. There is no way I walk away without running like a fugitive. My wannabe ninja butt already has to sneak around as is, just to keep out of range of their very active radar. The typical getaway back pack has been readied and hidden, just in case I slip and accidentally do something that gives me away in public. All I know is, there is no way in hell I will ever let anyone use me for evil! This makes it my responsibility, to make sure that never happens as long as I can still breathe. If they were to find out, I would run, but not if I can help it. Staying in the valley, at least long enough to figure out what the best course of action is, happens to be what I would like to do.

A confession will eventually be made! See there is something Zumies and humies have in common. Unfortunately, the lot of us can't wait to destroy ourselves in most heinous of fashion. It's something I know we both possess within us 4sure. Like fear, love, hate, despair, regret, joy, and pain. We are so very much alike it scares me, but in a good excited way. Humans call it having butterflies in your chest, or stomach. I get it now. Wow it really feels that way! Maybe that's why those humies didn't kill Dudes' girl? They saw that she was scared, and we both recognize fear when we see it. I mean Z-Bots do not feel anything but hunger and pain. Nothing else. Sometimes I wonder if the REALLY, REAL DEATH is the only mercy you can show these lost souls. (This is brain death, or the total destruction of the brain. For Zumies, not one piece can be left, or the brain grows back. We are hard to kill.) Then the soul can at last pass on to the next life, and go to whatever heaven or hell they belong to. This is the death not even a Zumie can come back from, it is for REAL, REALLY. Since the man saw her obvious fear, he had a moment of hope and let her go. This now gives me hope, even though I believe the humans are just as afraid of us as we are of them. No one really knows how a people would react to the likes of us. Between our paranoid Zumies, and the humans justified concerns they could definitely harbor towards us. I couldn't risk it just yet. A war of sorts might be the result of my arrogance. Fear of the unknown is usually the seed for hate and distrust if things aren't explained in an intelligent way. And to be honest, I'm not ready yet. So, keeping my secret for now is what I must do. For both mankind and Zumiekind alike. When the time comes, I must find a way to be the bridge that connects the two races together. Just as we are actually the physical culmination of that very notion, I must make it happen in everyone's mind. Not easy, no way man, no way.

'Til such a time arrives, I will prepare myself for the journey I must someday take. Somehow, the urge to see where the humans might be is very strong. May as well give in, knowing how the humans operate and live will only help me unite the races someday. Practicing my newfound skills in secret while gathering supplies and a method of oceanic travel will be my new mission. I have a friend that I haven't talked to since I fulfilled my dues to the city. He lives in the only cove that takes a ravine to get to the open sea from. If he has an extra boat I'm set! He is a good friend, and has offered to take me out on his boat many times before. Guess it is time to take him up on that offer. Amazing how things can change! How I've changed! Just a couple of weeks ago, leaving the valley would never have crossed my mind, and now... it's the only thing I seem to want to do. Hope I know what I'm doing...

JOURNAL ENTRY# DIEZ

*PREPARING FOR SOMETHING YOU HAVE
NEVER DONE BEFORE...
THANK THE HEAVENS FOR JAKE!
JAKE "THE PIRATE"*

Being an observer of sorts who records the world around him, is awesome. Except the world around me has now changed, and I find myself in unfamiliar territory despite reading countless books on exploration. Let's face it, reading about it, and doing what you've read about happens to be two different animals! I have not yet come close to petting either beast yet. To think I could command such an animal to do my bidding was an intoxicating challenge to say the least! See preparing for something you have never done before is tricky. Knowing what to store away for your journey, it's a guessing game at best. Narrowing it down takes skill, or help. Help from someone who might have some experience in what your about to embark on.

Fortunately for me I have such a friend, or at least the closest thing to one. There is only one thing weird about my friend, or you could say original about him. He believes that he has become a pirate somehow. That's right, I said a freakin' "PIRATE"! Like all the time a pirate, so I call him JAKE THE PIRATE... he seems to love it! So, why the hell not! Knowing that feeling comfortable around others wasn't his strong suite, made me feel privileged that he trusts me enough to let me into his world.

I met him when we surveyed the valley to see how much land we had protected by the landscape of the area. He was already fixing a boat and had fish cooking on a fire, not too far from a place built into the trees that he called home. The others wanted to move him and put him to work, but something inside told me we needed him for something else. Without hesitation, I convinced the others to let him be a lookout for any humans coming from the ocean. They agreed and I explained it to Jake. I told him that he would always get to live in this valley if he agrees. It took a few brooding stares at the now council, and "ONE CONDITION":

JAKE THE PIRATE: On one condition you scurvy land lovers... that ya leave me be to me self. I don't like rules, and I don't like company... Ye understand?

EDMOND (in his skeptical tone): AGREED... PIRATE!

And there you go! I made a friend. It became part of my tasks to visit Jake once a week and get a report on the traffic on the seas from the cautious pirate. If there was an emergency he has a crate of flares and four flare guns to warn us here in the valley. In fact once, he called me down here, and was very excited to show me an old pirate ship. After a big storm it seemed to have gotten wedged between some rocks near his paradise like cove. He fixed it up and called it "PIRATE'S DREAM". It wasn't long before he made it into his home, and still works on it 'til this day. Loves that boat, he does. Unfortunately for the massive schooner, it will never see the ocean again. That is unless another storm washes it back out to sea. Don't tell Jake though, he will defend her seaworthiness 'til his last breath. After a while we just used the CB radio to check in instead of me coming in person. It all stemmed from me fulfilling my duties and that's why we lost touch... well I'm a bad friend, and I haven't talked to him in about three months or so. Hope he isn't too pissed off at me. I really need his help! He uses a fleet of small gas powered boats to patrol the coast and I'm hoping he will let me use one.

So, I swallowed my pride and took a hike to the cove of JAKE THE PIRATE, or as I like to say JTP for short. It didn't take JTP long before he noticed my presence. I wasn't even close, and he gave me a nod from a distance as he raised his arm up to wave. When I got close enough he smiled and came at me with open arms! Nothin' like a big hug from a salty pirate who loves to call you young master Zack! It was as if I hadn't missed a visit! He was as hospitable as he could be; food, drink, and smoke was offered. We ate and smoked while talking about the council and its sacred notion of what a good life is. For a pirate he was a great guy to have a serious, or casual conversation with. He always got me, and could teach me a thing or two when I was lost. Maybe because we were both outcasts in our own way, and yet the valley depended on us both for important tasks to be done. Ironic if you ask me, but it is why me and Jake always felt like we understood each other. After hours of stories and memories it was getting late, and I finally got the courage to tell Jake about my ambitious plan to explore the world abroad. Not everything, but enough truth to keep even JAKE THE PIRATE from being weirded out by my secret skillset. He also agreed not to tell the council or anyone else for that matter, totally cool as usual. The only thing he asked for was an electric generator for PIRATE'S DREAM in exchange for a nice pontoon boat out of his small fleet of homemade ships. Perfect for me. A trip to Z-MART would solve all our needs, and we all know how I love that crazy stupid awesome store.

This was the break I had been looking for. A way out of the valley undetected, and into the unknown. All I had to do was come through on the generator. No sweat. In fact, I not only found his generator, but on the down low, I got some previsions for a trip that would last for a month or so! Everything I needed was there, and if I needed anything else I'm sure Jake would tell me. You know on a less serious note, well kind a serious... Z-MART is evil! I go in with a specific list of things to get, but almost always come out loaded down with a cart full of useless stuff. HOW? EVIL I TELL YOU... evil.

When I got back from the Mart, JTP was ecstatic over his new generator. I guess he has been waiting for a long time to finally turn on the lights that he has carefully installed on his PIRATE'S DREAM...

JTP: Arrrr... Master Zack thank ya for gettin' me a wee generator for me PIRATE'S DREAM!

ME: No problem JTP. Anytime I can get you anything you need from Z-MART you just let me know, ok! I got your back on supplies, equipment, or whatever!

JTP: Much appreciated Master Zack. I can now light me DREAM up at night, without burnin' her down. I happen to be a wee bit of a pyro around fire of any kind. So electricity should help me out. ArrArrArrArrrrr!

ME: I'm really glad you're helping me out with my secret journey. I hope I'm not putting you in any danger with the others!

JTP: No worries mate, ye be me only true friend Master Zack. No one will know unless ye wants them to know! Have me word on 'at ya do!

ME: Thanks JTP! I knew I could count on you, it means a lot to me.

JTP: Besides... nobody listens to me anyway! A benefit to being a scurvy pirate that smells like fish and bilge water... hehehehhahaha... ArrrrArrr...

ME: 4sure Jake! JAKE THE PIRATE! Thanks for the boat, she is beautiful. She has a sail though. I thought we were going with a gas powered motor?

JTP: Oh hold on to yer anchor there master Zack! She has a powerful motor under the ship that be foldin' up *when ya put her on shore. The sail is for emergencies, or if ye want to move about without makin' even a wee bit a sound to tip off those humies that you're lookin' for. No needs for thanks on that piece of fried sliced gold young Zack.*

ME: SWEEEEET! You are way smarter than you let on JTP, I'm totally geeking out over the whole ship! RIGHTOUS MAN, RIGHTOUS! It's more than I could hope for JTP. Thanks man, really.

JTP: Aye Master Zack, yer very welcome lad. Just be warned... although she is sea worthy, this vessel is more for traveling up and down the coast. A few miles out to stay hidden from the shoreline, but by no means can she handle the open seas. You must respect the limits of ye ship, or she will break apart under the might of the currents that open waters possess!

ME: Yes sir! I mean! Aye, aye cap'n! I won't take the sea for granted. I promise!

JTP: Ok, I'm not foolin'. Now here is the key to your vessel. I have named her "THE CURIOUS TURTLE". "THE C TURLE" for short. You will see, no pun intended, why that is its name. ArrrHarrHarrHarrrrrr...

ME: Thankz again Jake, Really!

JTP: Arrrrr... lad... enjoy her, a ship is real freedom these days. Just remember freedom be risky, and is very seldom safe. That's why we pirates love to be free. Never a dull moment, and always somethin' to reach for! Now that is livin' Master Zack! And that is why souls will die to protect it, or to have it. Freedom that is, and the ship for that matter. You'd do yourself a favor to remember me harsh wisdom. 'Cause it works lad, it just does...

ME: I will JTP, I promise... I will never forget.

Jake gave me a hug like only a pirate could, and walked away drunken from smoke and drink, feeling no pain, and looking for a nap. Since it was getting late, I headed back myself to keep up appearances, and gather more supplies. Choosing, or guessing what I might need for this leap of faith is going to be tricky. I must lead the local authorities to think that everything is cool as a cucumber. (Whatever a cucumber is anyway?) They have been a little edgy lately, and I want to stay ambiguous as long as possible. Invisible if I play my cards the right way. Because let me tell you! If they caught wind of what I was doing, they would shut it down immediately and detain me for questioning. Loads of fun for everyone...

See the Z.B.I. thinks that if a Zumie were to get caught, that they would eventually give up the location of this precious little valley. Then the world as we know it would be over. So, avoiding this is priority for the Z.B.I.

I understand why they are scared, but I am no ordinary Zumie. Not to mention that I would die before putting the city in danger. I love my people, and what I am doing is for our future survival. Funny if you think about it, I mean I bet that these silly, diluted, psychotic, loving, playful, curious, trusting, paranoid, and hopeful souls will ever know I am going to really miss them! For me, well before I can say where I truly fit in with the Zumies, I must find out for myself who I am. The only real way to accomplish this is to 'RIPP OFF THE BANDAID", "TRIAL BY FIRE!" (Last but not least!) "PUSH HIM IN THE WATER, AND IF HE DOESN'T DROWN, HE

OBVIOUSLY CAN SWIM!" Time to face my fears, and find out what the hell I'm made of. Why I need so strongly to leave is sort of a guilt driven feeling. As if a voice has been calling to me, or a force of some kind has successfully pushed at my will 'til I thought it was my own. No matter now... I cannot resist the calling. I must take on this task of finding others. Human or whatever! It seems to be getting stronger, and my budding powers won't stay hidden for much longer. So, north is where I will head. This may be my only chance to slip out, and do it without anyone but JTP knowing. I have a small window at best, but even though I'm still fooling everyone for the moment, with my powers growing, that could change any day now. If I don't leave now, I may never get the chance again.

I have the vessel! The supplies were gathered easier than I thought! I have my courage, and new found abilities to defend myself from the unexpected dangers of the outside world. I was given a good sized knife and pistol by my mate JTP. This is a gift I will definitely need at some point, but the hope is that it's just a precautionary measure. Something I would not want to need, but know that it is necessary to have in this dangerous wasteland of a broken world. JTP goes everywhere with an old colonial pistol and a small sword of some kind. This being said, a rite of passage was given to me by a man who believes he is the real deal. WELL DAMMIT HE IS A REAL PIRATE! WHY NOT? And now, so am I!! Arrrrrr!

Tomorrow is the day of putting my money where my mouth is. I have NO IDEA WHAT THAT MEANS!? But humans say it all the time in the movies when they are testing their courage or bravery. Always appropriate in a time like this. May the weather be kind while I'm out there navigating the sea. What could possibly go wrong? Maybe I should be scared, but I can't turn back now. My window of opportunity is small, so I must take it. The risk is worth the reward. I could finally find what I am looking for! Funny, it seems to be that this is what I'm scared of most inside the hidden places of the mind, and yet I feel it calling to me. It is deep seeded, and I will answer the calling. A calling filled by purpose, with a chance to change the lives of everyone, in a positive light. A chance to honor the scientist who never gave up, while securing the safety and future of my people. I hope that my good intentions don't lead to horribly justified actions. Sometimes these actions or events can bring even more suffering, just to accomplish a twisted goal that resembles nothing of what the hopeful outcome was supposed to be at its inception. The very planet we live on is an undead example of how those hopes lead to a cataclysmic, twisted outcome. The mission now, is to bring humanity and Zumiekind together, strengthening the two in unity! Giving them a leg up in a world that desperately wants to kill itself. I hope that little old me is enough to accomplish this ambitiously necessary goal! Unfortunately, I could be a total self-delusional idiot, and get myself killed expeditiously!

BUT IF! IF, I CAN PULL IT OF SOMEHOW, SOMEWAY!

I can find peace for the things I have done, and fulfill this promise to my people. Find a way to keep them safe, while securing a treaty of some kind with the humies, and start a movement to bring the planet back to life! And if this is to be accomplished, questions will have to be asked and answered. LIKE:

Can we both occupy the same space?

Live together in this new world, benefitting each other willingly?

Or will we kill each other in the process?

Only time will reveal the answers... truthfully, even the questions could change. Who knows? I must go and play it as it comes, be adaptable and think on my feet. It's an adventure, an unpredictable journey of sorts! There is also a strong possibility that nothing could happen, and I would have to go back to the drawing board. Gotta get some sleep and fill up my own batteries...

WISH ME LUCK!!!

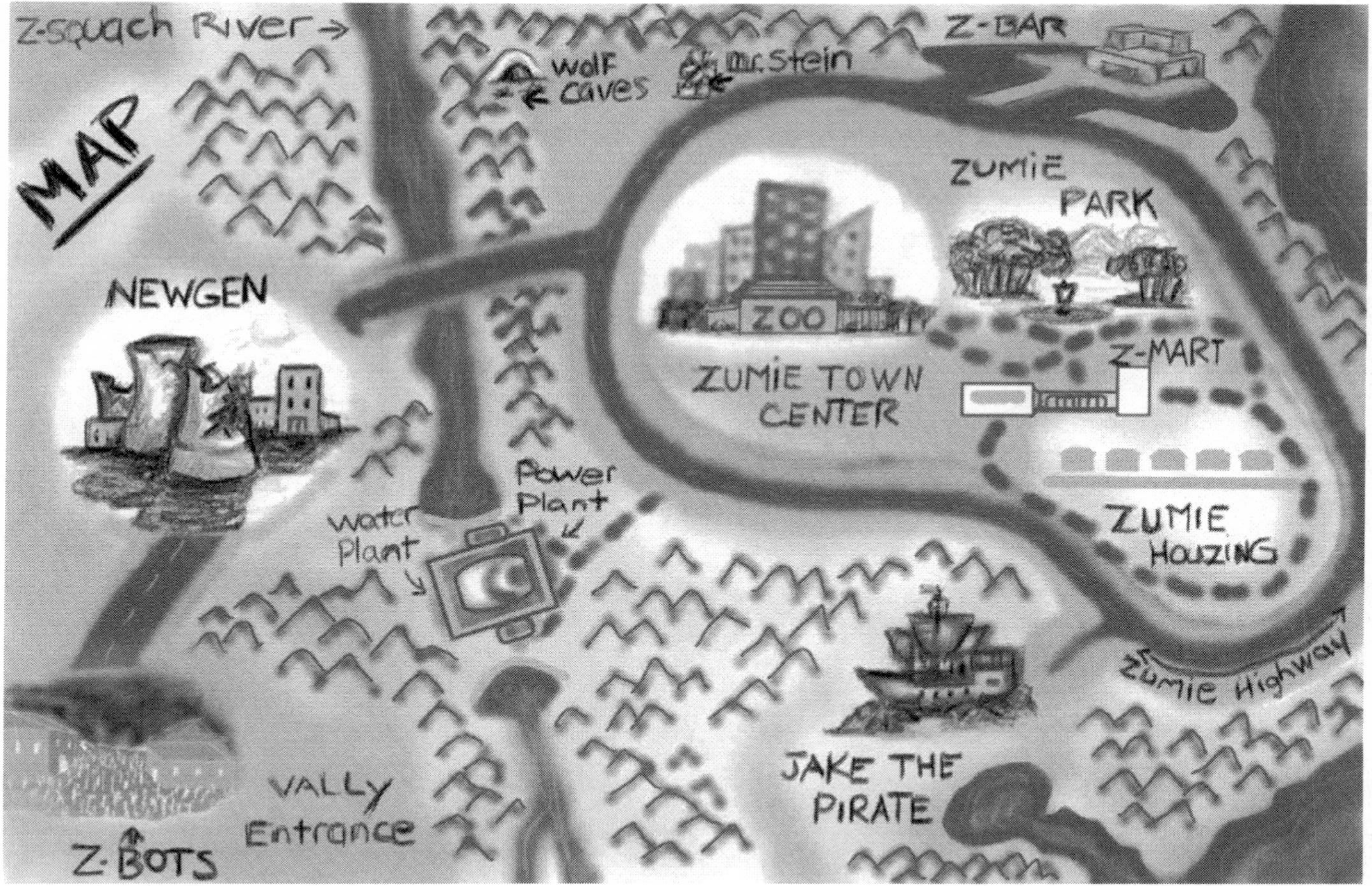

MAP
Z-squach River →
Wolf Caves
Dr. Stein
Z-BAR
NEWGEN
ZOO
ZUMIE TOWN CENTER
ZUMIE PARK
Z-MART
ZUMIE HOUZING
Power Plant
Water Plant
Zumie Highway
JAKE THE PIRATE
VALLY Entrance
Z-BOTS

JOURNAL ENTRY# ONCE

A JOURNEY, ADVENTURE, WHO KNEW?

Here I was, looking long and hard at the vessel to the unknown destination in the back of my mind. A mountain fortress, a stronghold, and man I swear it's calling to me. What am I looking for, without it finding me first? A journey, adventure, a voyage that would define me forever. My future, and my real purpose! Because now I'm not just recording a history of my people, but making the history as well. I guess it sounds narcissistic, but that's the human in me I guess. The only thing that makes it all worth the risk? The hope that I can balance the two sides of me enough to make a positive difference in whatever happens. No more fear, no more killing, and some real peace. These are my long-term goals for both humankind, and Zumiekind alike. My heart of hearts tells me that some real sacrifices are going to have to be made for these dreams to realistically come to fruition. The question is, who or what the sacrifices are going to be. Imagine! This is what goes through a man's head while checking off the list of supplies as he packs for the trip:

1. Compass
2. Radio
3. Batteries
4. Charging cables
5. Pens, pencils
6. Paper
7. Fishing gear
8. Pots
9. Water
10. Binder
11. Snacks
12. Music box
13. Greenleaf
14. Soda pop

MMMMMMM... SODA POP... it's ok 'n' stuff... I'm totally lying!!!!! It is the single most awesome consumptive concoction that mankind ever invented! Like I said... it's ok. Feeling ready to float right out of the cove and straight up the coast. Who knows what new undead life forms I might see, if any? Who knows where I will end up, or what challenges are waiting to be discovered? All these thoughts filled my head as I pushed off the shore and started the boat motor for the first time. Throttled forward slowly, making my way for the outlet of the cove. "BANG, BANG" my head snapped around!! Behind me in the distance was JTP!!!! Standing on a cliff, waving his arms, with smoking pistols tightly gripped in each hand!! Saluting me with comic enthusiasm, as I motor away towards the small river-like stretch of water that makes its way to the sea. I waved back knowing that I would owe Jake big time for everything he had done. He is a real friend, someone I truly care for.

As I navigated thought the small outlet, I wondered how that old schooner ever made it through untouched by most accounts. Amazing! Once I was past the final bunch of rocks, and the incoming waves were behind me. The sea seemed to calm down for me, making the experience almost therapeutic. Standing at the front controls of my vessel I closed my eyes, and felt the spray of cool sea water coming off the bow. Hitting me across my torso, neck, and face. It was absolutely incredible! The smell of fresh sea air, and the sight of a horizon that looms ahead, filled my lungs up with pure hope in the mist of the spray that hit me. Blasting into me a newfound love of the ocean, and all it represents, with the promise of the unknown in an instant! For me, it was at that moment in time that the wealth of experiences yet to come gave me energy, drive, and strength to push forward! (Even though fear was creeping up my spine, attempting the justification of me turning back.) For, the taste of food no longer pulled at me the way it used to. Now! My passionate focus on food, has been replaced by the pull of impending journey, and the discoveries it could bear. I throttled The C Turtle's strong single propeller motor, and forged up the coast with reckless abandon. The time seemed to pass by with the same quickness as the name of my vessel. Unfortunately for me I had traveled into what seemed to be barren waters. No life, movement, or even voices of any kind, resulting in an indescribably eerie, cold sort of silence. I have been forced into getting used to the noise of voices in the background behind me, or in my head these days. Now silence is scary, and I welcome some noise for once. If this is what traveling is like, it will take more getting used to than I care to admit. As the boat motors along, I check my food supply and the other things I brought for the trip. I had brought more than enough, and was prepared to scavenge, along with hunting if food supplies ran low. This is going to be successful, I know it, I feel it in my bones.

For now, I am happy to be a klick or so off shore, considerably far, but close enough to see the shore line and mountains just past the horizon. No fish so far, very disappointed! No whales, sea lions, dolphins, or sea turtles, except mine of course. Thought I would have to maneuver a few times to avoid them. Since there is no human boat traffic I figured sea life would flourish. I was wrong so far, and not an aquatic soul for miles of travel. Maybe they are just further out to sea. Smart if you want to avoid an apocalypse; I guess it makes sense. The wish for it to be safe enough to get close to certain shorelines, might outweigh the danger below. Since the sea bed was hundreds of feet down, there was no telling how many undead were entombed along the bottom of these coastal areas. Hope my dream about the humans is more real than my sea life dream. Really. The coast on the other hand was beaming with activity, and sights that had me looking in awe, as The C Turtle pushed north up the coast. Z-Bots seemed to have taken over most of the human ruins that once buzzed with life along the shorelines of the coast. Not even with my new skills would I attempt to go ashore in the areas that I happened to pass without a second thought. My favorite though was the burned out ruins of an amusement park by the water, a boardwalk of sorts if I remember correctly. Wishing it wasn't so overrun with undead, I throttled back and stopped for just a moment to look a little longer. I imagined it when it was full of life and happiness. The sound of skeet-ball, shooting the clowns nose with water 'til the balloon popped, while somebody's big sister throws baseballs at the bullseye so the clown gets dunked. Last, but not least, the sounds of the rollercoaster in the background, followed by screaming passengers at the mercy of the coaster roaring through the tracks! In reality, the roller coaster that was left was still in pretty good condition.

The screaming passengers were gone for a long time now, replaced by the moaning undead. The magnificent monstrosity of wood and steel would have to wait for me just a while longer. Due to the fact, that even though I was half a mile out in the water, the Z-Bots were falling off the boardwalk into the cold rolling waves, crashing into the shore, to come after me and the Turtle. I could try using my mind to make them go back, but why waste the energy when I need to move on anyway? I turned my head, and pressed on heading north, once again at full speed ahead. My day dream took too long. There was no telling how much time had passed, so pressing on was the only option if I didn't want company on my ship. My Bad! Got a tad curious, and drifted on the water while in my head. Definitely need to be smarter if I'm going to look for humanity, or I will be captured while trying to observe them.

Pushing up the coast I realized that the sun was going down on the horizon, and this prompted me to start looking for a place to settle down for the night. Since I hadn't slept in a while, even though I tried, my eyes were starting to get heavy. The anticipation of my journey kept me up at night even though I knew rest would be best. Just could not stay asleep, like a human kid on Christmas Eve (A human holiday where gifts are given to kids who are on the nice list. Saw that in a movie.) Yup, that was what it felt like. Kept on my heading for a solid hour, and finally noticed a little shore line surrounded by cliffs. Reminded me of Jake's cove, but smaller. Perfect! I knew that this was a safe place to rest for the night, and I could press on in the morning. As I steered towards the shore my mind began to wander.

The mountains were calling to me, in my mind this would be the safest place for humans to survive. The colder weather, combined with rough winters would slow the biters down, and the mountain terrain would make it hard for a Z-Bot to see or hear human activity. Another plus would be that the human population would sweat less, and that would kept their smell to a minimum. I personally don't think humans know how strong they smell when they are all together in one place. When I was a Z-Bot myself, humies smelt like big meat sacks, and we all know how much the biters love sweaty, smelly, sticky meat sacks. So being inside a mountain or up one would really help hide all those things the undead use to find their next humie meal. The undead biters would eventually give up, starting to look elsewhere for something/someone to eat, turn, or both...

I broke my train of thought, just in time to start throttling back on the Turtle's motor, bringing the small pontoon boat to a nice stop on the sand. I jumped out of The Curious Turtle, and immediately began pulling the 24ft vessel up the shore, assuring me it would be there when I woke up. Got into the weather cab and grabbed a few things. Something to eat, a good can of beans, a couple of pops, sleeping bag, journal paper and pencils, gun, knife, and binoculars to look out on the horizon if anything looked peculiar. During this small routine of getting firewood and building a small fire, my train of thought got back on track, the paranoid one.

You know I was wondering? If the humans saw me from a distance, would they shoot first and ask questions later? If it were me, I hoped that a closer look is what I would do in the same situation. SHIIITTAKI!!!!! WAIT! Undead do not wear cleanish cloths and carry a backpack. I should be fine as long as I wear my hat and shades. Oh, and I would be manning a small vessel. Z-Bots don't wear shades... right? Will I be able to hear human thoughts?... What would they sound like? I haven't thought that out just yet... CRAP! A clusterfluck of questions had flooded my mind, and I needed a lifeline!!! Oh man they're gonna shoot me 4sure... gonna have to be like the ninja I wish that I was, and just observe them from afar. Not making contact 'til I can find a way to do it peacefully is definitely key to my survival...

Crazy, here I am writing about meeting a human, and I still don't even know if I will find them at all. Keeping an even scope on my expectations has become almost impossible now. Even daring to not think about the moment I see a human for the first time is impossible. It just seems to make the nervous tingly feelings get even worse.

It seemed to be the end of the line for that train of thought when the fire finally started to stay at a steady burn. I kicked my socks and shoes off, letting the sand get between my toes as I moved the little pork chops up and down. Popped open a can of soda pop, (orange by the way) and cooked a can of pork & beans to perfection. In the scope of this time the sun had gone down and the night was beginning to settle in. My pork & beans had been eaten, there was only a sip or two left of my pop, and the sleeping bag had been laid out. Still it was hard to close my eyes, the soothing ocean air that was breezing, and the moonlight over the cliffs that reflected on the water was captivating. The smell of the water filled my nose as it rolled up the sand just far enough to keep you from getting wet. In this time after the apocalypse, it still amazes me how life finds a way to go on. I now think of it all as more of a new beginning than an ending of sorts. Especially on a night such as that one. The chill in the air told me I was close to the colder northern air. The mountains have grown larger in size with every mile I travel up the coast. Soon I will either find what I'm looking for, or a clue of some kind pointing where to head next. I have this relentless vision in my head of roads leading up the mountains, so that is what I am heading for. I wonder if there are more NEWGEN facilities where the Zumie phenomenon could have happened. What if that's what I find? NO WAY! Funny how your mind wanders when you are alone in a peaceful place such as this.

My hand slows as I sit here writing this journal by the water, and this wonderful fire, hidden from the undead and the rest of the world.

Like I'm in a kind of safe cocoon, right before some events change me into something else, someone else. We will see, getting tired now. Because I'm part human sleep is still necessary, and man for me it's kind of awesome. That is, when I actually get some sleep... it's hard to come by these days. Don't need more than a long 5 to7 hours for maximum recharge and recovery. We heal fast, but when we sleep for real, we heal like vampires in the human stories of old! Not that time is a huge concern for someone who can only die if your brain is destroyed, but 6 hours of sleep is equal to 48 hours of energy. Cool, huh! Also, recently... when I sleep, my skills, powers, whatever they are... they get more effective, and easier to control! This transformation is scary, but I can handle it. I just know I can. Oh, I know this has nothing to do with my journal, but Zumies would be great for space travel if the human's research was on point. Just sayin'! Gonna sign off till next entry, hope I have something exciting to write about!!!

JOURNAL ENTRY# DOCE

1st **Chapter**

THE STORM!!
AND THE BEGINNING OF THE REST OF MY
LIFE......

It's almost unbelievable what I am about to write in this entry. The time that has passed is not important. One week, two, or more, it doesn't even matter! What does matter, is what got me to where I am right now. The very event that I thought was a huge stroke of misfortune, was actually my salvation. A series of events in fact, that have changed my life forever. One big journal entry to explain it all!! K... K... OK!... K... K... OK.

The last time we spoke was right before I went to sleep on that cool breeze, clear sky, perfect night. When I awoke the next morning, the air smelt wonderful, but colder. I sat up and put my feet in the sand, which was still warm from the embers of the fire that must have gone out while I slept. It seemed to be a great morning, the first morning after I was out on my own and free. There was no hint or feeling that would have lead me to think that this would be the most challenging time of my short Zumie life. The weather was cool and clear, with some cloud cover in the distance to the north of me. Not one clue or gust of wind that warned of the darkness to come. Packed up The Curious Turtle and pushed off the shore. Started up the motor and backed The C Turtle up enough to turn around, getting me pointed back out into the open water. My mind was spinning, full of expectation and anticipation. There was almost no way I could not meet a human. YOU KNOW WHY? BECAUSE I SAID SO!!!! I steer my vessel with the heading of my destiny, north to the mountains, the same ones I have been dreaming about for a solid month now...

OK! That sounded dramatic when reading it back to myself, I know! Although these experiences warrant some of the dramatic flair I've put on them. See what had happened was, that I went through some dramatic shit so I could even be here to write this entry at all. K! Sorry, I'm done. Had to be said...

On a less drama driven note, I totally get why Jake the Pirate named my vessel The Curious Turtle. Emphasis on the turtle part of the name! Speed is not what she was designed for, but being able to land on shore with ease was pretty damn awesome. I mean we were moving at a good steady 22 to 24 knots up the coast, and making some headway. The wind at that time was just not on our side yet, so pushing against it was slowing us down. Otherwise, The C Turtle would be pushing 27, 28 knots steadily like yesterday. Fuel was good, plenty in the barrel inside the cab. Also the supplies were in check, and I was loving every mile that was added to the gauge that only had 47 miles traveled on it when I left the valley. Now it read 287 miles traveled. For me that was a moment. I was out in the world and no one or nothing was going to stop me. Just as my ego was stroking itself, I remember the wind shifted in a direction coming from the southwest. Thinking to myself... PERRRFECT the sail could go up and give me a boost! I opened the sail and engaged the parallel controls from inside the cab. The Turtle was flying now, like a supercharger was turned on. NOW! Pushing through the tides would be a breeze, no pun intended. From the way it felt you might have thought I was pushing 40 knots. It was 39 freakin' knots, and it was wonderful. The shoreline was not as interesting as navigating the Turtle through the waters. Unfortunately, I stopped paying attention to the conditions around me, and the price of this ride was about to get theme park expensive, real quick like. I just wasn't aware at the time.

Since my sail was up, controlling the Turtle had to happen from inside the cab. This shielded me from the cold, rough winds that were pushing me and The C Turtle like we were the wind itself. It also kind of gave me a sense of, well no sense at all. This cab also shielded me from the fast moving storm that was heading right for me. It was dark and massive, but did I notice in time to prepare?... Noooooooo... I was too busy enjoying the feeling of 39 knots in a Turtle that was pushing its limits. Besides, the harsh winds couldn't bother me from inside the cab was my thinking at the time. Just as my thoughts ensured my ego to keep speed and heading, the wind shifted right before my eyes. Not just in one single direction, but the wind was changing all around me. Hitting The C Turtle from the north, then southwest, and so on... SAILS DOWN!! I thought aloud in a panic. My brief supercharger had to be shut down or it could capsize the vessel and it would all be lost. I quickly put the Turtle on autopilot and made my way outside to pull down the sails. HOLY FROZEN NIPPLES!!!!! It was 30 degrees colder than when the sails were put up, and I was in shock. The wind was slapping me in the face, the cool sea spray was now a firehose of freezing ass water. The cold crippled me as I fought the sails, trying to bring them down without ripping them to shreds. I was losing miserably, and The C Turtle was off course pushing further out into the rough, violent waves. Things were getting worse with every attempt to save my boat. Waves were crashing across the deck of the vessel as I finally got the sails down in a last-ditch effort, before having to cut the ropes with my knife. Scrambling back to the door of the cab I finally looked up at the storm; it was massive and angry. The wind that was once my source of pure exhilaration, was now sending a different kind of chill that ran up my spine. Just as I grabbed the controls of The C Turtle... CRACK! BOOOOOM! RUMBLE, RUMBLE, CRACKLE! BOOOOOOOOOMMMM!!!!

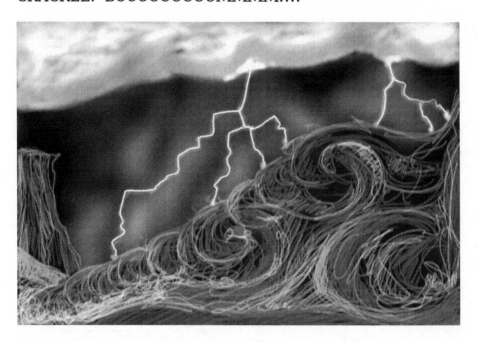

My goose bumps tried to fly south for the winter, and my jaw dropped when I realized that I was in the middle of a real-life storm. Like the ones you see in movies!!! Winds, rain, thunder, unbelievably sized waves on the horizon, and lightning! Not to mention that I was being forced out to sea, and I couldn't even see land anymore.

Thinking to myself:

> *ME: Self, fine mess you have gotten us into, how in the hell do we get out of this debacle now??*
>
> *SELF: We don't stupid! Either you steer us back to shore, or we drown. Over, and over again, 'til madness takes over and you lose your mind completely... thems yo' options fool... deal wit' it!*
>
> *ME: You don't have to be an ass about it! Screw you! We are gonna survive this, and then I'm gonna rip off my own arm and beat you with it!*
>
> *SELF: Well you sound like an insane asylum candidate, you've got my vote man! Go for the primary, I'm sure once you've pulled yo' arm off, and begin beating yourself with it you'll get everyone else's votes too! Maybe unite the two parties in a unanimous landslide vote!... HAHHA!*
>
> *ME: UHH... well... when you put it that way!*
>
> *SELF: OK Mannnnnnn! Pull it together, and face THE STORM!!! Before we drown, K?*

LIGHTNING LIT UP THE NIGHT SKY FOR A LONG SECOND!... Had to brave the storm and head back to shore. Wait this out, then continue when the bad weather passed... LET'S MAKE IT HAPPEN! If I concentrate, focus my everything, and don't hold back. I WILL MAKE IT HAPPEN! It almost seemed like the wind was pissed because it lost its chance to throw us around like a ragdoll. When the controls began to vibrate in my hand I could remember feeling real fear for the first time. I thought out loud:

ME: HOLD IT TOGETHER TURTLE!! YOU GOT THIS!... DON'T GIVE IN... YOU CAN TAKE IT!!!!

I said it out loud to make myself feel better I guess. I think it worked? It felt like it made a difference at the time, but in retrospect... not really. Remembering the feeling of helplessness as the controls of The C Turtle became useless. The both of us were at the mercy of THE STORM. The motor struggled to keep us moving, and heading to what I hoped at the time was any kind of shoreline. The crazy part of it all, even if I had made it to shore in one piece! Who knows if it wouldn't be crawling with undead, and then I would have been in a whole new shitstorm of... well shit! What a day it had become. Just as I was taking in the situation, looking to find some way back to shore... A FLASH OF BLINDING LIGHT!!!! CRACK!! SMACK!! CRASH!! THUNDER, CRACKLE!! BOOOOMMMMM... BAAAAANNNNNG... BOOOOOOMMMMMMM!!!!!

The Turtle shook like there was an earthquake, but just on The C Turtle itself! Couldn't tell if it was the sound of my mast breaking in half, or just the thunder that blew out my ear drums instead. The lightning that hit the mast cracked it good, and knocked me on my buttocks. Under the pressure of THE STORM the mast just cracked, and crashed down on the deck with force! Not completely in half, but awfully close if you ask me. The top half of the mast was holding on because of the sails' ropes and a 2x4's worth of twisted, splintered wood. You think that talking to myself, and The C Turtle was bad? Well now I was screaming at THE STORM ITSELF!:

> ME: WHAT MOORE DO YOU WANT FROM UUUSSSS!!!! HUH?! COME ON STOOORRRMMM... BRING IIIIIIIIITT!!! BRING IT YOU NAMELESS WUSS OF A SUNSHOWER!!! ONLY STORMS WITH NAMES GET RESPECT!! AND I WILL NEVER NAME YOU AS LONG AS I LIVE!!! YOU WILL NEVER GET THAT RESPECT... SO COME AND GET ME ASSSCLOWNNNN!!!!!

I took a huge breath in, and prepared to curse THE STORM out one last time. I say that because a tsunami like wave that really didn't belong was coming right for me and The Turtle!...

ME: OH YEAH THAT'S WHAT I'M TALKIN' ABOUT, BRING OUT THE BIG GUNS EH?! GOOOOD! 'CAUSE WE CAN TAKE IT YOU...

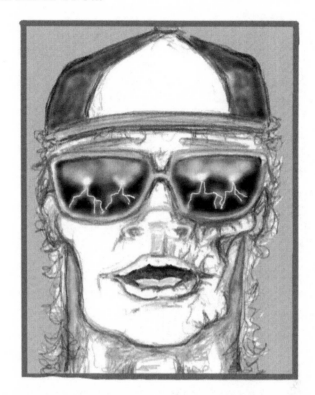

And because I literally asked for it, a huge flash of light and... NOTHING... THAT'S WHAT I SAID NOTHING!!!! I remember nothing after seeing a flash of light so bright it was blinding! Never ask a storm what it's made of. Chances are you will get a swift answer!

STILL ENTRY# DOCE
2nd **Chapter**

REALLY WAKING UP, YES PUN INTENDED!

Well, it's safe to assume the storm answered back! However long I was out, it only felt like a quick nap. The event was like one long confusing set of small dreamlike visions. Let's say, the mini coma was filled with dreams of humans, and a mountain fortress at the end of a long winding road? These dreamlike visions always seemed to be accompanied by an aging, but comforting feminine voice...

> *DREAM VOICE: When the time is right, you will know all you need to. Don't be afraid, and never give up. YOU ARE MORE POWERFUL THAN YOU REALIZE! INSIDE YOUR SOUL IS THE KEY TO HEALING THE WOUNDS OF THE WORLD. THE AWAKENING OF YOU AND YOUR PEOPLE HAS SET OFF A SERIES OF EVENTS THAT WILL UNITE US ALL!!...*

I never had the pleasure of seeing the face behind the voice of inspiration inside my subconscious. A very comforting tone to her words, made it easy for me to remember them, and absorb the hope they were successfully attempting to invoke. The vision of the mountain fortress had more of a feel to it, rather than visual keys. A warm sense of acceptance, with feelings of purpose coupled to the notion that hope was the theme of it all. Music trickled in the background like a psychedelic music video for a movie, or short film of sorts! It repeated a few times, leading up a road. While being filled with excitement and nervous expectations, I recall hearing the voice of the wonderful wise older lady one more time before my coming out of my three weekish coma!

> THE VOICE (opening the pathway to who I was meant to become): Oh, young Zack. It is time for you to see the world in a different light! YOU ARE ENLIGHTENED! And the way you see reality, will forever be changed. Just let it happen. Do not fight it, and everything will play out as it should. This is the first day you are truly AWAKENED!... NOW AWAKE ZACK!... WAKE UP!... AND BRING BALANCE TO OUR WORLD ONCE AGAIN!... Wake up! Wake up! Wake up!

I did just that. I woke the heck up. Straining to open my eyes, I slowly got myself to sit up. Lucky for me, my fully healed body was still in the cab of The C Turtle. Covered in a few of the supplies and equipment that got thrown around the cab during uhhhhhh, wait!... I couldn't remember for the life of me anything about how the Turtle and I made it here. Focused my eyes and noticed the dried blood covered clothes that still happened to be on my person. At the time I couldn't tell how long I had been out of commission inside the Turtle mending my obviously broken body. (I've guesstimated about three weeks or so). I slowly pushed off the cans of beans and other crap that had left imprints in the skin on my arms as they rolled off my rising body parts, since they have been sitting in the same place on me for some time now. Just sitting there, like I was an organic shelf at Z-MART... (Wonder if I will ever see that magnificent place of everything my half human, half undead heart desires again?) I stood up slowly, grabbing the backpack at the same time. Looking to find some clothes that didn't make me look like I ate the living for lunch. It was right then, I realized how far inland the storm had taken us during my little nap. The tsunami like wave, which didn't seem to belong, had taken us miles into the heart of this coastal area. A wall of mud and whatever the water dragged along with it, blocked my view of the land in front of me. Behind me was a cleared path of wrecked forest, and washed out land left over from The Storm with no name.

I packed a small pack with survival essentials like, my gun, knife, dried brain jerky, rope, poncho, lighter, and (Last but not least!) a small tool kit for scavenging. I then forced open the mud blocked door to the cab. Jumping down from the elevated Turtle, safely jammed between the two trees that were cradling her 'til she could be fixed. It was at this very moment I noticed the change in the smell of the air, the sounds that seemed louder than normal. Everything seemed to be heightened for some reason! The elements themselves were visible to me. Each one with its own color, along with a signature, as if everything had a spirit that lived within. The colors of this newly visible world right before my eyes was magnificent. Life was all around me, and I felt it! Like it was flowing through my veins, replacing the very blood that occupied them at one time with life itself! How can this be? Stumped where I stood, only the words of the wise older lady could sooth me. Just let it happen she said, don't fight it, and that is what I did. I shook it off and went about the business of assessing the damage, seeing where I was, and finding people if they existed at all. I took a few steps, and quickly turned around to scope out how much damage had been done to The C Turtle.

She must have gone through hell before being forced to rest between these two well-hidden trees from the looks of her. Hidden from the world by the wall of mud and shit, I scoped out the damage to my vessel. Some major work was needed to make her sea worthy again, but definitely doable despite our circumstances at that moment. If my memory serves me right, and it always does, photographic and all... The world around me looked like it was once above sea level. And now... well it looks like it was once below sea level, and now back to above sea level again. That makes sense, right? The area looked like a recently dried out muddy river bed, almost everywhere you turned. Dried walls of mud, and more mud covering the base of everything in some way shape or form. Debris scattered all along the edge of the tree lines like a wall leading you to the base of what looked like... THAT'S RIGHT! I craped my pants when I realized how close! Not even a mile or two away from the wreck, very faintly, there it was. Showing itself at the bend of the curve near the end of this wall of debris.

It was almost frightening, but it looked just like the beginning of a winding road, like in my dream visions.

My eyesight was keen, and crystal clear! Even though it was far away, I could see just through the brush at the bend in the curve of what had to have been a small highway to the coast. I was feeling super lucky, and defeated all at once! Was this just dumb luck, or were the hands of destiny pulling strings, like some puppet master? Flicking and manipulating the strings to make sure I ended up where the puppeteer intended all along? Paranoia was starting to fill my head with bull-crap notions of things that just couldn't be. I got a hold of myself, and focused on what could be. The air was cold, crisp, and clean. No sounds or smells of any intelligent life, but the evidence of what was once occupied by intelligent life, happened to be just a good football field away. (Could I really be this close to the mountain fortress of my dreams?) My current situation had to be handled first if I was to have any business in exploring the dream like visions I experienced in my deep, deep sleep. First fix The Curious Turtle! It was the least I could do for the vessel that held together, keeping me from the fate of becoming a drowning mess! (For drowning is the worst form of imprisonment for us Zumies. Due to the fact that we need to breathe air, meaning we can still suffocate! Feeling nothing but the pain of needing air, with a serious side of madness, as you drown over, and over again for what could be an eternity.) This gratitude, with a love for my true source of freedom, drove me to take care of the precious vessel. The trees and bushes, along with the wall of mud and debris have my Turtle well hidden. With her fixed, I could explore the mountain and have a getaway Turtle if things got rough. Hmmmmm... Getaway Turtle sounds like a fail, but it seemed like a good idea at the time. Let me tell you... I just told you... that makes no sense... why do humans say stuff like that? Never mind, where was I?... Ohhhh, yeah. I was so sure that humans were in the immediate vicinity, that being able to run had to be a readied option, just to be safe. Think of a plan, then make it happen... like a ninjaaaaa...

I immediately started to gather debris and fallen branches to cover my wounded ship even more than it already was, just for positive reassurance. Some of the pontoons were showing so I covered them with a generous portion of whatever I could scrounge up. Feeling confident, I remembered this wasn't just a place where the undead could be! The very real possibility of human contact was closer to happening than my mind could compute at the time, and it made my adrenaline pump on the mere thought of its possibility. For not too far away was a small mountain town, looking abandoned and ripe for scavenging, which was something I was very good at.

It was in the opposite direction of the other road that seemed to go up towards the mountain. Perfect, this way I could do some reconnaissance, and gather supplies before making the journey up the mountain. Careful, but adventurous was the mindset as I set out for a small group of buildings just above the flood line, less than half a mile from where I happened to be. Looked deserted, and gave me cover to look around without being too vulnerable to an attack from another scavenger, or undead. This little one stoplight town would also give me plenty of opportunity to grab what's needed to repair The C Turtle:

> Some metal panels to weld onto the holes left in the pontoons from THE STORM should do the job, maybe some rivets or bolts if I'm lucky.
> Big frickin' nails, and anything else to mend the mast if I can find it.
> Railings of some kind, to keep me from going overboard. (For the next time the sea wants to bring it.)
> Any ammo or food I can scavenge...

As I got closer to the little cluster of buildings, I could tell that they had been deserted for a long time. The Storm never to be named beat up what was left of the tiny rest stop of a town. Even then, you could still see why this little watering hole might have flourished in its time, before the undead walked the earth in hoards. I cautiously entered the back of the town, making sure that if someone was here, it wasn't me that was gonna be surprised. Taking caution, and traveling with light feet seemed to come effortlessly now, so that's what I did. It was a very small, one pub kind of town. A tad bit on the creepy side if you'd asked me at that time. It didn't take long for me to clear the area and gather that not even one Z-Bot was roaming in its buildings or streets. Totally abandoned... not even a cadaver, or a half-eaten animal in sight.

I slowed my breath, and concentrated with my mind. Attempting to hear any voices or thoughts that could have been within a mile of my position... Nothing but silence of the 3rd kind. Here, let me explain the different kind of silences I have experienced:

> 1st Kind: Uncomfortable silence... when people run out of things to say. This results in a short period of quiet (Even though it feels like a long time!) that feels awkward and weird, until someone says something to break the silence.

2nd Kind: A silence that is deadly... this is for the unsuspecting innocents that looked confused in the silent but deadly moment, right after someone lets out a Zumie fart rumored to have level packed rooms!

3rd Kind: A silence that is defining... finally the silence that is so present and constant, that you start believing there is no sound at all... until the first sound you hear is so loud that it scares the undead right out of you!

Finally, I snapped out of my internal bantering upon seeing some metal shingles from an old storefront. Perfect medium for patching up the pontoons on The C Turtle. Pliable, yet solid enough for the rough waters off the coast. Just one problem! How in the hell was I gonna get the stuff I found back to the ship? Had to figure this out first. Then I could get together the things I need and get The C Turtle back on its feet. My butt sat down in the belly of the old store and ate some cow brain peppered jerky. The last of the best brain jerky that Z-MART had to offer, and man was it hard to come by. Taking a bite of this petrified piece of Zumie heaven calmed me down, and allowed me to think. At first my mind wandered back to the days of rebuilding the valley. The streets were covered in dirt and brush, kind of like this little town. Back then, I was the man! Everyone needed me to help figure out how to bring life to the sleeping giant! Then I proceeded to instruct them in the ways of maintaining the beast once it had been awakened. The important people needing me to show them the way. Now I've taken on the simple notion that somehow, I was supposed to show them the way again. I can remember thinking that maybe this was my purpose. That no matter my gifts, I would be the one who could show my people a better way and without pushing them even further down the rabbit hole than they already were. (Yup I read that madd cat dude's book too!) Fortunately for me there is a point to this thought pattern. I came to realize, I'm still that guy! Just now, I'm instructing myself, and it is all up to me. This is where my photographic memory stuff started to really come in handy! If I can sift through and memorize a library full of instructions, books, and visual media, then scanning through a memory I had just an hour ago, that is 45mn long, should be a piece of cake. See the cool thing about my memories, I can look through them as if I was a third party. Traveling through the memory and seeing details that I may have missed in the moment. This ability is awesome when I need it, and it makes me look really, really, smart while using it. Since clearing all the buildings and the town in general!!! All I needed to do was close my eyes and sort through the memories until I found a solution to the heavy load issue. In that moment, I closed my eyes and began slowly walking through the town one more time. Not even 9mn in and WHAM!!!! There it was! An old boat with holes in it. Tie a rope on the front of the old boat and pull the parts to the other boat with holes in it. Huh... now that just sounds funky, but it happens to be what I said in my head unfortunately! Without haste I rounded up some old lifting straps from what looked like an abandoned moving van... then secured them to the front of the boat... taking those straps and putting my arms through them like they were straps belonging to a trusty backpack... from there I went back to the old store front, and loaded my metal shingles into the holy boat. After scanning the memories some more, there seemed to be some old wooden fences with nails sticking out. Like they would be perfect for attempting to mend the mast of The C Turtle. (That's if they weren't rusted out completely.) Put my arms through the straps which had cleverly turned the holy boat into a would be mud sled. It was then I began to make my way to the wet, bent up fences along the washed-out road. When found, I was shocked at how big these old nails were that stuck out of the wooden fence. THEY WERE GIHUGIC!!! (favorite made up word.) Since the wood was still damp, removing the nails with my trusty knife was easy-peasy. To my surprise, they were not too rusted out, and with a little effort I collected a good number of them. So far so good, got two major components towards being seaworthy again. Still a bit to go, but feeling good about the chase.

While scanning through some more memories, I remembered some security window bars on a few of the small businesses in the town. There should be more than enough to make The C Turtle safer in extreme situations. I felt like a mastermind because I had determined that these could be used as railings on the sides of my vessel to help me when The Storm with no name comes back for vengeance! I will be ready for the damn thing this time! Like before, I focused on the task in front of me, and executed the plan with ease. All that is needed is some tools to finish off the future railings that are protecting the windows and I would be in business. Time to head back to my ship, pick up some more tools, drop off the stuff I have now, and get these sweet ass railings for my boat.

After grabbing a few more things on the way back to the river of mud, I decided to take a different route to get to the Turtle. This way I would be dragging the broken little boat through the woods along the mud bed, instead of through the mud to save time. This would also keep me hidden, not so out in the open, just in case! It didn't take long for my mind to wander. Hunger set in, and I was already dreaming about my soda pop, and a can, or four, of beans to satisfy my Zumie sized appetite. Unfortunately for me before those dreams of beans and soda pop could come true, they were quickly shattered as The C Turtle started to come into sight. The chilling streak of fear traveled down my spine when my mind figured out something wasn't as it had been before! When I left earlier, the Turtle was camouflaged! But now the Turtle was revealed and uncovered! I remember dropping the straps on the ground and using my ninja skills to get closer and find some cover. Hopefully whomever discovered the Turtle is gone, or hasn't seen me yet? It was my only hope! Clinging to this hope I closed my eyes and focused my mind to listen for any thought, or a presence of any kind. Nothing, not one soul, but a couple of undead who hadn't even noticed me. For a second, I was surprised to feel disappointed that there was nobody for me to observe or confront. The timing of it all was impeccable, and it had been hours since I went out for materials to repair the ship. I stood up a bit, aggravated I grabbed the straps of the mud sled. Made my way towards The C Turtle, and then proceed to SHIT MY PANTS!!! (not really, ok!) My Zumie heart stopped as the sound of an engine belonging to a sweet looking pickup truck started and then came to an idol for a minute.

Just long enough for me to hide as it started to creep out from behind some broken trees.

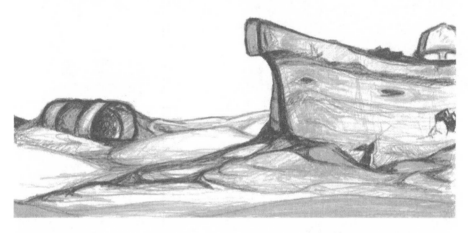

YYYYYYYYEESSSSSSS!!!! My chest filled up with fear, excitement, and a sense of curiosity. Was I really this close to actual survivors of the worst event human kind had been subjected to in this planets lifetime? Stopping for a moment, (that seemed like hours!!) I could see their faces and hear them talking. Not clearly, but the bass and treble of the voices were clear. Only the sisss, tees, and puhs were hard to interpret as they conversed. Armed to the teeth, and ready for any situation is the impression you get when you looked at these battle born examples of humanity. It rattled me to the bone, I wanted to say something but it was just too overwhelming... I would have sounded like an undead just because I was so awestruck. I would shoot me too if I where them... It just wasn't the right time!? The two men were smiling and exchanging puffs from a small pipe that looked like... that's when I saw it... They were smoking greenleaf, out of my pipe, and then I remembered. The greenleaf was mine as well! The humie thieves had more than that, soda pop, cans of food, and my tools. They were gonna take it all!!! THAT'S WHEN I ALMOST LOST IT ALLTOGETHER and without thinking I stood up while saying out loud:

STUPID ME: HEY! THAT'S MY STUFF MANNNNNNNN!!

I quickly got back down, quietly peeking at them through the thick leaves of a fallen tree. I froze like a child whose parent came home early, not knowing their child skipped school. Then the parents began to have sex! What does the child do? Run and risk being seen, or just hide and wait till the event is over? The two men stopped, looked at each other, and dropped my pipe as they went for their guns like it was go time! They got out of the truck while it was still running and began to look for the idiot who yelled out without thinking of the consequences. Boy I'm a dumbass sometimes. This was attention I didn't want to get. What was I gonna do now? While panicking in some thick brush, the humies started to walk in my general direction. Just then I remembered the two undead that were close by, minding their own business so far. If I focused hard enough, the biters would come this way, and they could be a distraction so I could sneak over to the pick up and get something back at least. I had to hurry... every second counted as the two men got closer:

ARMED HUMIE #1: IS ANYONE OUT THERE? COME OUT WITH YOUR HANDS UP AND WE CAN TALK THIS OVER.

ARMED HUMIE #2: If this is your boat, it's damn cool. No worries man we won't hurtcha... too much. Hahahhehheheh!

ARMED HUMIE #1: Stop that ... what if there is someone out there?... Look at all the stuff we found. Has to be someone's ssshhht... did ya here that?... Quiet fool!!!!!

Yup, every second counted. This is when I closed my eyes and concentrated 'til I was certain the undead would come to save my dumb ass. As I instructed my biting distractions to come my way, a crack of a close branch snapped me out of my concentration. HE WAS SO CLOSE I COULD SEE HIS SHOE LACES THROUGH THE BUSHES! I was so done for... UUUUUUHHHHHHH... just then... a sound I never thought I would be glad to hear. My biters were coming, and in the nick of time. Humie #1 was using the barrel of his semiautomatic rifle to look through my bush. Never thought a Z-Bot would save my tale, but that's just what they did!

HUMIE #2: OH YEAH... TIME TO GET OUT MY BOWIE KNIFE!

HUMIE #1: Not too loud dammit!... We don't want to attract any more dead walkers! Lead the mindless bitches away from the truck, and then we can take them out, ok?

HUMIE #2: Ok man, sounds smart, you got it... this way!

They lured the undead heroes away, giving me just enough time to grab some things (lightning quick!) and bolt for cover once again. The two guys high fived as they came out of the woods, and got back in their still running vehicle. Picked up my pipe and began to puff and pass. I was quite jealous, but if I had taken it back, they would know there was more than biters out here. So, my pipe became collateral damage. A small price to pay for staying hidden 'til the time was right. It's all good, my favorite and most used pocket pipe is in my pocket right where it always is. That was my spare stash. Oh well! The two proud men drove away in a cloud of mud and dust, along the road leading right towards the mountain, and then vanished around a bend. I could hear the cool looking pick-up accelerate as it hit the pavement that I now knew lead up to the road of my dreams! Wow! I thought to myself, as the dust settled from the strikingly cool truck that sped away. The very mission I was here for is real! I wished right then that Jake the Pirate could have been there to see it, but I doubt he would have survived the human bad-asses without getting himself shot. A few times even, if I know him. Dammit, they took all my food, water, only one can of Zumie cola remained. Oh, and did I fail to mention that my tools were gone! That's right! The very tools I needed, not only to get the railings, but to fix the Turtle herself! My welding kit, hammer, and saw. All gone. Not even a scrap of stuff left. They got it all. My options went from few, to a tiny window that had to work or else! The town had been picked clean, even before The Storm with no name made its presence known. My only option was to wait for nightfall, and track those two humans back to their sanctuary, cave, fortress, or whatever is their base of operations. I know! This is what I came all the way out here for, but man this was not the plan! Starving to death was not part of the plan! Crash landing the Turtle into a bunch of broken forest trees was not part of the plan! Stalking humans to get back my food, and supplies... NOT PART OF THE FREAKIN' PLAN!!!!!!! Little did I know that this was the decision that would change my world, and how I would see it for the rest of my days! WHOOOOSSSSAAAaaaaa... Consumed by these thoughts, I pulled myself together and let out a big sigh. Looked up at the mountain one more time, and let it sink in. THIS IS WHAT I'M HERE FOR... THIS IS MY FATE... I MUST ACCEPT IT, AND LET IT HAPPEN! Camouflaged The C Turtle one more time, looked at the mountain and said:

> ME: Ok! Show me the way, you big beautiful beast of a mountain, and I will confront the humans tonight! Somehow, someway.

Just then the moon light pierced between the clouds, and there it was! A break in the trees in the distance, resembling the pattern of a road... the road.

The choice was made easy now, and I remember thinking, pack for anything. Because anything will happen, and it will happen tonight. As I was thinking these things a weird sort of calm came over me... like a cool breeze, or a change in temperature. In that moment, I knew everything would work out somehow. Packed light, but smart. Got on my feet and started towards the mountain. The winds of change were blowing, I could feel it... even then!

STILL ENTRY# DOCE...
3rd **Chapter**

"THE MOUNTAIN OF HOPE"

I stayed out of plain sight, which was not hard to accomplish. The debris and plant life left everywhere in ruin, made it surprisingly easy to stay hidden. It looked like a huge filthy pool filter that was stretched out flat for miles. Woven into the tree line where the tsunami like wave had finally lost the steam needed to knock down trees as it rolled over the lands. Tires, broken doors, signs, a vehicle, wood, paper, seaweed, and so on and so forth. Everything that could be carried by the might of the wave was packed into this wall, which seemed to point towards the muddy base of the road that I swear has haunted my dreams for some time now. (Somewhere around three weeks, give or take a few days.) Hard to make it out completely, but there it was! At the end of the stoic wall of garbage and miscellaneous stuff that was left behind by the tsunami like storm I will never name. A real man-made road birthing out of the mud, like the mountain herself was showing me the way. It would be reality in a matter of minutes. I must stay hidden, but man there it was, there it finally was! At that moment, it took everything I had to contain the tornado of butterflies in my stomach and just move, just move forward... Looking back now the mere memory still gives me butterflies as if it were happening all over again! Such an exciting time for me, for everyone involved!

The mountain seemed to be full of life, and green trees covered almost 60% of the massive piece of artwork produced by millions of years' worth of evolution. Absorbing the vision of hope before me, I kept moving forward. Animals like squirrels, all kinds of birds, and the sounds of life filled the air as I got closer to it. The Storm was no match for this magnificent feet of nature, weather, and time. If I were a human survivor, it would be a great place for a new start. Not even The Storm with no name could hurt it. Perfect for starting a new race for humanity to run. Nobody would even know you were there, unless you wanted them to. HUH?... A head start, and a view of all who oppose its position. And yet! Something keeps bugging me. I couldn't feel the minds, or the presence of those two humies, but I could feel the undead? Maybe I can only read the minds of the undead, or half undead? This means that the advantage I thought I had with reading minds was not an advantage with humans at all. When I began accepting this fact, the doubtful reasoning that could kill the courage of even the most courageous hearts started to fill my mind with fear and doubt. Had to pull back on the reigns a bit, and as I hid behind some debris the debate in my head began:

ME: *What if these are not good people? What if they just want to torture me and experiment on what we have become!!!?*

SELF: *PULL IT TOGETHER MANNNNNNNN!!!! WHAT IN THE HELL IS WRONG WITH YOU!!?*

SCARED ME: *I'm not sure. I feel needy and panicky all of a sudden! THIS IS NOT HOW I PICTURED THIS HAPPENNING, OK!*

SELF: *Ok, ok... let us look at this in a fate destiny sort of way. Ok?*

FEELING BETTER ME: *Okaaay?*

SELF: Look! It all started with a dream... right?

CURIOUS ME: Yeah...

SELF: A dream about your purpose... about this very mountain! Then we discovered we had powers. The dreams became a nagging voice in your mind pushing you towards the north... We made A FRICKIN' BOAT!... Then we blindly went north and got caught in a storm... You let me tell the storm off and it knocked your ass out!!!

AGGRAVATED ME: HEY! You were out too!

SELF: No, no, no, no, no... Yoooouuuu were knocked out. I was AWAKE THE WHOLE DAMMN TIME! As I was saying... THE STORM then landed us a couple of miles away from the very spot we are hiding in. Last, but not least! We have a wall of trash showing us were the road starts and you still have doubt!?

CONVINCED ME: OK, OK, OK, ok... I get it, really... This is where everything we have done over the last 8 weeks has led us to. It is meant to be, even if it means my end...

SELF: Nobody said anything about dying... stay alive fool... damn!... I'll be watching.

While rounding the final corner before getting to base of the mountain road, I came upon a pleasantly chilling realization. This was no coincidence! That was the moment I accepted my fate, and began to believe. Someone, or something was leading me to this place. Just because I felt this way, it was not gonna change how carefully I would approach the humans. But, my confidence was right where I needed it to be. My goals were clear, and my mind was sharp. Seemingly ready for whatever it needed to adapt to, however difficult the challenge may be. Not every human is gonna be thrilled to see the likes of me, and I don't blame them. I'm a threat, and this means having to show them I can be useful. That my presence would be an asset, and really, that's what I want to be to them anyway. Hopefully I am the man deep inside, I believe to be.

My eyes had finally adjusted to the moonlit night, and I began the journey up the mountain road. Staying in the tree lines so no one could spot me, but keeping the road in sight so I could stay on point. The wolves, owls, and night creatures all sounded off, to let the day dwellers know to stay indoors. For the night is theirs, and the hunt was on. Loved the way I felt, it never scared me, the night, always thought of it as an old friend. There, by my side, when I walked the streets of my little world back home. In this moment, that same familiar feeling seemed to guide me while making my way alongside the two-lane road. A welcome companion on the journey up a mountain that had filled me with hope and expectations I desperately needed to be real. Despite my abstract thinking, I was gaining a significant amount of ground! To my surprise, before I had noticed how far it was, miles had been covered while stuck in my head, reminiscing about the world I had left for this one. The sound of a wolf calling out to a full moon, illuminating the forest that blanketed the mountain's base, drew my focus back to the now. The wild sounds that filled the night air with character was loud and clear. Yet, a familiar sound began to overshadow the sounds of the forest, because it was in my mind. Stopping me in my tracks, and diverting my attention momentarily, because it was so loud. I had made some good ground, but I just couldn't ignore their call. It was that dreaded sound of my past horrors, the severe and painful hunger. I closed my eyes and focused the mental radar that had been newly acquired... There they were!... A mile or two out of the way... A HUGANTIC herd. Deep beyond the trees of the mountain forest, but for me it sounded close enough to touch. Had to check it out, something began to pull me towards them like a hunger for knowledge that rivaled the hunger for you know what. It became a 10mn jog out of the way, no sweat, but WOW! As I got closer the voices of the massive heard of lost souls just waiting to be awakened began to grow louder.

The herd was completely hidden from the rest of the mountain by rock and caves carved out of its side! I could tell, as I quietly crept closer in order not to awaken them, that it was an old silver mine. You're wondering how I could tell? It said so on the rusted-out sign condemning the mine in 1969! Abandoned long before the events of the apocalypse, these undead had to have been brought here after said apocalypse to stay! But by whom? I mean if somebody were to stumble on this sleeping giant, well!! It became clear why I needed to see this. Like, I might have been sent here (in the nick of time!) to save the humans from this disaster just waiting to be unleashed. It is only a matter of time before someone stumbles on this holding cell for the undead. An amount of undead, that thrusted a wave of chicken bumps up my spine! In fact!! To this day, whenever I recall the event it still gives me chills. It was that massive of a herd!

Even a large densely populated city would struggle not to succumb to this angry tortured hoard of undead biters. From this distance, hidden behind a very large, old tree, I could hear them clearly in my mind. Unfortunately, I figured they were too far away to influence in any way. My plan was to quietly sneak away and warn whomever I find on this mountain. That was, until the unexpected rocked me to the core! The herd went silent! Silent! In that moment, my eyes could not believe what I was seeing. The entire herd began turning their heads in one specific direction. My direction!

I remember wondering, can they feel me? Did I do this?! Was it me? The event was simply mind-blowing, and I still couldn't grasp the severity of the moment. The silence and stillness of the herd was bone chilling! Just knowing they couldn't physically see me was warping my mind, at best maybe my scent was strong! BUT STILL! They kept looking, never uttering a sound, not even in their minds! I froze, and stopped breathing all together. I have never been so confused, and scared to this degree in my entire short existence. The concept of a herd working in unison?! Unheard of 'til this very moment, and I have observed the undead in great depth. Every sound was crucial, and because the heard was so still, if I were to so much as moved a millimeter they would have found me. The air flowing through the trees and crashing against the rocks was almost as loud as the ocean, it was so quiet. Small animals oblivious to the unstoppable threat just lying in wait, as if the undead were awaiting a sign from their GOD! All I could do was wait, wait patiently for the chance to leave without a trace. No way was my presence going to be the reason for the mayhem that this new kind of undead would bring upon the human's heads. For this new unusually frightening kind of flesh-eater would definitely be the one factor that could really turn any kind of fight for survival against the undead into a bloody massacre. It was intoxicating and dangerous at the same time. Never had I felt so alive and affected by the adrenaline that came with the fear that seemed to turn into strength. I knew what had to be done, even though it was all happening so quickly. When I look back, it was the first time I had ever really felt this way. I snapped out of it as the 10 thousand plus undead began to go back to their original state. It took a good amount of long minutes for me to feel it was safe to attempt fleeing! Then, another stretch of moving extra carefully slow, in order for me to place every step! Not a stick to step on, nor a branch to brush against. Silence was my ally, as I hid, and moved to another close place of complete cover. Not one would know I was ever there, I made sure of it. Finally, my ninja ass made it back to the edge of the rock face beyond the vision of the biters'. NOW! I will huff it running with haste back to the road that leads to what could be all that is left of humankind! Smack dab into the base or whatever it is waiting for me up the mountain... I remember the anger, and the inevitable unknown that I now had to face faster than planned, pushing me to run, and man did I run! The woods I had already traveled through were etched into my memory. Once again having a photographic memory saved the day, or at least it felt that way at the time. I knew where every branch and tree were, even in this night sky which created a maze of endless shadows! Not a detail wasn't used to my advantage as my ninja like reflexes, with the aid of my memories, guided me like I was a ghost in the wind. It was no time at all before I was back to the road. I looked back at the path of impending doom, knowing it was only a matter of time before this new kind of threat became real enough to pose a challenge to the humans' very existence on this mountain. The responsibility of having this information did make it hard to ignore the haunting fact, that I was about to gamble with my life in an attempt to save theirs. I knew in my bones, the human condition was close. Just how close kept me hungry, and I pushed on, followed by a pace that was now quickened with a new purpose. A true mission of actual importance to the survival of a people. I was up for the challenge, or at least I thought so. It wasn't long before signs of humanity started to fill the air. Things human beings always had difficulty keeping hidden, because it was familiar, and comforting in some secure way. I smelled them cooking and making coffee, and it smelled like home, like us... the Zumies... smells of garbage and the buzzing of activity close by. Just like Zumie Valley, wow it filled me with hope. They had to be close, very close indeed. My senses were tuned into the radiation of the lives that every cell in my being could feel. Inside me fireworks were exploding with excitement and fear. To my amazement there it was!... Just like my dreams!... Gates of epic proportions!... Just built right into the side of a mountain rock face. As if to say! WE ARE HERE... BUT WE WONT TAKE SHIT FROM ANYONE!!!... If anything, I was in shock, and impressed all at the same time.

This impressive, massive, strong, and intimidating gate did not disappoint my sense of dreamscape in any way.

It was even more than I fathomed. If I'm careful, maybe some observation could yield some way to sneak in. Giving me an opportunity to leave a note telling them about the time bomb in the abandoned mines about 3 or 4 miles from these very gates. (This was what filled my mind at the time of this debate, on a strategy to stay alive, while still warning these people about the impending danger that lurked around the bend... LITERALLY!) Could it be possible that they would want to communicate with me? Feels so stupid and risky. I mean in their eyes I would be the very thing that got them here in the first place. A reminder of a lost world of sorts... The very representation of the monsters that wrecked the world they remember from years past. Except now I'm alive! A new soul in place of the original like a body snatcher, Mannnnnnn. Even writing this now makes me feel guilty about the soul that was originally meant for this handsome mug. It's not really mine, so I promise to make the best of this life. To honor, whomever was in here first. If only the humies inside these gates could see the truth in my memories, in my mind. Only then would they see the world I come from, and have no doubt about the intentions of my presence here. (Maybe I could have gotten my soda pop back... Naw, I would have enjoyed myself consuming the fizzy goodness if I were them... 4sure.) The history of the NEWGEN plant, and the emergence of my people. Maybe then it would be easy to accept my kind. Being a handsome Zumie, but scary to a humie, doesn't help me in this situation at all. The spinning in my mind stopped, and I forgot everything. The world came to a halt, because I was about to hear her voice... THE MOST AMAZING VOICE, OR SOUND THAT EVER WAS CREATED!!! It was the first time I heard it, and man it was life altering!

THE VOICE!!: Don't worry stupid head, we are not all afraid of you! You are welcomed by me if you pass a test. That means it's me you should be afraid of. Ha! Just Playin'!

This sent chills down my spine! I paused and didn't hear a thing for what felt like an hour, but wasn't even 2 seconds... and then it happened:

HER VOICE AGAIN: Wow! I can hear your thoughts Zack, you've figured that out by now I hope? I mean, not at the moment! Since you are quiet as a church mouse. (A FEW LONG SECONDS GO BY!)

THE VOICE: OK! Not talking I see. Well, let me tell you about myself. I am part of a small group of children born after the apocalypse. We were given the merciful gift of speaking without words, by evolution herself. In a world where a single word could attract a herd of soulless biters. It has made us very useful, and helped me and the others find purpose in this world of death. Some call us blessed, others say it's a curse. What say you, Mr. Zee?

I paused but was compelled to answer. See your thoughts can betray you, so I took a deep breath, and let it fly...

HOPEFUL ME: Well... I think it is both.

HER SOFT VOICE: Really! And how do you figure that, Zacky?

ME (taking a risk): See... when you communicate in this way... Hey how do you know my name?... Duh... anyway, as I was saying! There are no secrets, nothing to be surprised about on a later date. No mystery to discover about the person you are connected to, in his or her mind. Hearing the good, the bad, the embarrassing thoughts that you would never say out loud. And how someone really feels about you on a first impression can really leave a long lasting scar on the one who hears it all. This is a very good way to keep you from the evil lies people can tell, however, it also subjects you to the ugly side of the truth. And it hurts hearing the truth sometimes. Even though you put an endless amount of voices in the back ground, sometimes you still get lost. Lost in the drama of the mind pouring out thoughts, like a used bucket of soapy water you toss into the street. You are alone by the time you figure out how to use your gift properly. I'm almost there?...

HER VOICE: Very good! I must say, you pass with flying colors... HMM. Zack Zee, what a name... you will find out mine later.

CONFUSED ME: What does that...

HER VOICE: I am obligated to go now! I will find you in the woods in one hour. Don't be late... Just kidding, I will find you whether you like it or not, K? Naturally, since I can her your every thought. You are so loud to me! See you soon Zacky...

ME (in a panic): Wait! What's your name... you didn't think it!... Come on, you know minnnnnne!

HER VOICE: It's Kami! K... A... M... I... with a K... k!... k. For your journals, if I make it into them that is.

Wow!... Who?... Who... Mannnnnnn... I was electrified! Overwhelmed with nervousness. I wanted to burst, but wouldn't dare for fear that someone would hear me, and regardless of my test results, blow my head clean off!!! If the wrong kind of humie saw me, it would be over Mannnnnnn, over for sure. OH shit! I was hoping that Kami with a K wasn't still hearing me... knowing my luck she was laughing right at that moment somewhere inside the fortress. I can still remember geeking out like a young man who just discovered girls. I couldn't contain how she already had me wrapped up in her little web. HER VOICE was like music, and man I couldn't wait for the debut album. Just then the gate began to open, like the slow moving giant that it was. The sounds of the generators turning on, and the gears begging to sound off as they clacked together. This got me thinking about one obvious fact that had hit me when light began to pierce from the opening in the giant gate. Kami with a K was not wanting to announce my presence to the rest of the group. Run came to mind... so I turned around real slow like, and ran like a ninja in a race to the sword rack. Like there was a pack of WereZumies chomping at my heels... I thought to myself in a panic... WAIT! STOP! Not too far... the biggest, most important moment of my life was about to happen, in ONE hour's time! NO problemo! Just one, long ass, forever driving me crazy with anticipation 'til I want to shiv myself in the forehead, HOUR!!

The anxiety of waiting to meet the person behind this voice from the heavens was driving me to a frantic, pacing back and forth kind of guy. Right before my 57th pass by the broken trail, I remember hearing a SNAP!!! AAAWWWWW SON OF A Bit!... #%$@#!... CRAP I STEPPED IN A MOTHER F!@$#$$%N BEAR TRAP!! Really, a bear trap of all dag-gummite things to step in, and what timing to boot!

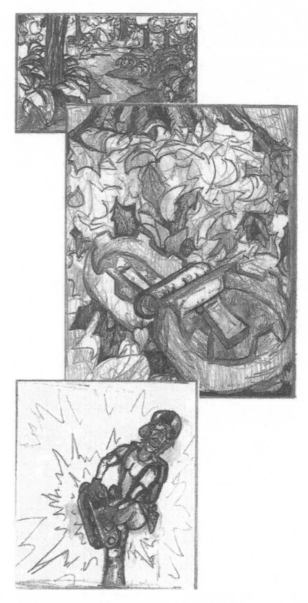

The panic driven thoughts started rolling in like a fog at the beginning of a damp, cold morning on the coast:

ME (freakin' out): AAAHHHHH COMON MAAANNNNN... My frickin' leg!!!! OK, let's breathe and... AAOOOUUUCH! Never mind, who am I kidding *this hurts like a !#@$#%... How could I let this happen? How could I be so stupid?? To top it off there is no telling how she will be able to find me. What if I missed her already?*

ME (talking to myself in an unhealthy way): Please stop this whiny display of self-doubt... Either she is gonna be cool. OOOOR... She will bring guys with guns and blow your head off... Simple, right? Riiiiiiiight.

KAMI WITH A K: Stop complaining silly butt!!! I can hear you crying from miles away... I will be there soon, just relax and tell me what happened.

ME: Like a dummy, I stepped into an undead trap. It got me pretty good!

I remember this conversation like it just happened. Every word, every tone...

KAMI WITH A K: Oh Dammn, ouch! That must hurt in more ways than you probably want to explain.

HUMBLED ME: Yes, it does! Yes... it does.

I remember thinking to myself freely, as if she couldn't hear me. Slowly she came down the small broken path and the moonlight cast her in a wonderful light. I was surprised in a new sort of way. My eyes could see a feisty, yet strangely attractive figure, behind the intoxicating voice.

I expected horror in her eyes when she finally saw me, and wondered if she would change her mind, and run. But to my surprise she had a concerned smile on her very pretty face. Mannnnnnn!... She was sexy and cuuuute!... Maybe 19 or 20 years old. She wasted no time in releasing me from my dilemma, trusting me totally. I recall thinking this is sooooo cooooool! Then she politely interrupted my thoughts by reminding me of a well-known fact by now, that I had so haphazardly forgotten:

KAMI WITH A K: You do remember that I can hear your thoughts, right? Hello?

I obviously had a moment of DUUUUHHHHH!!!!!

ME: OH CRAP! I forgot Kami, sorry I didn't mean to put you on the spot like that. Still getting used to someone hearing my thoughts. I've only ever heard thoughts of others. For me it is a rare event that someone can read me as well. It's going to take some getting used to.

KAMI: It's ok Zacky. I understand I am quite the hottie, but less thought on how I look would be appreciated in the future. If you can help yourself... that is?

ME: Well, it's not my fault you look like you!!!! Nice to finally meet the person behind the voice by the way.

KAMI WITH A K (playing hard to get in an unbearably attractive way): Yeah, I guess! Besides Zacky Zee, you're not as hideous as you think you are.

ME (hanging my head low): But I'm a... well... I'm half...

KAMI (feeling sympathetic): It doesn't matter what half you once were. What matters is the half that is in control, and that half seems more like just a whole person to me. I'm sure once my people meet you, they will feel the same. They too will be interested in this whole person, and not the half that you once were... K?

ME: I really appreciate you getting me out of that trap. I just wasn't in my right state of mind. Freaking out is not usually my first response, it's just that I...

KAMI: I know half undead-half human, not quite Z-Bot, not quite Humie... Ahaaaah! Zumies that's what you call your people. They don't even know you left... risky Zacky Zee. I'm impressed that you trekked all this way to make allies with us. Really impressed!

ME (feeling a little violated): How much can you see? Is anything sacred, miss rude ass?

Just then the sound of a branch breaking drew my attention away to the west of our position. Not thinking, I put my hand up at a right angle, and closed my fist. Kami snickered, and again I was painfully reminded, that she was already in my head. So, I thought to her instead of speaking out loud.

ME (finally getting it): I heard something in the distance, we should get going. I think the road is this way, or is it that way?

KAMI: Don't worry, just follow your photographic memory back to the road. I've looked, you know the way. I will follow you, ok! My memory is not as good as yours, plus my night vision sucks.

ME (in a stern voice): Ok! You got it, Kami. That, I can do. I'm not helpless, I just lost myself for a minute or two-enty. I've got this, follow me... this way!

As we made our way back to the road, our conversation continued. I just couldn't help myself. She was just, well, she was infectious, and for me there would be no cure.

KAMI: So... You gonna ask me to help you fix your boat? Let me seeeeeeee... mmmmmm... THE CURIOUS TURTLE.... SO lame!... Yet cool at the same time! Just like you Zacky! The C Turtle for short... huh!

ME: Mannnnnnn!!!!! I don't know if I can handle being one step behind every time. You might wanna take me out on a date first, before raping my brain any more than you already have! You rapist!!

KAMI: You're such a baby, stop crying and listen, ok?...

ME (with a grunt): Ok fine...

KAMI: Just get us to the road and I will take it from there!... Mister, I can't help myself around an attractive woman...

ME: AAAAAAAgain!... Not my fault you look like you and talk like YOU... all the time YOUR FAULT! All the TIME!

KAMI (with a look of satisfaction on her face): I know foolio, just come on. The road is just ahead, I can see it from here now.

We found the road, and Kami looked around to see if the coast was clear. I closed my eyes and listened for biters... it was clear. Kami also scanned the area for biters, she heard nothing either. The sky was still, quiet for a change, and the moon was very bright. There was about 5 more hours 'til morning and I was encroaching upon impatient. My mind was racing, it seemed doubt was creeping in once again. Kami wasn't saying anything, but I'm sure she heard it. Then she turned around abruptly, and put her hand on my chest. The air stood still as she looked into my eyes and said:

KAMI: Why are you freaking out, Zack? I won't let anything happen without warning you. I'm taking you to an emergency storage shed with supplies and things to help fix the C Turtle. This way you can leave if things gets heated with my people, which I doubt very much!

ME (with a sigh): OK, that sounds great. This way I can relax, fix the boat, and get my mind in the right place... don't worry, I will be just fine.

KAMI: You don't have to worry. We won't encounter any of my people out this late, and this far down the mountain. By the time we get the supplies we need and fix your beloved C Turtle, you can decide whether or not you still want to be introduced to my clan, my people.

ME: Oh, that's right you can hear even my deepest fears too, huh?... I'm a little worried about how everyone will react to me! If you looked like me! You might understand what I'm feeling, and why it's hard to trust. What it really boils down to, is that I am worried about being able to manage all the feelings, thoughts, and fears of those who see me. It's not easy to absorb for me!

KAMI (making sense of it all): It's all right, Zacky... I understand   better   than   you think... LOOOK!... Understand this Zack... YOU CANNOT MAKE EVERYONE HAPPY ALL THE TIME,... but if you are honest and sincere. I know they will eventually like you, or just tolerate you so I don't hypnotize them, and make them jump in the mud with our farm full of sweet, sweet swine...

ME: And if they hate me... a bullet to the head won't hurt too bad, RIGHT!... Ppsssmmmmhahhahhahah!!!!

KAMI: Or maybe a hand shake and a machete to the skull... Hahahhdhahhahshshsajissaiitttahahh

We laughed out loud, and took a second or two to catch our breath...

ME: If it's a disaster, a shotgun to the face has always been a reoccurring dream for me anyway!... WIN-WIN Mannnnnnn!

Kami looked at me with no expression, and then... (UNCONTROLABLE LAUGHTER!)... PPPSSSHAHAHAHAH OHH HAHAHAH WHOOO OOHA AHAHA HAHA A HAH SSSS-S-S-SS HAHAHAH! We lost it altogether, and had to stop walking so we wouldn't walk into a tree or something.

KAMI (with tears in her eyes): OK, OK! Zack, you win for now... I won't talk about the intro mission until you're in your right mind, ok? Remember, I know what your mission is so don't think your gettin' out of it without a fight from me, ok?...

ME: I won't, Kami. I would be disappointed if you didn't fight.

KAMI: All right, let's go get you some tools-n-stuff, and get that Turtle fixed. No strings attached, I promise...

ME: THE MOUNTAIN OF HOPE? That is what your home is called? Very clever, and yet simple.

KAMI: Yeah! Because that's what it took for us to get where we are now, a mountain of hope! If all goes well, we plan to hang around for as long as the mountain lets us. I know it happens to be a little corny... THE MOUNTAIN OF HOPE... but to us "Humies", she will forever be...

ME: Uhh... yeah, that's what we Zumies like to call you guys. Sorry, hope it's not offensive. The Zumies are really laid back and casual, most of us.

KAMI: Noo worries Zack. I'm sure I'll get over it somehow. Now lets' get moving, we've wasted enough time chatting it up. There is a three hour window in between the patrol that comes by here to make sure it stays hidden. If we hurry and get to the hidden cache of supplies unnoticed, you can load up what you need!... HIDDEN! HA!

Kami had a smug, confident smile about her, as she described the audacity of her peers in trying to hide things from her at all. No secrets, no surprises for the mentally gifted in this new reckless world.

ME (hanging on every little detail of this young woman's existence): Do you ever wish that you couldn't read minds anymore? Even for just a day?

KAMI (pausing, because the answer didn't come easy): I've thought about it many times over. And you know it is utterly amazing, but every time I have convinced myself that I would want to give up my powers, some event, or a life that would have been lost otherwise shows me the way once again!

She really came through for me, everything she said she would do, she did. We walked along a patchy path, and then came out to a hill on the side of the mountain. Before I knew it, there it was. Plain as day, even though it was night. A door forced into the side of the hill, hidden amongst the rocks. She stood in front of the door and began slowly tapping the wall a few times to start the sequence on what seemed to be a trick lock... "TAP... TAP, TAP... TAP, TAP, TAP"! She then used her index finger to push one of the small pieces of wood; it moved with ease. Sticking out of the door just waiting to be manipulated, it then, with a click and a tug became the handle of the door itself. Clever if you ask me. The door opened with a firm two handed pull, shaking off some dust and moaning like it wanted to tell on us.

It didn't seem so vast, but it was after all an underground bunker. Kami picked up some dirt and threw some on the top of the door, making it appear as if no one had opened it at all. Then she slowly closed it, and lit a candle waiting on a strategically placed ledge as if she has done this before.

ME (looking confused, again): But don't we have to get back out, Kam?

KAMI (smiling as she thought to me): Silly Zacky... Of course there is an alternate exit, it happens to let you out not far from the little town at the bottom of our mountain. No worries, this isn't my first time borrowing from bunker #3!

I walked down a steep set of stairs, as spider webs made themselves known by sticking to me like I was a web-magnet. My eyes were focused on Kami walking down the stairs like a post-apocalyptic badass, as I followed her like a love-sick puppy. It took me a moment, and a look of pathetic nature from Kami before I realized we were in an apocalyptic utopia! An underground buffet of dry goods and tools. Water bottles, liquor, soda pop, and supplies enough to feed an army, or start over if they get overrun... again, very clever. Even a small torch to weld the patches of metal shingles onto the pontoons of the Turtle were available at bunker #3!

ME: I wish we had a cart or something! This place reminds me of my wonderful "Z-MART" store in our valley!

KAMI: OH MY LORD!... I can see it in your mind, its HUENORMOUS! You guys are even worse than us when it comes to hoarding goods, aren't you!

ME: I cannot deny the truth woman... YES... YES, WE ARE WORSE THAN HUMANS WHEN IT COMES TO THIS CRAP!

KAMI: HA AHAHAHAHHA KKKKSSSSAAAHAHAH OOOOOHHH MY GOOODNESSS!!!!! If this all works out, YOU must take me there someday, K?

ME: You got it Kam... No worries at all.

KAMI: Cool, 'cause your valley seems amazing in your memories... would love to visit someday.

ME: Yes, we are not perfect in any way, but we sure know how to make the best of any situation. Even if they aren't the sharpest knives in the drawer, they always seem to get things done, and I love them for it. Despite our obvious faults, we get along, have purpose, and live every day to its fullest. This way we won't take this second chance at life for granted.

KAMI: Sounds like my people, if I think about it. We are very similar in our goals of life and living Zack... Maybe meeting my clan won't be so bad after all... I know, I know I said I wouldn't say anything... but you know I'm right...

ME (with a, I know your right but I am not ready to admit it tone in my voice): Ok... OK already! I get it... I'm stressing for no reason. I get it Kami... really!

KAMI: Well, ok Zack... I found another knapsack. I can carry your torch and some more food to replace what the Raiders took from your ship.

ME: OH yeah. By the way?... Why can't I hear the minds of the other humans?

KAMI: Oh, that's right you came up on a couple of Raiders... They scavenge, take big risks to get medicine and rare items that are hard to come by. Not to mention protect the Mountain to their last breath. They are cool, and their helmets are made from a special alloy. With lead as its primary element for the Kevlar metal compound that binds the metals. It also blocks gifted ones like me from seeing what they have seen in their very "things you can't unsee" life moments. All of this for reasons you can see if you look into my mind. I'm one of the gifted who requested it. Due to the fact, that sometimes you can't handle what someone else has seen. So, these helmets are good for a lot of different reasons.

She wasn't kidding either, I dared to see what it took for some of the Raiders to survive their duties to the mountain. The deaths of countless comrades... Having to kill friends who had been infected. The cowardly things humans had done to each other thinking that it was the only way to survive. I disconnected from the read and had to breathe:

ME: Wow... I get it now... Are you ok, holding on to these memories?

KAMI: Sometimes I must ignore the nightmares when the helmets are off. It's difficult, but I get through those rough nights.

KAMI: Well enough about that, we must get moving before daylight catches up to us, and makes us very visible.

ME: You got it Kami, let's move out!

KAMI: Cool with me Zacky Zee, let's move...

After loading up Kam's backpack, we headed down the mountain with vigilance. The mud bed was upon us so fast, the bunker was so close the whole time! We were so close to the C Turtle, I could swear it was only a mile or two from the boat itself.

> KAMI: So, what do you think of the wall of debris the flooding left behind?

> ME: It looks like an advertising history of mankind, and the old world.

> KAMI: I know, right! The way it used to be. I've been told many things, but venturing out on my own has taught me sooooo much more!

We were rudely interrupted by the discovery of the Turtle which we came up on rather quick. Not that time was my concern, but when I'm with Kami, it just flies by... She was impressed with The C Turtle and how it was designed. Being the quality soul that she was, she put on some gloves and assisted with fixing the Turtle. All this while talking about nothing, and everything at the same time. Her voice was simply music to my ears, and I hung on every chord.

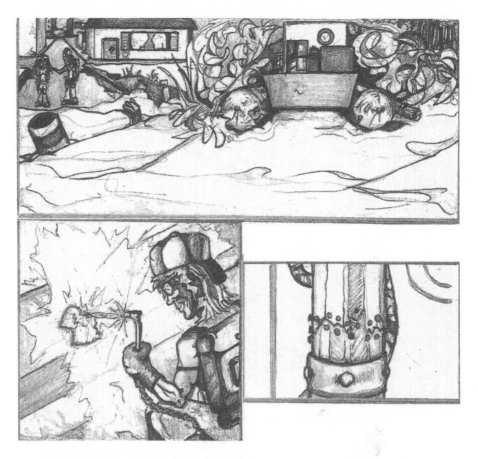

KAMI: So, how does it feel being the so called bridge between our two worlds?

Since I wasn't ready just yet to answer her question... I pulled the classy move of comedy and diversion...

ME: OH Kami... I'm livin' the dream ova here! Can't you tell... speaking of how does it feel... How did a 19/20 year old young woman become so intelligent and resourceful? You answer that, and I will answer your question seriously this time!!!

KAMI (with a grin on her pretty lips): Well... since your wussing out on my question, and because you asked sooooo nicely... I will elaborate on that notion. Oh, and by the way, I'm 22!

ME: Ok smart guy... I mean girl?...

Kami put her head down, and picked up a small stick on the ground... I could hear her contemplating if she should tell me in her thoughts... She started doodling in the dirt below her and began to say...

KAMI'S STORY (word for word): So... Some of us born post apocalypse have been gifted with talents... as I explained a little earlier. Like great strength, or speed for some, others were given great mental skills as well. Invention, and ingenuity, even medical smarts have been found beyond measure. The amazing thing, is that these people are barely teenagers. Performing surgery and helping the community in more than average ways. For me it has always been the ability to pick through people's minds, as if it was an open book or magazine. Like you said, a gift and curse all in one. In short, I'm older than I seem. Not because I was forced, or it was what I wanted, but 'cause it's just what was necessary to cope with the images that haunt my dreams. While my eyes were wide open...

ME (with awe in my eyes): Wow!!! That's impressive, all of it...

KAMI: I KNOW!

KAMI: The other kids with gifts like mine... they can read thoughts well enough to aid the Raiders and hear what you're thinking. But none of them can feel the pain, and the reality of the memories. The visuals that are hidden in the deeper parts of the mind, where only I seem to be able to go.

ME: Wow being around people must have been seriously intense at times...

KAMI (sighing as she got ready to speak): That's mainly why I spent so much time outside of the walls of the fortress. The time alone felt like heaven compared to all the voices inside of the mountain. It's not that I couldn't block them out, it's just that, well it's relaxing not having to do it all the time. Feeling weightless is what I could compare it to, if that makes sense at all...

ME: It wasn't like that for me... It happened really slowly, and I had to really practice to accomplish small feats... until recently... THE STORM... the lightning!

KAMI: WHOA... I CAN SEE THE STORM AND YOU CURSING ITS VERY EXISTANCE... Brave, but dumb as rocks... OHHH MY LOR...

ME: I know I was knocked out for a while...

KAMI (with awe in here tone): Uh, yeah! Like three weeks you were out! That's how long ago, THE STORM, as you say happened... over three weeks ago, Zacky.

ME: Wow, no wonder... All that sleep must have super charged my batteries...

KAMI: That's right, your kind doesn't need much sleep. So, you being out that long must have boosted your gifts.

ME: You think I might be as good as you are some day?

KAMI: NOPE...

ME: You know you are so confident... do the undead even scare you at all?... Or can you suggest things for them to do besides eat people?

Soon as I said it, she looked at me with a stare that just... well it exited me. Those eyes have a captivating quality that cut right into me:

KAMI: You already know the answer to this 'riddle', but ok, you not so smart, ass.

I loved every ounce of her 'tude......

KAMI: I can't control them like you will be able to someday, but I can hear them like you can. Their tormented minds are very loud, and sad. Effective warning system included in this package baby!!! Keeps me out of reach, if you know what I mean...

ME: I do! Miss package!

KAMI: They really suffer, you know. All the undead sound the same... hunger, pain, and sadness. You know... I kind of feel sorry for them. Tormented souls looking for something they will never find, unless we give it to them... Peace... That is what you call it, or is it the really real death?

As she said these things to me, a warm new feeling came over me. This is when I realized, that I have found a friend. Not the, I see you at the store every time I shop friend... but the real thing. A person who gets me, and gets what I'm going through. Because in her own way... she is going through changes like me. It all makes sense! Like me, she has had to hide herself, but with me she doesn't have to. Never would I have fathomed, that meeting a person could feel this way. She is... well, exactly what I hoped for and more. Forgetting, once again... about the telepathy thing... Dammit man...

> KAMI: Don't get so sappy Zacky boy! We just met, and I'm not that easy silly butt!

She shook her head and smiled with a look that confirmed my suspicions... She thought I was cool, and she felt it, too...

> ME (with a gulp): Uh... right... my bad! Keep forgetting about that part of the mind reading thing again. Not that I'm great at hiding things anyway, but I will try to control myself... or not... it depends.

> KAMI: Not to change the subject, but I'm gonna. You need to know that there is some real power inside of you. I've seen it, and it is real and present. I know you feel it, there is no way you don't Zack, no way!

> ME: Guess it's obvious that I really haven't owned that yet. The pressure is mounting, but I have no real clue on how to control it. So, the fear of hurting someone, or myself has held me back. To be honest... I've felt it since waking up after the storm.

> KAMI: That's why you have this big question mark in your brain. Makes sense now!

I paused for a hot second, and asked her to reach deep into my mind to see what caused this jolt of power in my being. Maybe she could see what happened when I was knocked out from the storm. She wasted no time in telling me:

> KAMI: I wish that it was possible Zacky, but you were passed out. All I can see is darkness. You must have

gotten a huge jolt of electricity from the lightning strike that knocked you out. The ship probably insolated it from frying your circuits completely, but you were still affected somehow. It amplified you in a positive way. You got a power boost my friend, use it wisely Zacky Zee.

ME (with doubt in my voice): YEAH... A regular super hero of sorts, I'm sure?

KAMI (with conviction, and well, she was a little pissed at me): LISTEN!!! Your mind is so powerful. That from the moment you woke up, I felt your presence! You are super gifted, and not exploring the boundaries of that power would be a mistake. What if your power could have saved someone who was hurt, if you just took the time to test yourself? Wouldn't you feel like an ass?! The regret would destroy you, or even worse. Turn you towards the evil side of power... If you do not choose, the choice will be made for you. Pushing the limits of who you think you are, and accepting who you could become. It is the only way you can have the power, and not lose yourself within it. You should be able to move objects with your mind, maybe even manipulate the thoughts of the weak minded, once you own the power inside of you...

ME: BUT...

KAMI (more calm now, same amount of conviction): LOOK! It all depends on how brave you really are. If you don't learn how to control it, you will do more harm than good. I know you desire to make amends for when you were all the way undead. Remember! You gave me permission to look deep, so I know how you really feel Zacky. This is your purpose, just let it soak in.

ME: Yeah... you're right. I want to do good things, I want to protect my people, I want make up for the awful things I was a part of when... well when I was sad and hopeless... what if I mess it up though?... What if I just make things worse?

I paused and thought without being able to control it:

ME: What if someone forces me to use it for bad? I'm not sure if I can control what I might become, and this alone has scared me away from letting the power come alive.

KAMI (trying not to laugh at me, and doing a bad job at it): FORCE YOU?? HA! HA!

KAMI (realizing she needed to reign me in): You will be able to yield a power that could change the world forever! They? Whoever they may be, will fear you first, and then try to destroy your power. Once they realize that they can't destroy you, you will be forced to decide.

ME: Decide what Kami?... What?

KAMI: Whether to rule them, or protect them with your life. Either way, they will never be able to make you do anything that is not your choice, PERIOD! That's why power is so volatile! It will either save the world while watching it flourish, or enslave it indefinitely while witnessing its demise!

ME: How can you be so sure Kam? How?

KAMI: 'Cause... that is what they did to me once my gifts were found out. I figured it would be the same for you.

I couldn't help but feel her pain... It poured out of her like a fresh wound! Every ounce of me wanted to fix it.

ME: I'm sorry they treated you that way! I will remember your words, and if it is up to me! NO ONE! No one, will ever treat you that way again! Ever!

KAMI: Thanks Zacky Zee, I know you mean it. Maybe I will call you Zee... Yeah that sounds strong... Zee it is from now on.

Kami looked around like she was searching for something and she quickly answered my thoughts:

KAMI: Sleeping bag foolio... Well since you don't need to sleep as much as I do, you can stand watch 'til mornin' K!... K.

ME (with a confused look on my face): OK sleep! That's appropriate after a meaningful conversation like that, right? Right! I will keep an eye out 4sure!

KAMI (with the quick dig): Not literally, I hope dead boy.

ME: NO, not tonight anyway smart ass.

KAMI: That's right, better to be a smart ass then a Zack ass... oh I meant jackass, or is that dumbass I forget...

ME: Ok that's enough humie, why don't you go to sleep so I can curse you out without you hearing it for once!

KAMI: You got it Zack ass. Nighty, night Zee.

ME: Night Kami with a K... sweet dreams.

As she fell asleep I could only think to myself, wow, what great fortune bad luck has brought me. (I remember checking one time to make sure she was asleep. She was, and the thoughts started to flow.)

Once there was a time when meeting a human seemed a farfetched notion. Now life without this person is unfathomable. She has captured my imagination, hope, and heart. I truly care for her existence. I have just been exposed to a whole new adventure! Fate has led me to something I never thought possible in my wildest dreams, and there is no debate needed on what my choice would be. I knew that meeting her people and showing them what I am made of, had to be my best chance for both of our kind. Success would be essential to the survival of both species. Even though I still felt a little unsure, the thought of not being there for Kami felt worse. So, I had to make it work, because life is good, but life with Kami in it? Well, the word "GREATASTIC" comes to mind. This was the punch in the face that got me thinking. It's time to own it! My power, my destiny, whatever it may be, I must be ready for it. Not just for Zumiekind, or for mankind, but for all who still cling to life, and the hope of really living it once again! Even if Kami doesn't know it yet, which I doubt. She is my secret weapon. She gives me power, and makes me want to be a better version of me! The me I have always dreamed of being, but was too naive to accept. Funny how things work themselves out sometimes. See, the power had been inside of me all along.

YUP, IT'S STILL ENTRY# DOCE:

4th Chapter

BECOMING MORE OF THE ME I WAS MEANT TO BE!
OH AND BY THE WAY!
YOU CAN CALL ME ZEE!

Watching Kami fall into a deep, deep sleep, was a whole lot more fun than it should have been. It made me feel content and happy. Letting her get some good sleep, a sleep without fear. A slumber without waking up every few minutes in a nightmarish frenzy, checking frantically for her legs due to worry a threesome of undead creepers were having her limbs for a snack. In today's world that can sometimes be extremely hard to find if you're a human. For Kami, it was my pleasure, and honor to give her that small gift. Besides, as it stands I have a large debt to pay for all the help, and supplies she has given me! It is the least I could do. 8 hours or so of guard duty is a piece of brain cake for a Zumie anyway. Besides, this gives me time to test my newly acquired abilities, powered up by The Storm that shall not be named. An unexpected, but awesome side effect to being electrocuted by very large bolts of lightning. Hmm. Think maybe I should call them powers, but it just doesn't feel right! Is this really who I am now? She believes in me, it's time I believed. What did I have to lose? I knew it was there, because when I close my eyes and still my breath, I could feel it coursing through my veins. Mutating and working with the very serum that brought me back to life in the first place. At that moment standing there looking at the night sky, the breeze of chilled air gave me goose bumps just to make a point. My naive brain finally started to believe. Pure energy struck me... and now that is what runs through my body. Like a powerful current that hums in the street lights in the dead of the night. The energy from this planet itself charged my tiny little gifts into full blown powers, or as my humble nature wants to say, "GIFTS". The recent attributes of strength and speed upgraded, it was happening right in front of my eyes! I just wasn't paying attention. The quick healing became super healing, the ability to hear thoughts was now powerful and easy to control. What was I becoming? For me it was frightening, and exciting all at once. Overwhelming, but it also made me feel like I COULD be the bridge for humanity and Zumiekind to exist as allies! I mean, even the ninja skill set was like... freakin' AMAZING!!! The salad bar of unforeseen side effects, were freakin' me out, but not in a bad way. It was time to test my new powers, and I remember hoping I wouldn't blow myself up!

After putting this together, it became easy to believe in what Kami was so sure of all along. So, I separated myself enough from Kami, so if anything happened I couldn't control, it wouldn't hurt my friend. Far enough to keep her safe, but close enough to react in case she was in any trouble. I remember clearing my mind, relaxing the muscles, and breathing with a purpose behind each rhythmic breath. When the body was an afterthought I closed my eyes, and let the power in, completely. When I achieved this for the first time, a clarity washed over me, like a familiar blanket, and it actually felt right. For the first time, I understood... the power was always there, it was just waiting for me to give it permission to come on in and show me the possibilities that were right in front of me. The Storm that shall never be named amplified the intensity and strength of my gifts. Giving it a presence all its own, like a second consciousness created to protect me. It was time I learn how to master the bond forming between me and the power coming alive inside of me. A growing part of me, evolving quickly, and adapting to the new sense of all the unavoidable challenges in my immediate future. Eventually these gifts will help me atone for all the death I was responsible for when I was a mindless bringer of sorrow...

As the power took over the parts of my brain that wasn't being used, this blanket of clarity covered me. I stood there and reflected on the nightmare that was the driving force behind my absolute need to be the best person I could possibly be... for them... for my very soul!

"It was before I wandered into the valley where new life had found me. I can remember it clearly because it was the first time I tasted human flesh. Right after a deadly virus consumed my brain, and killed me with a relentless fever. Killing the human being I once was, replacing it with an emotionless monster! The first time I opened my eyes as the undead was utterly frightening, filled with confusion, and mindless instinct. The hunger was attacking me without mercy, like a

demon clawing me to shreds from the inside out. With no energy to drive me, only the hunger, I stood up... FLESH... It was close, and the closer I got to it, the stronger it seemed to make me. Not thinking or reasoning in any way, I was on my feet hell-bent on satisfying my insatiable hunger for the flesh of any warm blooded, salty meat sack that I could find. This hunger was the driving force behind my every move, and the smell got stronger. Filling my lungs with its intoxicating presence. I yelled out a horrible moan, and could hear the screams of the people in the room as I rounded the corner of the hallway. The looks on their faces as I limped through the doorway to devour them, will haunt me forever... I was someone they knew, someone they... loved. Frozen in their shoes, crying with horror and pain in their eyes. It was obvious that they were devastated at the possibility they would have to end my suffering, and face who I now was. I stood there drooling with anticipation of my first bite, not caring about the room full of loved ones and friends that had no clue in how to handle the chaos that was about to unfold. (My heart breaks every time I relive this awful memory.) I can still hear them calling out to me, desperately trying to reach the person that was already gone forever. Hoping that I would snap out of my spell, but there was no hope! The demon of hunger dug its claws in and ripped the humanity right out of me. It was horrible... I lunged for the person nearest to me without any care as to who it might have been. As I bit down I could hear the screams of horror, as panic fill the room like smoke in a blazing fire. Surrounding me with the pain of the realization that it was a child... and that is where I can go no further... I basically killed my entire existing bloodline that had survived the first wave of the apocalypse, in one fell swoop. How the guilt of this memory hurts me. I don't even know their names! What I do know, with every fiber of my being, is they were the people who loved me, and I got them all killed. Bit every one of them before they could even digest the death of the *young one that I had mercilessly killed with one ripping bite to the throat. She bled everywhere... and as they frantically tried to save her, I picked them off one by one. They tried to fight back, but they were surprised by a hoard that were attracted by the screams of the women who lost their baby. It was very apparent that they just gave in... The trauma due to the loss of the smallest beacon of hope. The future of the family was gone, and the will to fight went with her. Remaining family members and friends, one by one... They just let go and let it happen. Whether it was me, or the girl... it broke their spirit, and the rest is my waking nightmare. Forgive me if there is no drawing for this memory, it's hard for me..."*

With that painful memory in mind I opened my eyes... to my shock and awe... The rocks and other small things, like leaves and even a mouse frozen from the shock! Well... they were floating in the air! That's right! In midair...

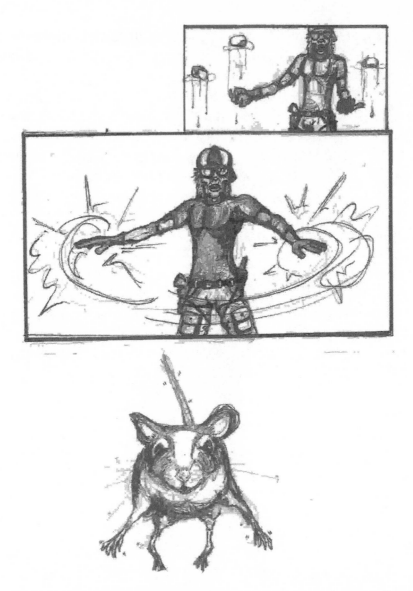

I stood up lightning quick, and everything dropped with a thud. My hands! Sweaty and shaky, but I was physically unharmed by this surge of energy. It was as if reflecting on my guilt and regret opened the door even more for the gifts to become one with me. Now... I can feel every molecule, every leaf, every tree, and every undead in the area. The air itself felt pliable, like I could move it, just by waving my hand it the direction I needed it to go. The ability to feel emotions from my past, and use bad memories to do good! Excited me to the core! I thought to myself as the leaves were circling me, not because of a dust devil or crazy winds, but because I willed them to circle me. The very earth beneath me is alive with energy, energy that I now can feel. It flows through this earth like the very current of the ocean itself. Except now... I can see it everywhere... the energy of life, of our souls. In the trees, the water, the air, and in anything that is still alive. This energy is the reason for it all, a brilliant balancing act that allows the soul to inhabit the earth through a vessel of flesh and blood. You know... our meat sacks! Looking back now I realize... my body had to be strong enough to handle the power, it all makes sense. IT FELT INCREDIBLE!!!!!! THE POWER WAS INTOXICATING!!!!!! Dealing with my past has opened me up! I can do this, I can really do this!!!!

The memory of this moment still gives me chills. It was the moment that I let the power fully into my consciousness, and realized that my life would never be the same. The possibilities were endless!!!! This powerful gift was now a part of my life, I was all about embracing it for what it was... a GIFT! I must have reveled in my newfound sense of self for hours, who knows? The power was like second nature now, it was just a matter of pushing limits, and breaking into new territory to see what I could accomplish. Moving objects, reading thoughts, sensing danger, and who knows where this could evolve as I learn to use this potentially lifesaving power. The difference between today and yesterday is... that I had Kami... and I now believed in me. I was finally ready to be me!

After practicing levitation and all sorts of other neat tricks, I stopped to relax, and calm myself, maybe even humble my mind after realizing I was now, a bona fide badass. My mind raced, and the only thing that stopped the tornado of thoughts in my head was a bunch of trapped ants! Trapped on a stick that was stuck on a rock, in the middle of a small stream. The very one I was using to relax next to. I decided to start levitating the stick that happened to have the line of ants on it. I could have drowned them, or killed them in any way I imagined, but that would have been so cruel.

I then floated the ants over the small tranquil stream to the other side, and watch them scammer away to find safety...

It was then I heard:

KAMI: Already playing hero, Zee? I knew that I was right about you Zacky! Sweet through and through, just how I like 'em...

As I soaked her words into my heart like a dry sponge that was sitting at the edge of the water, but couldn't quite reach in... "BOOOOOMMMMM, RUMBLE, RUMBLE, RUMBLE, CRACKLE CRACK BOOOOOOMM!!!!!! The sky struck down glorious lightning in the distance up the base of the mountain on the far side. It was in the distance, but still too close for any kind of comfort. There it was... THE STORM... but how? As if it was still mad at all the things I said in anger when it was trying to sink me and The C Turtle. Leave it to a monsoon with a side of tsunami to hold a grudge. Closer and closer it seemed to get, like the wind itself had a will or master behind it, cracking the whip without relent. Unfortunately, we weren't the only ones who had noticed the light show heading this way. My senses mapped out thousands of Z-Bots heading for the mountain road. The very road that could lead them right to the gate of the mountain fortress, and Kam's people. Now I know this sounds a bit like bonkers is my middle name, but the undead were following the storm like it was the leader of a tour group in Las Vegas or something. There was no rain, or any precipitation of any kind, but clouds were everywhere. This was THE STORM'S electrical sister, and man was she pissed off!! Kami instantly turned to me with concern on her face...

KAMI: It's my duty to get back to my people Zee!! The floods have washed away several of the barriers we had in place to stop such hoards from being a threat. If I don't warn them who knows what will happen? Besides, we won't last long out her either. We need to go now!

ME (frantically): BUT, BUT! What about The C Turtle, we just fixed her!

KAMI: We have time to cover her and tie the pontoons down, but quickly. They won't touch it if they're chasing us right? It's the storm that we need to worry about. Otherwise nothing else should happen to it.

ME: Ok, but I'm not understanding why we need to leave so soon. I'm pretty sure they aren't fast enough to beat us up the mountain!

Kami looked at me bearing the stare of someone who was about to open a wound, and it was a revelation on how brave humanity has become...

She didn't speak, she just opened up her mind to me. It may have been only a few minutes to the rest of the world, but for me it was an education into the mind of the survivor. When it started, I could her voice guiding me through her thoughts and memories...

KAMI'S (dreamy voice/w echo): Zee listen carefully to all I say before you judge. When one of the mountain people die, we turn into an undead regardless of a bite or not. So instead of just laying down and dying... twice. We choose to go out taking a shit load of those biting bastards with us if we can. Now every once in a while, someone gets to go out a huge hero and live on forever in our written history. This very thing happened not too long ago... A very old warrior that was well respected got a very bad stomach cancer. Instead of living in pain for a few months longer and dying in his bed. (Which would then result in a loved one or someone else takin' his undead life to give him the true death.) He chose to end a longtime problem that plagued our mountain safe-haven. We gave him an old truck... with his favorite beer, and some music for attracting the population of dead walking, that had trapped us inside our own walls. He barreled out of the fortress gate, and got the whole heard to follow him and his drunken karaoke singing until he got to the old mines that were in the middle of the mountain. He drove into the mine itself. 'Til his tail lights could no longer be seen. Gone forever. We then closed the undead meat-heads inside and sealed them in the mines to rot. Unfortunately, the storm broke the seal to the mines and undead have been pouring out for weeks. We managed to keep them there by blocking off the entrance to the mining camp itself. BUT... this storm will destroy that blockade... and my people will once again be trapped in the mountain they call home.

I took it all in and thought aloud...

ME: WOW... Your people are full of brave souls ready to sacrifice for the survival of their loved ones... So very brave in the face of death!

KAMI: Yeah... we really do. Sometimes things do not go well, and this last time was a costly example of good intentions coming back to haunt you...

ME: Oh crap... I saw what you are talking about... They are already breaking through, combined with the hoard coming with the storm... and there is something else!

KAMI: You got it Watson!!!! The gate you came upon is the only way in or out of the mountain. We have attempted to tunnel out, but cave-ins and setbacks have kept us from success. It will happen someday, but who knows how long that could be.

ME (feeling like I was about to pull the rug out from underneath my beautiful Kami): I know this is going to sound crazy, but for a small amount of time, not sure how much, the undead in that camp heard me break a branch and all at once they turned slowly! Like they were more than your everyday dead-heads. I mean... I get it!... If you want to sleep at night in this world, a perfect enclosure would do it for me too. You have no other choice, you're the hunted. What I am saying is these undead seem evolved in some way, and we can't take that for granted! If they get to your home, there is no telling the damage they could inflict. My grasp of this was horrifying, because not even the hunger was in their minds. It was as if they were one consciousness, of one clear mind. It scared me to the core Kam!

KAMI: I know Zacky, it's ok! I can see your darkest secrets, your pain, and the way you felt when the whole thing went down. Not to mention the gore and carnage that you inflicted when you were once an undead. The reason you were scared to the core Zee, has to do with it reminding you what it was like to be undead. Like a flashback or something! Through all of that torment it amazes me that with all the power you now possess, all you desire to do is make it right somehow, someway. I really admire you for that Zee. It's a great quality in a person. Don't change that part of you, OK?!

ME: OK... I promise Kam.

Me and Kami got dangerously close. We smiled and gazed into each other's souls. She wanted to kiss me, and I wanted to kiss her... My whole body was charged with anticipation. My first real kiss... I know it was hers too... it was as if we were of one mind, and we both could not resist the obvious attraction that was there from the start. Our faces got close enough for me to smell the sweet scent of her breath, and her hair smelled a faint hint of berries, with a mint finish. Time stood still as our lips got closer, and closer... she never felt this way before... neither had I... It felt like the life force of the world itself was pulling us together... there was no resisting her allure. Irresistible is not quite enough to describe the pull this young, beautiful, sassy woman had over my everything at that moment. The truth! There was nothing I wanted more, ever! Timeless anticipation made it even worse as our lips were about to touch... The most unexpected, fate driven act, forever connecting me to another's soul without an ounce of hesitation in the move... Her lips felt firm but soft... slowly slipping slightly this way and that way, pushing back and forth as breathing no longer mattered. Then it happened... our minds being one, we opened our mouths slowly, and slid our tongues together as if they knew what to do before we did. Nothing was thought out because we thought it together. Together, every breath-taking touch and squeeze of our bodies were meant to happen as they did. Not only did we feel our own sensations, but because our minds were feeling each other's experience as well, the passion was amplified like a "12" inch sub-woofer in a compact car. Even now I can only describe how it felt, not what we did... it still hits me that way, affects me as if it just happened. Wow!... Amazing... SHE IS...

CRACK   BANG   POW...   CRACK
BOOOOOOOOOOMMMM!!!!... The sky lit up like it was

daylight outside even though daylight was still an hour or so away! Abruptly bringing our glorious first moment to an end, "THE ANGRY SISTER STORM" had caught up to our moment and we had no time to waste. Nothing had to be said... we knew what to do!... BOOOOOMM... CRASH CRACLE... BAANNNNG... CRACKLE... BAAAAAAAAAMMM!!!! We snapped out of doe eyed lost in each other's moment stuff, and finished securing the Turtle. We started to worry and for a good reason... Kami! A.K.A., meat sack to all undead A-holes that were not too far behind, was a beacon for every hunger driven Z-Bots to follow! If they caught her scent there is no telling what would happen. Not to mention, this crazy display of an electrical typhoon like storm surrounding the base of this mountain. (Looking back, it almost seems as if the weather had purpose in its existence. Like it was being driven this way by some other presence!) See by myself I could maneuver without being noticed, but as soon as they got a whiff of my berry mint beauty over here, we would have both been dead! Did I mention how dead we would be? Pretty damn dead let me tell ya! Then without warning Kami remembered something...

KAMI: OH CRAP!!! When I said, we better go now... I have another good reason for that revelation... memories

ME (with a question mark): What do you mean?

KAMI (with concern in her voice): Ok... see the gates that you saw in my memories will be sealed in the event of a hoard, or multiple walkers of any real numbers. Soooooooo, if we don't hurry... we will be locked out of the mountain with the biters... And we don't even know how many there are!

I closed my eyes and concentrated on the undead I could see...

> *ME (feeling proud): There is roughly 10,000 biters being led this way in total, from several directions. 2,017 more if you count the mines... equaling... 12,017 undead floating our way, give or take a few.*

> *KAMI: Really... really Zee that's what you say when I say we are in trouble... Good pep talk mannnn! Thank you for freaking me out even more!!!!!*

I held out my hand, and thought to my girl:

> *ME: Take my hand... I will carry you to safety and nothing will happen... I give you my word... Look into my mind and experience last night with me. I'm not*

sure where this power I have will take me... but wherever it is, you will always be there with me. I will never let anything happen to you while I still exist, in some way, form, or fashion!

Kami took my hand and I picked her up in my arms. We smiled and knew... that no matter what happened that we would do it together. She gives me strength, and I give her clarity. Together there is nothing we can't do, her beauty to my beast... always. I took off frantically, making my way to the wall of debris in seconds. The sounds of the undead were ringing in our heads as we made our way to the road at the base of the mountain. Kami's worry that the undead would follow us anyway kept me on the fringe of the road, in the trees that lined the road. Like a ninja, I went from cover to cover with Kami in my arms. We were thinking as one and my body was the conduit. If she felt them coming one way, we would go another. Zig-zagging all around the undead until we were ahead of them somehow! Together we were magnificent...

KAMI: Wow Zee... very impressive, your strength, and anticipation while being in tune with me was Godlike!!

ME: Well, it's not over yet... we still need to get passed the mines!... So hold on Kam... HOLD ON!

As I ran up the road with Kami she propelled herself onto my back holding on for dear life, giving me a better center of gravity to run with. She noticed how fast I was running, trying to act oblivious to the speed with which I seemed to be able to run up the mountain. Not even breathing heavy, or needing to slow down, I ran from one hiding spot to another. To me it was as if everything was in slow motion, and darting from cover to cover was easy and second nature. The terrain was diverse enough, and plush with plant life for us to keep hidden... but her sweet smell, and I do not mean the berry mint in her hair, was about to give us away. Undead were being drawn away from the lightning and thunder! The sweet smell of a mind reading, young, wicked pretty woman was too much for the hungry undead army to ignore.

Kami, being the type person she was, thought of being a decoy so I could save the mountain fortress. The Mountain of Hope... I totally get it now, totally!!!...

ME (with authority): NO WAY LITTLE MISS SUICIDAL!!! I will find a way... now just stay here while I pick a fight...

KAMI (with extreme worry): NO Zee... what...

ME (with confidence): Stop, calibrate, and listen!... No really, trust me Kam... I have a good plan, K?

KAMI: Ok, I trust you Zacky

With that, I sprang into action! I used my ability to get in the heads of about 15 or 16 undead and did something awesome. I used them to fight the other undead, got in their brain and turned them into allies. It was epic... Some I made do martial arts and fight like ninjas, while some I made pick up rocks or big sticks and attack other Z-Bots heads for the true death. It worked well enough, since the other undead were so mesmerized by the storm they didn't even notice the carnage ensuing not too far away. Then I made it happen! Closed my eyes! Concentrating with all my might! CRACKLE, CRACK, POP! The biggest tree I could find, broke its base, and down it came. Taking 10 of the Z-Bots out as it came barreling down out of the night sky. As it fell, The STORM let out a huge bolt of lightning in the worst of places, the perfect spot to redirect the Z-Bots towards the gates! You would think genius move, right? Knocking down a tree? This way the tree would have blocked the view of me and Kami slipping away, hopefully unnoticed. The tree itself felt weightless. To my mind it was like a huge sturdy piece of cardboard, with pompoms at the top of it all. That's what I thought to myself anyway, and it worked! Wow, I really just wrote that? Yup... Anyway, the undead were dazed and in combat with each other (Kami and I both wanted to geek out about that, but it was a stressful time... so we thought it instead!) Normally you would think things weren't going too bad considering the circumstances, except there was one thing I happened to overlook. The lightning had set some of the tree tops on fire, and now... not only do we have to deal with the undead, THE STORM II, and the metal doors closing. We also have been given the "JOYOUS" task of dealing with a forest fire! Happily working its merry way up the side of the mountain! JOYGASM! I remember thinking to myself as Kami yelled in her mind... FIRE ZACKY FIRE!!!!

ME: *Thanks Watson, I think THE FIRE is pretty apparent. I don't need your heads up on that one!*

KAMI: *IT... wasn't my idea to knock down a tree that was about to catch fire! NOW WAS IT, SHERLOCK!!!!*

ME: *OK, OK, OK!... Let's not lose our heads, it's my bad! NOW... how do we get around all this Kam?... It's your mountain... THINK!*

Just as Kam's memories of the mountain flashed through my brain, the undead now stared back towards us and the blazing fallen tree. Courtesy of yours truly, my brilliant maneuver of getting the tree to fall, snapped the fighting Z-Bots out of their spell. Now we were the only thing they were focused on, and they were closing in fast. Unfortunately for us, a huge wave, or mega heard of undead were also coming up our juicy left in no time flat. A FRICKIN' ARMY WAS KNOCKIN ON OUR BACK DOOR!! Either way we needed to move, and fast, before we became overrun! Had to get Kami out of this predicament and find a place to make my stand! Maybe I get Kami to the gates... they would let her in while I fought off the biters that were about to take over the mountain. Keeping her safe no matter what... No matter what! Those happened to be the perfect choice of words, because Kami heard every thought, and screamed out loud:

KAMI: *No way Zack Zee!! I'm in this with you 'til the end. We can do it together... I know we can!!*

I stared into her mind... and didn't even have to think a word. She basically downloaded the map of the mountain to me in her thoughts... All I had to do was think, where should we go... where should we go! The fire was so hot we were sweating like it was high noon. The undead were closing in so fast I could smell them, and feel there hunger all around us. I wasted no more time... I picked up my Kami tossing her around to my back, bracing for warp speed, and ran for it!!!!... Mannnnnnn... whoooooooooeeeeeeee!!! I never ran so fast in my life!! If everything went in slow-mo before, well let me say this... the earth stood still. I was a blur of Zumie super awesomeness. Running as if each step was the sum of twenty normal steps!

KAMI: *Wow you're even stronger than I thought. You finally calmed down and let the power inside... didn't you Zee?*

ME: *Maybe... wait you gazed into my mind! You know the answer smart ass!...*

KAMI: *Not allowed to hate me 'cause I beautiful, aaaand smart, boyee! Besides, you can do so much more. More than even my visions could have ever revealed. Even the Elder felt you coming, and her power isn't what it used to be. Like before I was a little one, she became the leader of what was left of mankind here. She has been the warning beacon, and advisor to the council of our people. Some say she has used herself up to save us. My grandmother doesn't want people to know that the truth is... well... That is why her power is fading, and fading with every awakening of a future telepath.*

ME: *You mean... I am the reason for...*

KAMI: *Yup... it seems to be that with every telepath that comes of age... well, it drains some of her power... just a tiny bit each time. She is still all powerful, but holding onto your position was really hard for her... so I figured it was the Elder thing and all... You know?*

ME (*not breaking a sweat while having a full-blown conversation, running up a huge ass mountain*): *AND YOU? DID YOU SEE ME COMING TOO?*

KAMI: *YES... I waited forever for you to show up. Ever since THE STORM. It took you weeks to find us, but there you were, finally! Rambling on in your head, wrestling with your own destiny... mental case that you are.*

ME: I never thanked you by the way... for pushing me in the right direction. I was a bit lost, and you were so what I needed...

Under normal circumstances, Kami putting her hand over my mouth and ordering me to stop would be surprisingly stimulating, but this was serious:

KAMI: STOP!! NO REALLY... STOOOOOP RUNNING ZEE!!!...

My feet slowed down, and the blur that was all I could see came into focus. Man, what a ride!! It was simply fantastic! My legs were like the engine of an auto. I couldn't believe it, and I was the one running if you can swallow that malarkey. Even though my writing may make it seem like minutes had gone by, IT WASN'T!... 57 seconds... uhhhhhhh-huh, you read correct, I said 57 seconds! According to my Passenger watch that was right in front of my face as she held on like I was a teen-Idol or something! Kami showed no hesitation and grabbed me by my shoulders. Before giving me the skinny on the situation, she told me to only talk to her through thought. She didn't want to freak out the Pack any more than they already would be upon seeing me for the first time. Let alone having to deal with all my powers 'n' stuff. That's when it hit me like wet fish in a shirtless fish slapin' contest. ("Fish Slapin'", is something that we Zumies invented. I will elaborate another time.) I looked up ever so slowly, and there it was! The Gates of the Mountain of Hope, the fortress of Kam's people! BIGGA-GATE!!!!

KAMI (in a whispering voice, even though it was in our minds): We are here Zee, and they can see us... see you. Some of them are cool, curious, and opened minded! But, there are those who are scared, and want to lock you up, check you out, and see what you're all about. Listen to me... don't say a word Zacky Zee... not one!

ME: But the biters are coming... they will be here in a matter of minutes... seconds. What is the hold up?

KAMI: By the way... You run super-fast! Nice upgrade!

ME: Thanks, Kami... I was wondering when you'd notice.

I smiled at Kami with my new cocky little grin, and looked back at the gate. Ironically here I was, exactly where I've always wanted to be. Except, now I am the one who can change the world if it comes down to it. I am finding the weight of the responsibility, overwhelming to say the least! It is just unbearably hard to bury my self-preservation, and just be the hero. The undead were slowly getting to close for comfort, and THE STORM II that will never be named was just darkening the sky enough for everyone to notice. Including thousands of undead, flocking in from miles around, like it was a free rock concert! I knew that Kami would not leave my side... so I did what any man who cared about his woman would do. I took off my hat and waved to the guards, screaming about how they have time to save her, and to just leave me behind!!

KAMI (screaming in her mind): NOOOOOO ZEE!! I won't leave you...

I ignored her cry and persisted to plead for her life...

ME: Good morning, I'm Zee. If it's ok, can Kami and I please come in? The road will soon be filled with the undead that you all left in the mines. They were unfortunately freed by the storm's winds and lightning. These strikes resulted in knocked down barricades, letting loose a small army of hungry biters! Not to mention, all the undead following this unusually placed storm! You see, I made this young woman a promise!... That no harm would come to her if I could help it... SOOOOOO! If not both of us!!!! Then just Kami should be let in!!! I can hold them off while you seal the doors back up! BUT, YOU MUST HURRY!!!

KAMI (with sincerity in her eyes): ZEEEeeee!... I won't leave you!

ME (*with a look she hasn't seen just yet*): *You have no choice... you will survive no matter the cost! YOU UNDERSTAND?!*

VOICE FROM BEHIND THE GATE: *Kami? Are you harmed in anyway?*

KAMI: *Duh! Look at me, I'm fine... He is quite harmless to us, a lost puppy if I have ever seen one!*

ME: *Hey...*

THE VOICE: *Kami, these doors are sealed shut. It will take a few minutes, just hold on...*

ME: *We don't have a few minutes. They are close now... I can feel them.*

THE VOICE (*sounding panicked*): *No way... they are already starting to come around the bend... TAKE COVER... HIDE YOURSELVES!!*

KAMI (*with a look like she is about to give up*): *If something happens Zack... I want you to know that there are no regrets, and I would do it all over again just to kiss you one more time!*

Her lips didn't move. This way only I could hear those words... It was exactly what I needed, and somehow I don't think it was an accident. Man... LIKE I SAID... it was exactly what needed! With every moment that had gone by, the circumstances continued to mutate into something extremely desperate. Many more undead were getting closer and closer!

Soon... soon they will be faced with making the decision of letting us in, or leaving us fight the hoard alone; giving the people inside a chance to survive. Sacrifice the few, to save the many. Translated into Zumie that means, sacrifice us to save the fortress. If the leaders inside the gates were any good... they most certainly have come to that conclusion by now! Without words, the look on Kam's face confirmed it.

She thought we were dead! But she forgot about something that I saw just a few hours ago; the ropes hidden on the top of the gates. She would use them from time to time, making sure that she could sneak in and out of the fortress at night without being noticed. When Kami let me in I was shown inside her good memories, of little parties out in the woods with other teens. This was our salvation!!! She was just too panicked and scared to remember! With no hesitation, I picked up my angel and made for the corner of the gates. Set down Kami and proceeded to calm her down, while I used my ability to move objects to bring the rope down to us! Well, it fell on us. I barely got them to move; I was super lucky, trust me! The ropes were tied to the bases of huge fresh air ducts. Unfortunately, they had big fans inside, drawing fresh air into and out of the front area of the fortress. I can remember Kami snapping out of her panic state when she saw the rope coming down. She looked at me and KISSED me right on the lips, hard...

KAMI (blowing my mind): I could kiss you to death, but you're half there already Zee... SO fantastical... can't believe you saw, and remembered everything so well.

ME (while rolling my eyes): DUUUUHHH! Kam you have looked in my soul, surely you remember my photographic memory?

KAMI (rolling her eyes, but doing it more effectively than I ever could): Of course I did... so that means you remember everything? Wow, and I thought I had it bad! OH! And don't call me Shirley!

ME: Yeah... You're a regular comedian 'n' shit! You do realize, that it also means not being able to forget the memories you wish could be erased forever!...

KAMI (looking like she was not impressed): I'm sorry it's me who is the one bursting your bubble Mr. Zee! Memories that suck, have a way of haunting the mind, even if you don't have a photographic memory. Unfortunately, even the strongest minds have issues letting go!

As we were flirting in the middle of a hugely dangerous moment... the rope got stuck, due to a knot that was stuffed in the grate of one duct...

ME: Aww shit bags!... Ok, hold on Kam!... We are going for a ride!!!!...

KAMI: Oh boy!

With that I put Kami on my back, and concentrated on my legs, then focused on the rope that was a good 35 feet above us. I envisioned me jumping to the rope in my mind, took a deep meditative breath, and... THEN IT

HAPPENED! WHOOOOOSH... I flew up towards the rope... even with her on my back I shot up like it was something I did all the time... until we got to the rope... WHOOSH... right past it, about 20 more feet. I landed on my feet... me and Kami just looked at each other with our mouths on the floor. We were there about 10 seconds just talking in our minds at the same time:

ME: Did you...

KAMI: YEAH, OMG mannnn.

ME: I can almost fly...

KAMI: I KNOW... so cool, so cool!!

ME: I'm so geeking out over this...

KAMI: That was GIHUGIC, you're like a superhero or some...

Our geek out moment got rudely interrupted by the banging of countless undead slapping, and banging their hands and fists frantically, desperately!!... to get at the people inside, to devour us all. The wall wasn't affected at all by the angry, hungry banging the biters displayed without relent. The people inside the wall though, were vastly affected by the sound of death knocking at their ONLY door! These people were now scared, and full of blame. I could feel it like rain down all around me, like when the clouds themselves first opened up and poured all over the valley to awaken me. It was so overwhelming it gave me chills and I started to lose my nerve, but she was there to catch me. We were there for each other... Still, the feeling was so dominant. I had to shut out everyone but Kami, and she understood.

BANG... POW... BAMM... The biters were piling up, and an endless sea of them were still coming for the electrical show of a storm. Pushing them up the mountain as if THE STORM II was the master of these new kind of undead. As if a whip was cracking behind them without mercy. Then it happened... Me and Kami completed the memory of her sneaking out of the compound to have a party in the woods. She looked at me as if to say oops, I'm sooooo sorry Zee, and I saw it... In conclusion, Kami and the popular youth of the mountain were having a great time. The result of this good time?... People died! Music was being played on a working computer tablet and speaker set! This being somewhat rare and valuable in this time, all the kids were extremely distracted. Dancing and singing around a small, but blazing fire. In normal times this would be harmless, in post-apocalyptic times, it possibly, and most certainly could end up fatal. This good time was no exception, and the reason, I couldn't see it...

> KAMI (with her head held low): I was supposed to be listening for them, you know the undead... I drank a little too much... and my gift got cloudy! I... I couldn't hear them!... 'til it was too late! The music attracted about 10 to 12 of them. We had 11 of us, but two were surprised... Aggie and fanboy. The rest of them we handled with ease! It only made it even worse that I let them down, and I hid the memory so you wouldn't hate me. The way my friends felt after it all happened. To this day, they still won't speak to me! I deserve it! Their safety was on me, the whole group depended on me!! I let them down because of a few too many! They speak to me now when they are forced to, but things will never be the way they used to. They have tried to forgive me, but because of my gift their true feelings are no mystery to me. Knowing how someone really feels? Well, we have discussed it, and I agree with you, a gift and a curse indeed.

Right after, she revealed why she said "she was sooooo sorry"! Due to the two teens dying, the hatch was sealed from the inside by a weld of some sorts. We were trapped, and there was no way into the fortress from where we stood. I can remember feeling Kam's painful guilt flushing over her. Then something wonderful happened... without her even realizing it she said to herself in despair...

KAMI'S DESPERATE HEARTFELT CONFESSION: I got my friends killed, and now the man I think I love. I am truly cursed... truly.

As a single tear fell down her cheek and goosebumps came over me like fans at a stadium doing the wave. There it was, my powers guiding me to remember WHO I FREAKIN' WAS! Like a power bar in a video game, mine was at max power and it was time to strike. Her thought charged met with rage. All I wanted to do was end her pain!... And no... NO-ONE HURTS MY GIRL... physically or emotionally! My hand became heavy, like an anvil or a wrecking ball. Except to me it was as light as a piece of wood! As the rage built, and Kam's tears began to fall like a monsoon, it took over! That side of me, still me, but not the me you would ever expect from a 170 pound, scrawny, barely six-foot version of myself. This other side, where my eyes glow light green; I feel decisive, and invincible at the same time. AAAAAAHHHHHHH!!!! Without warning, I jumped into the air, down towards the pile of hungry moaning drooling bags of death... Swinging my hand down to the ground right through the biters as if they were butter. SLAAAMM!!! A shockwave emerged from me hitting the ground, pushing the air as if it were mine to command. I said, "BAAAACCK!" As countless undead were forced back, or to their knees from the shockwave of power no-one could see but us! I stood up from my superhero landing stance, and the power bar was still at max. Remembering what I could do just a couple of hours ago, inspired me to believe that I could use the very air molecules themselves as weapons. I cleared all thoughts, and concentrated on the air as if it was all that mattered. The undead that had been knocked out by my sweet mega fist strike were starting to get back up and a herd was almost on me. I could faintly hear Kami screaming something, but because I was in the ZONE her words were muffled, and had no weight upon my actions at that time. I could feel the power swelling inside of me. Bodies started to lift off the ground, rocks and anything that wasn't nailed down began to float with a shaky twinge to their aerial independence. Even Kami tied herself to a steel beam with the rope when she realized what was about to happen. I couldn't contain it anymore. Holding in any longer felt agonizing, so I let it all go... WHOOOOOOOOOOOOSSSHSHHSH!!!!! It looked like the aftermath of a concussive blast. Z-Bots flew back like they were leaves being blown away from a leaf blower on lawn day. Flying back into the onslaught of incoming undead that were still being pushed by THE STORM'S will itself.

I recall thinking to myself... "How can I save Kami? That just stunned them, and I'm not sure what to do next." It was just then that I heard a calm wise voice telling me what to do.

> VOICE: *Use your power and concentrate on the latch. Open the gate, and have Kami jump into your arms. Bring her inside, and you will be safe... I promise Zack... you can do it... concentrate, it is the only way to save her!!!*

With that I turned to the gate. I began to see the gears and tech inside the gate, as if I was a little bug flying through the huge mechanisms of the latch. Found what was needed in the nick of time, as undead were gettin' up slowly, and more were making their way to the gates of the fortress. I drowned out the world, and forced the latch to open... it took 20 seconds of grunting and pushing in my mind, but I finally did it! With no time to lose I called out to Kami. She was already falling as I stretched out my arms to catch her. She knew what was going on with everything that I did. I pulled the big door open with my power and rushed into the gates... put Kami down and turned towards the giant gates, quickly getting back to push them closed with my bare hands. I then put my finger to my temple and proceeded to close the latch mechanism until it was secured and locked. It took all the energy I had left. Spent would be an understatement!

ELDERMUM or "MUM" For short

Just then a calming silence fell over me. It was as if time itself had come to a standstill, and then I heard her. The Eldermum!...

> ELDERMUM: *At long last, Zee... I am the voice that guided you in just now... It is my pleasure to meet you. I am known as the Eldermum.*

> ME: *Kami told me much about you without having to say a word... It's my honor to meet you Ms. 'Mum.*

ELDERMUM: *I want you to be prepared for the way things will unfold. The soldiers will point their weapons at you... they are going to be insecure and scared. Let them do their worst with no retaliation on your part! I will plead your case and in time they will see you are the only person who can save us from being entombed inside of this mountain.*

ME (with a shaky voice): *Okaaay ma'am... I will... I promise.*

ELDERMUM: *I will explain everything to Kami. You will see her again soon, but for now just go with the Pack peacefully, okay?...*

It was then that time came back into focus and I heard that old sound. The sound of guns being readied, and boots stomping behind me. When I was an undead, this was a familiar sound that I knew all too well! Even when it was my own people doing their military thing, it would always give me chills.

MAX (the leader of the Pack): *We want this to go peacefully, so do as I say and your head won't explode in an expeditious manner!... UNDERSTOOD HALF-BREED?*

ME: *Yes sir, I want no trouble!*

MAX (with a cigar in his mouth that looks like it has never been lit): *That's good! Since you saved Kami, I won't behead you on the spot, but the things you can do has scared some of the locals. The result is, that I will need to detain you until they can discuss what to do with you... about you! Since the hoard they think you brought here on purpose is only getting bigger, your chances of survival are not exactly awesome right now!*

ME (with sincerity in my words): No way... I would never! I came here to bridge the gap between your and my people. Not to hurt anyone... but to help you... (ZAP!... zZzZzZzZz... NAPTIME!)

MAX

Right HAND
MAN, and "protecter"
of "EIDERMAN"!

(YUP, HE SHOCKED ME WITH A TAZER-GUN......big jerk.) When I came to, everything was hazy at first. It took a minute or so for me to blink my eyes enough to even see at all. Finally, the fuzzy haze like tears were rolling down my cheeks instead of blurring my vision. It was only then the room would come into focus. Without knowing that I could get out of any restraints whenever I wanted, they shackled my feet and hands. My head hurt a bit from the shock, but I was feeling pretty good considering I was being held captive in the very place that I have spent months dreaming about. Felt rather ironic.

At the same time I knew that this was where I was meant to be, almost as if fate helped me along. Whatever it was that got me here, here is where I was, and I had to make it work. The air smelled of piss and fear, like some seriously messed up things had gone down in this room to get at the truth. I had no problem with the truth, whether or not they would believe me, was another question. It was cold enough to give you the chills, and the split pea paint job could depress even an optimistic fool like myself. A single cup of room-temp water, with just enough left over condensation to let me know it was once nice and cold, sat in the center of the table just to make me thirsty. Clever making someone who is alone sitting in an interrogation room, think about something they could see, smell, and fantasize about, as their mind festered over the inevitable events to come. This might break a normal human, but they haven't a clue who they're messin' with. The silence was maddening! So, instead of going mad, I decided to use this time wisely and practice spying on those who aren't counting on how fast I am adapting to my newly acquired gifts. With that thought I focused on the little holding area I was in, and listened to people talk about what was happening all around them. Some couple in the supply closet having sex... The Pack walking into a room to discuss my fate... Guards eating in a break room and complaining about the coffee being barely drinkable... A guard smoking with another female guard, talking about how the storm is threatening to kill the generators. OOHH! SNAP!... Now that was a good place to start, because the female said if that happened they would suffocate in a matter of days. Those generators provide the power for the fans that deliver fresh air to the fortress, and the pumps that moisten the air with water vapor. This system, and the juice that runs it, was the key to the mountain's sustainability. I then heard the Pack arguing over me. It pulled my attention away from the guards, it was so loud...

MAX (in a loud assertive voice): OK, CLAM UP YOU FAIRIES!!!!

DIRK THE SNIPER A.K.A. ONETIME (because that's all it takes for him to kill ya): If it weren't for Kami, he would have been shot on sight...

MAX: Yes, Onetime... but he is special. The Elder told me herself that the half-breed must be spared. In fact, I was told he is the one who can save us all.

B-BEAR THE HEAVY HITTER (big burley African American man, who hits like a truck! Uses a very large hammer to kill his undead, and that's it. No guns, hates them... and he is quite gentile and wise, until lives are in danger!): I say we listen to the... whatever he is. He don't eat flesh, and he's got gifts. An ally is what we should make of him, not an enemy.

MAX: I agree with B-Bear. He seems like he has a good enough head on his shoulders. Besides... despite Kami's one mistake, she is a great judge of character when it comes to new peop... or whatever he is. She swore the guy is good inside. She has looked deep from what I understand!

PYRO (no explanation needed. Not very forgiving, or playing with a full set of batteries in his controller, if you know what I mean): I say we blow him up and ask questions later hehehahahohwee!

MAX: NO!... Pyro... absolutely not! You saw what he could do, just like the rest of us!

PYRO: Ok... Ok, don't have a cow... We hear him and the Elder out... Then we blow him up hehehahahohwee!

JOHNSON A.K.A. SMOKE (cool, laid back, and believes in The Elder and her ways. Ex-Army Ranger/Special forces recon... a real badass): Shut up asshole. This kid is gonna change the world forever, and we are gonna help him. It's our destiny, and I'm not hiding in this tomb forever.

MAX: I agree with Johnson, after watching him selflessly save Kami... I doubt he is here to hurt us in any way. I hope he can help us when the storm knocks out our power source. We could really use a man with such talents... AM I RIGHT BOYS?!... I mean come on, anyone who can push back a herd like that is worth the air he breathes at least... so let's chill-out, and hear what the Elder's reasoning for all this is. Then we will make our decision! Until then, keep him right where he is! Unfortunately, the Elder is caught up calming down the flock. Once she assures them he is not the cause of all this, we will let him out. B-Bear...

B-BEAR: Yes my man Max...

MAX: *Go watch over 'Mum until she is done. You know how bad those people can get. Your presence will keep the peace... go now big man, she will need you.*

B-BEAR: *You got it... I'm out.*

After hearing that exchange, the anxiety lifted. Knowing that I was in no danger from this group of warriors let me calm down and focus on the one person that was on the back, front, and every other part of my mind no matter what I was doing. I then pushed my mind out past the walls of this little building, and brought my consciousness to the place where Kami was, and listened in on the speech The Elder gave to her people:

THE ELDERMUM: *MY PEOPLE... CALM DOWN... NOW LISTEN TO ME... The young man you saw today is the one I have told you all about. He just doesn't know it yet, but soon he will realize his true potential. Upon this revelation he will embark on a journey. This willing soul will then put into motion the events that will free our world from the Evil that has infected us all, forever! We all become undead when we die, and he will free us from the curse of our forefathers. Letting the souls of the dead rest once again, the way it was always intended to be. You must be patient, and not let fear of the unknown infect your decisions from here on out. It would be our downfall if you were to do so!... Evil is behind it all, and soon this unnamed evil will unveil his end game. Through this half undead, half human we will have the weapon to combat this end game whatever it may be! In this game for which we must all play a part in, the stakes are most high. Whether we like it or not, this evil has focused on us! There is nothing to discuss, except what part we choose to play in this psychopath's game!... We can wither and die in its presence, or FIGHT! I am ready to give my last breath to win this fight! Are you?!!! (THE PEOPLE CHEERED, AND ANSWERED WITH A UNAMAMOUS YES, THIS WAS A COMMUNITY OF FIGHTERS, AND NO-ONE WAS GOING TO TAKE THE MOUNTAIN, WITH-OUT A FIGHT!!) Go on home, and gather your gear. Tell the ones you love how much you really care for them, for it well may be your last chance to say the things that need to be said. For a good death... THEN! GET READY TO FIGHT FOR OUR RIGHT TO EXIST IN THIS WORLD! ONCE AGAIN!! FOR WHEN THIS IS ALL OVER!... THE BLOOD OF THE EVIL UNDEAD WILL FLOW AT THE HANDS OF OUR DEFIANCE!! WE WILL LIVE!! WE WILL BE SLAVES TO NO-ONE... EVER!!!*

The people begin to fall into denial and yell out... "NOOOO... IT CAN'T BEEEEEE!!!... NO ELDERMUM YOU AREN'T RIGHT ALL THE TIME!" Eldermum's chest puffs up! She looks at her people with the kind of look that could humble the most agitated of the angered. As she begins to speak her truth, you could feel the shift from fear to anger and disgust. Not towards Eldermum, but towards the hoard of Evil undead that were trapping these people in their home. As she spoke these words... the heart of every one of her people filled with hope and determination. It was inspiring to say the least, and still is to this day, I close my eyes, and feel inspired by this woman.

ELDERMUM: LISTEN TO ME... QUIT NOW AND LISTEN TO WHAT I AM ABOUT TO SAY!... HE WISHES TO USE OUR UNDEAD BODIES TO DESTROY THE REST OF HUMANITY... AND THIS IS WHERE IT ALL BEGINS! HE WANTS TO INFECT US ALL, TAKE OUR CHILDREN AND MAKE THEM HIS SLAVES... (The crowd begins to rumble once again, now realizing the importance of the moment. The people stopped talking, and looked to Eldermum as they now were hung on her every word.)... I KNOW THIS IS AN AWFUL BURDON TO A PEOPLE WHO ONLY WISH TO LIVE IN PEACE. BUT NO MAN OR WOMAN, CHILD NOR ANIMAL... WISHES FOR THE FIGHT OF THIERS LIVES WHEN IT IS FORCED UPON THEM. JUST REMEMBER!!!!! WE HAVE EVERYTHING TO FIGHT FOR, AND THE ONLY REASON EVIL WISHES TO DESTROY AND ENSLAVE US, IS PURE ENVY IN THE WORST OF WAYS! IT WANTS WHAT IT CAN NEVER HAVE. SO, BECAUSE OF THIS, IT MUST DESTROY US, OR FACE THE UGLY TRUTH OF WHAT IT REALLY IS. A DISEASE, A STAIN ON THE GOOD NATURE OF THIS WORLD. THE ONLY ADVANTAGE WE HAVE IS THIS... HE DOES'NT KNOW THAT WE NOW KNOW... I HAVE USED MY GIFT TO BLOCK THIS POWERFUL EVIL FROM SEEING OUR HOME. UNTIL NOW HE DIDN'T KNOW WE EVEN EXISTED, LET ALONE US HAVING THE POWER TO FIGHT BACK. WE WILL

WIN THIS DAY!... HE WILL BE WEAKENED... AND THIS WILL BE ENOUGH TO BUY US TIME! TIME TO AID THIS YOUNG WARRIOR OF OUR WORLD TO GET READY FOR THE BATTLE... THE BATTLE THAT WILL DECIDE WHETHER GOOD WILL NURTURE THIS WORLD BACK TO WHAT IT ONCE WAS... OR DARKNESS WILL PREVAIL... FOR YEARS AND YEARS TO COME. THE CHOICE IS CLEAR MY CHILDREN, WE WILL DESTROY THESE MINDLESS DRONES CONTROLED BY HIS POWER... OR WE WILL DIE TRYING!!!!

Just then I heard the Eldermum in my head:

ELDERMUM (with a tone of sympathy, and caring): I know this is a lot to take in, Zee... but you must understand that I have no choice in the matter! I will always be honest and up front with my people, or I do not deserve the power that has been bestowed upon me! In time my words will make more sense. What I am about to say to my people is our business, so please don't be offended. It will all make sense someday when you are sitting somewhere not even thinking about these dark times. It will just come to you, and your training will be complete. I'm sending Smoke to come and release you now. Don't give him too hard of a time. He is a little sensitive to people like us, okay? Relax young hero! It is not as bad as it sounds... well, it is that bad, but for you it will feel natural. This, after all, is your destiny Zack. Do not worry, you will not let Kami down... I have seen it in my dreams, and my dreams are never wrong...

Just then my concentration was interrupted by a room temp cup of water being thrown in my face...

SMOKE: HEY BOY! Time to go see 'Mum... she has something to ask of you.

I gasped for air like I was under water. Now understand I wasn't drowning or anything, but man he took me out of the outa body experience, and I was a bit startled if you know what I mean! I could finally open my eyes without water stinging them, and Smoke came into focus slowly. His rough unshaved face was seasoned with confidence and understanding. You knew he was a bad ass even though he was inviting, instead of scary and intimidating. It was similar to meeting an old friend, or someone that I had once known very well. He smelled of greenleaf and gun oil, and when he smiled you had to smile back. He was a person who wasn't going to be bested by anyone, unless he wanted you to. Luckily for me, he was totally on my side, and knew more about my future than I did. For him, I was going to save his people, and that made me super alright in his playbook of honor... He in no way was going to tell me or show it, but well... I knew, and had to play dumb. Didn't want to give away all my advantages just yet!

ME (with a timid, but brave tone): O... OK Mr. Smoke, you got it.

SMOKE (with a look of surprise on his face): How do you know my name kid?

ME: Eldermum told me sir...

SMOKE: Oh yeah... I still forget about her ability to always be a few steps ahead of even the likes of me... You don't look like much... (He stared me up, then down, and let me know how he felt.) But from what 'Mum tells me, you're here to help. I will admit that your dead half is a little unnerving. Your muscle tone is absolutely fantastic though! (Squeezing my arm, he comments with disbelief in his voice.) I mean you're supposed to be half dead, but instead you look like a skinny powerhouse, or resemble some kind of cut up kung fu master.

ME (feeling a little bit hurt): What do you mean my lesser half man, c'mon man...

SMOKE: Hey... take it easy man, I'm just busting your balls. Don't get all "Neanderthal" on me, ok? I'm just here to cut your throat... I meant your restraints... hahahhah!

ME (with a smart-ass grin on my face): You having fun Smoke? Because my hands aren't restrained, and I am a little tired of your attempt at witty banter... if you must know.

Just then I sprung on the unsuspecting Smoke, and threw the zip-tie cuffs in his face... By the time he caught the cuffs I had spun around his backside, while simultaneously grabbing his bowie knife that was secured on his back. (FLASHBACK TIME... cool huh... Picture my zip-ties coming undone without me moving a muscle. That's right, I used my powers while my would-be captor was monologuing and having way to much fun at my expense. This was just to prove a point that I could leave anytime I wanted, but I didn't flaunt it in Smoke's face. No way... I was clever like a... a... Who cares! I was clever and it felt good for once.) I held it in a defensive stance while watching for a counter by the Army-Ranger. Letting him know I was ready for anything. I then stood down, and laid the blade of the big sharp instrument of death on my forearm, exposing the handle for the hardened soldier to grab with no worry in toe. It was just a quick reminder, that I was also a badass, and my hope was a glimmer of respect from the soldier in some way. Smoke smiled like it was cute or something, and then said:

SMOKE (with a nod of approval): Not bad kid. Just don't think that pulling a stunt like that on the others is going to go over as well, ok?! They won't quite get your oh so subtle message, if you know what I mean.

ME (with the denial squirm): Oh there was no mess...

SMOKE (cut me off quick and let me know): Stop!... You are a terrible liar, and I threw up in my mouth just a little while listening to you try to attempt your awful shitty fail of a lie. OK?... Good...

He then put out his hand and smiled at me. I placed the big bowie handle in his gihugic hand and backed away. I waited patiently for him to show me the way, figuratively and literally. He opened the door and gestured for me to follow, so I did.

TOLD YOU THIS WAS A LONG ONE, SO STAY WITH ME! IT'S ENTRY# DOCE!

5th Chapter

TIME TO PUT UP OR SHUT UP!
NO TURNING BACK NOW!
BESIDES, EVEN IF I COULD, I WOULDN'T
WANT TO ANYWAY...

It all reminded me of a scene from a human adventure or sci-fi movie, where the rebels and their people were getting ready for the against all odds last stand of some kind. Not to sound like I was desensitized and not aware of the severity of the situation, but I felt as if this was my comfort zone. During all of the mental oohing and ahhing, a strangely familiar feeling of the power within me began to meet me in the middle! An instant upgrade of ultra-heightened senses, my wit, and mental capacity. It was the wisdom of this power that has found its home in me, and comforts me with the gift of confidence. It was so strong that not even Kami, or Eldermum for that matter could read my thoughts when it communicated with me. As if there is a conscious ally inside me, or an alter ego that has processed all my knowledge. The plethora of manuals, including a few years of reading human history, philosophy, and anything else my photographic memory could retain. Basically, the whole city library, including the CD-ROM shit! This alter ego now aids me in my moments of need. Whenever I need to be lucid and present, it processes the vast amount of information obtained. By doing this, my conscious self can make decisions and maneuver through the situation at hand while using the info the alter ego has waded through for me to make the best decisions in the quickest amount of time. The physical muscle memory to execute any task that I have been educated in. It is there, ready to back me up, basically adapting, then aiding in whatever the situation at hand may be. The sweetest part is that after I'm done, the info gets compiled in with everything else! This makes me stronger mentally, for knowledge is power! Really, there is no way of telling where this will cap itself off, and I'm here for the long hall. (I mean... I'm almost immortal. No telling how long I will live... Can my brain handle the massive amount of information that will ultimately be stored in it? I hope so.)

So, here I sit. Smack dab in the middle of an emergency council meeting of warriors, leaders, caregivers, and anyone else who had been deemed worthy of this room. A room with pictures of warriors who made a difference, and beloved leaders who gave their last breath to save the people they loved. As my mind recorded the debate, my consciousness scanned the room, and all who sat in it. Reading thoughts, and absorbing the fears while trying to wade through the insecurities of those who doubted me, while my new partner gathered intel. I drifted off to where Kami was, patiently sitting outside the doors of the soundproof council chamber. That was set up as a neutral place for the leaders of the mountain to convene without interruption. She was thinking of me, and hoping the people would see me for who I was, and not who I resembled. I remember feeling her presence like a cool breeze of fresh smelling air. She inspired me just by thinking about me, and not even realizing it, she helped me once again. Reminding me that her people needed to see the real me, and know I was there to help, not hurt them.

It was then, as the Leaders of this mountain barked in the background of my mind, that I put it all together. A plan! Waiting for resources to become a problem was not the answer, we needed to secure the connections to the power grids, and I was the only one who could do it. All my knowledge of how to power up a city!... What a dumb ass, not only can I save them, but I can quadruple their energy output, and help them create an alternative exit in the process! That's right!!!! Because of a little plot by the miners, and structural engineers to get a bigger share of the fresh goods. My mind has come up with a little old solution on how to motivate the people without it being just my idea. And it is all due to the information I had just stolen out of the minds of the mountain engineers, who hadn't been telling the whole truth.

See even though they are actually a few dynamite blasts away from a safe alternate exit on the south side of the mountain underground, they have been slowing it down to gain more rations, clinging to the argument that they need more due to the hard work it was taking to burrow out of the mountain side. They recognized the value of this new way to travel, unseen in and out of the fortress. In their minds, they would not be needed as much when they were done. This led them to believe, if they were to stay relevant and survive, it would be necessary to stock pile nonperishables for trade. Living on the fresh produce the farmers have been providing, helped them acquire a nice sized hidden stock pile of goods. Wow having these powers gives me such an edge it is almost unfair. I understand how knowledge, with power can corrupt, and right then I vowed: TO ONLY USE THIS FOR GOOD, STAY HUMBLE, STAY ME, BUT NEVER REVEAL JUST HOW MUCH I KNOW OR HOW I KNOW IT! Or someday, I could be the one that people would be in a room plotting to defeat. Having become the very thing I once fought to end, a bitter, bored, and jaded old mind. The trick was to not make the engineers look like crooks, but to make them look like heroes instead. Not only did I have to deal with the engineers, electrical, structural, and the waterworks. (Waterworks, the gang who brought water to the upper levels from the underground river under the mountain.) There were also the ones who protected the mountain, which consisted of the Mountain Security Reserve, Raiders, and the Pack. First there is The Mountain Security Reserve, a scrappy group of brave men, women, and young adults whose responsibilities consisted of keeping the peace in the compound itself, and defending its borders when necessary. The Raiders have the dangerous and honorable task of recon of the surrounding areas all around the mountain. Other duties involve escorting the gatherers on missions outside of the compound, while scavenging themselves. The Pack runs them all... Doing what is necessary to make sure it all works, or picking up the pieces when it doesn't. That includes fixing any mess a bad mission could make. The Farmers, and those whom represented the crews that farmed the greenhouses also had a seat at the Council. But there were also the workers, teachers, custodial, cooks, and everyone else you could think of. Every faction had a witness that would represent them in this big, big room. Now at the head of the big, big table was Eldermum, and the Pack leader Max. Followed by Spike the leader of the electric engineers, Rockface the structural and mining engineer leader, and me. The rest of the room the remaining leaders were seated around us observing, adding comments here and there. The leaders who were needed most at this time were sharing the floor and speaking without interruption so everyone could hear. Now Eldermum has told the people of the mountain that I am, and have always been the one who was prophesized to end the apocalypse, and change the planet forever. The one who was going to save them from this evil that has infected our world. So, until I prove otherwise, the people have accepted that I am not evil, not here to eat them, or turn them into one of me. That being said, it was necessary for me to sit at the main table, this way I am involved in all the planning of this huge event. She won't let me in to see all her dreams about me, but I trust her word and intent. Although I was not fully onboard with being a savior 'n' stuff, it was finally sinking in that I was the only man for the job. These powers weren't just a coincidence that fell upon me. Not sure who, or what is behind it. Just know that whatever happens now... it is on me, and it's time to put up or shut up! No turning back now! Besides even if I could, I wouldn't want to. This is what I was brought back from the undead for. It just took a hot minute to accept.

My plan was complete, and while the room was deliberating the fate of the mountain, I whispered through my mind an invitation to look inside and see what my plan was. Eldermum closed her eyes, and to my delight she smiled. Then she answered back with a giggle on the edge of her words:

ELDERMUM: HMMM HMM HMM... Oh, yes young man... it will work. Just sit back and I will help you plant the seeds of those memories in their minds. Then I will justify the planted memories with statements that will solidify them with my positive reassurance. You can handle this massive of memory meld already Zack? Very impressive young man... very impressive indeed...

ME (with confidence): YES, Eldermum. In the mean time I will plant the seeds of those ideas that you saw in my mind earlier. This will help fortify the power grid, and push back the hoard while we secure this mountain's life line for years to come. I promise, you will see!

ELDERMUM: I believe in you Zack. I always have. I will follow your lead... but know this. These are the minds of my people, so I will plant most of the seeds, and alter their memories, okay?

ME (with deep respect): Yes ma'am... I mean, 'Mum... I mean, Eldermum!

ELDERMUM: Calm down young man. You will need to relax, now relax and breathe...

I then began creating the nudge of an idea, to push people into helping themselves. While I was doing that, 'Mum started creating fake memories for the engineers, their families, friends, and anyone involved in my little plan for the alternate exit, and air vent project. With Eldermum's help, the memories would be planted in the most respected of the structural engineer team first. Then the electricians would be next, followed by the Raiders, and the Pack. This idea of "solve the problem before it becomes one" must also be put in place alongside the memories. If done right, a proper sequence of events can evolve enough for the memories to support the idea. This would assure me a place where I can show worth by throwing in my ideas on energy storage and power boosting techniques. The very same kind of networking that I used to get Zumie valley's power grid back online. All of this had to happen within a moment of time that would be unnoticed. I left that up to 'Mum. I know she wanted me to lead, but in our combined wisdom, it was only right for her to plant the bulk of the memories. I will be the support and assist that she needs. For me, the only thing that mattered was the success of the plan. No ego was involved on either of our parts. Her mountain, her people, and she loved them dearly, truly a great woman! It was in that moment I winked at Eldermum in my mind, and the plan was set into motion. Piece of cake, right?

SPIKE
Leader of electrical engineers.

SPIKE (head electrical engineer and major ego maniac): OK PEOPLE!! OK!... Eldermum wants to speak, everybody shut up!

MAX: Order, order everybody!!! (SMACK!!! Went the gavel!) It does no good if everybody speaks at once!

You know a man is respected when the room quiets, and the focus of the people adjusts to his every spoken word. As I looked around the council hall, I could tell that Max had the attention of every member. 'Mum then stood up next to him and put her hand on his shoulder as if to say, "don't worry I have it now." He stepped back slowly, and you could feel the mood of the room shift from despair to hope in an instant. She may not be the biggest person in the room, but her charisma was undeniable. A quick but subtle look at the people sitting at the long, oval, wooden table, and you would see hardened survivors who seemed worry free and under control. Unfortunately, on the inside so very well hidden, they were trembling like children who were waiting for the teacher to tell them what to do next during a fire drill. 'Mum looked over the room and took a deep breath. For within her single, but long breath of air, time stood still for me and her, and every memory, every savory seed of how to save the day was planted. The skills of this woman were sick, and I knew she was the real deal. I helped, and let me put the emphasis on help, ok. My part was to implant little seed ideas, the hope was that these ideas would push the most respected council members in the right direction. This was crucial to the success of our mission, everything had to happen close to our visions for this to even work. Eldermum on the other hand, had to plant memories in anyone who was connected to the people in our plan, in two long seconds. Pretty kick-ass if you ask me!

It was done, and not one soul had even noticed it happened. Except me and 'Mum of course. Now, it was just a matter of time before the inner workings of our plan would show its stripes in the council and its members... any minute now!...

> ELDERMUM (with a confident smile): It is not up to me alone to decide our next course of action in this dark moment of our people. It must be a conglomeration of ideas, and actions taken together. Even though our talents are all different, if we combine those talents in an effort to save our home, there is not a thing we cannot overcome. I cannot predict an outcome unless we are all honest, and set towards the same goal. Even though the situation looks grim, we must not despair! We will find a way to save the home we have painstakingly fought to create! We are here, and this is who we are! The MOUNTAIN OF HOPE is here to stay, and so are we! Remember our way of life, and how we have become so strong. It is not our numbers, but the quality of the people that live within those numbers, that makes us stronger! This philosophy has made us stronger, confident in our ability to adapt, and to overcome any challenges we may face. BUT ONLY! Only, if we face them together! Together we are unstoppable!

The room filled with positive thoughts of saving the mountain! The amount of inspiration to be selfless and come together as one team of talented minds was hard to explain with words alone. But I will try. It felt like going from 0 to 100 mph in 6 seconds, over and over again. Until that is all you could feel, the rush, long lasting and sustaining. I felt it too, her words were perfect, and it showed. It was obvious in everyone's faces, not to mention the instantaneous standing ovation she received from the council and small audience that was fortunate enough to be there. That once again the time has come to live for something more than your own interests, but for the common interests of your kind. A much needed reminder of what had got them so very far in the first place.

It was just then, as the clapping started to subside, I could hear the seeds growing in their minds. Like a flower that would not be denied the chance to grow, they sprouted, and the ideas started to flow. The first to speak was Team Electric...

> SPIKE (stepping forward with his mobster accent): My team will collaborate with Max and his trustworthy warriors. Together we will find a way to the generators outside the mountain. This will assure the foothold we have on the mountain's gate to keep the undead at bay. We must make sure those undead can't shut down our party, if you know what I mean.

> MAX (giving a nod of respect to Spike for his contribution): Sounds like a plan if the council agrees. The Pack and The Mountain Raiders would be honored to escort and help these brave souls of Team Electric secure the power grid to the weapons and our home.

With that, Eldermum asked for a yea or nay to sound off in agreement. It was an overwhelming yea for the mission to be a go. Just then the farmers and gatherers clan offered extra rations for all who participated in the fight for the mountain, and others chimed in as well. The culinary clan offered high protein provisions to keep the soldiers muscles in good repair, and carb heavy bars to give them long lasting energy for the fight to come. The doctors and nurses then offered to work around the clock, keeping those who were injured attended to, and prepping for the influx of those who would need immediate attention when the fighting began. It was incredible how everyone almost didn't even need the push to want to be a part of the mix, lending their talents and resources in any way that they could. The only clan that didn't stand up and declare themselves willing to help were Team ROCK EATERS. They were not in the mood to share. I was surprised that the seed of being a hero to his people was not enough to move Rockface, a man who had the fate of his people in his hands. What else could I do to persuade him to help open up the south entrance to the mountain? He must do this to allow Max and his Pack to lead Team Electric into the power grid generators. By doing this, it will also give the Mountain Raiders an opportunity to flank the undead army just outside the gates.

Then in a cheer like a break from a football huddle...

> ROCKFACE (the hardcore voice of a well smoked out set of vocal cords, optimist that he was): What if you cannot all deliver on what you say... (His pause was intended to incite some sceptics to chime in out of order and begin a conversation about a plan that would cause more separation than unity.) I mean, maybe The Rock Eaters aren't down with these ideas you guys are tossing around.

I knew something had to be done, so I told Eldermum to follow my lead, and maybe the two of us could get the truth out of Rockface without making it look like he was holding back. If there was a way, I was going to find it. I came up with a clever lie that exposed the truth in a non-condemning way.

> ME (with a soft questioning tone about me): Well, I was waiting outside for the ok to join all of you heroic

people, and well… Well I overheard two of your clan get out of a vehicle and say:

FIRST GUY: Hey man do you think we should bust in an' tell them about the breach in excavation of the alternate exit project? We have finally punched through! I mean it could change everything!

OTHER GUY: I know, a day or so and we could open it up enough for the trucks and big rigs to fit through!

ME (now feeling a little confident): See I have a photographic memory, so my account of the two men is very accurate. In light of this totally new information, how long do you think it would take your Rockeaters to make all of this a reality?… (Long pause as Rockface stared me down with a "F U" expression on his face.)

The council room rumbled with chatter as Rockface stood in silence with a look of defiance about his posture. Just then a welcome ally sounded off! Now this was significant to my acceptance into the mountain, and I will always be in his debt for this leap of faith.

SMOKE: I vouch for young Zee… (The room was so quite you could hear a mouse fart. Apparently, Smoke has never spoken before at any meeting, ever!)… He is a talented young man. His heart, integrity, and intentions are on point. I know, because my interrogation of him was extensive and thorough. I would gladly fight by his side in any battle.

ELDERMUM: I have also spoken and communicated with this young hero's mind. He is honest and should be taken seriously. He helped revive a small city near the southern coast for his kind. Sewerage, electricity, and even a Wi-Fi communication system using old cellphones for the valley they call home. He can help this mountain run with more power and efficiency. In fact, if it wasn't for Zee, his people would still be living in the dark to this day.

ME (with a humble nod): Thank you, Eldermum... Smoke! You have my utmost respect, and I really appreciate how you see me. I offer my wisdom to you all, and will answer to Smoke and Eldermum. Whatever they agree on, I will follow suit.

ROCKFACE (not buying it for a second): HA! You expect me to trust a half dead rotten corpse to help save the day?! You must be smokin' the good stuff, because I'm not even sure he isn't the one who brought those bone munchin' assholes to our front door in the first place. If you get my drift there, "brotha" Smoke?

SMOKE (not flinching, best poker face ever): Not a chance crater face, I mean Rockface. Besides, if you can't take my word for it, Eldermum's should be more than solid enough for y...

 *ROCKFACE (ready to retaliate): Whatever! You should just disappear like your name! You ain't even a member of this council, so shut your face jarhead!*

ME (taking charge of what I started in the first place. Puttin' up and not shuttin' up): HEY!!! Both of you! The fact still remains! Rockface, you hold the key to our success. Whether you trust me or not, your council has put together a plan that will actually work. You can either be the hero, or the man who condemned his people to starvation and death. Which in my opinion would really suck badly. In fact, if the council wants, they could start cutting out all rations to your people, which would cause the inevitable in fighting for control of the rations. You know! The way it was before the success of the mountain, and your people. If that's what you're after? OR?... You could blast the hell out of that alternate exit, and become an instant cause of the mountain's salvation. You would be one of the many heroes that saved the mountain's future, and get your people more rations and cooked food for the effort. The whole shebang-bang hinges on your decision now Rockface! So, if you really need to hate me, or whatever it is, do it on your time! Because this is everybody's problem, and it's time to man up!

The look on his face softened but was still entrenched by his strength and stubborn nature. Except now it was starting to sink in, and he took a deep breath in and sighed a big sigh.

ROCKFACE (not looking defeated, but looking like a leader who was ready to throw in on the plan): Ok... ok, I will have my best on the completion of the new exit to our home. Besides, it's about time we had a back door to this death trap.

The council room thundered with applause, cheers, and feet stopping. Not a single member in the room wasn't cheering for the personalities that had always clashed in the past. But now, finally in agreement on something that they knew would change the way the mountain would operate for generations to come. All while saving their lives in the process. Not bad if I do say so myself. Eldermum heard my thoughts and couldn't have agreed more. Though it took more coaxing than I originally thought it would, the whole thing was a success. And man! That Rockface was a challenge, and she warned me he would be.

Right away the council began making plans, laying out the timetables that were essential to the success of all that had to be accomplished. People that had drifted apart because of the lack of needing each other in everyday life, once again appreciated the gifts they all needed to share. Now, because of this event, the tone had shifted for everyone to come together. It reminded me of my people, and the teamwork we displayed to get our valley working again. In that moment, I missed my Zumies for the first time in a long time. In fact, watching them plan and offer to do whatever it took to secure the power grid and compound really made me wonder. What happened that caused the destruction of the human race in a matter of months? They all seem so resourceful, and strong willed! How could the undead take over without being annihilated by the technology that fortified the backbone of the military? The same military that blew up whole cities with a single weapon at one time in its history. All of the armies that have battled on this world, and nobody was able to knock down some flesh eaters? Never mind all the people who had guns, according to all of the literature that was available in the city library. One out of every three humans carried a fire arm in this country alone! I then heard the voice of an angel, standing in the doorway of the hall. Patiently waiting for me to exit the scene, and make my way into her arms.

> KAMI (with a smile that made me feel ten thousand feet tall): Stop calling me an angel, it's gonna go to my head silly ass!

> ME (feeling complete and sure of one thing): I couldn't wait to see you again!

> KAMI: Yeah, 'Mum made me promise not to interrupt you while you were being... Well, AWESOME! I can't believe you two pulled that off so well. I'm so very proud, and a tad jealous of your sweet skillset!

We both stared into each other's eyes as this conversation went on, and the world slowly melted away. No one cared out loud, and it felt amazing to feel so connected to another soul. The one thing that had been unknowingly missing from my world was here, and I was cherishing every moment. A kiss was on our minds, but we knew it was too early to shock some of the people whose mental opinions were being blocked out, so we could just be. Nothing felt so right and natural. I went over to Kami and extended my arms so that I might put them around her small but strong frame. She looked right at me, and we hugged, rocking back and forth as if there was no one there to see the disrespectful PDA that was being forced upon the unsuspecting council of the mountain people. 'Mum grunted as if to say, "AAAAHHHHEEEEMMMM!!!!!!" We looked at her... smiled and looked back at each other.

ME: Please, carry on, our bad?... I will be right there, one moment.

I told Kami to give me five minutes and she smacked my butt as I walked towards the door of the council hall. Everyone, and I mean every single person in that hall saw it. There was a long pause of blank but scowling stares in my direction, and then the place was a buzz with planning and ideas. I slowly made my way to the leader of Team Electric and opened my backpack. Inside was plans I had written earlier for a new, stronger, and more efficient power grid. I put them down on the table and Spike looked them over while grunting and making noises that could only be described as... Well, unsettling at best... After a long pause he looked up at me and smiled a GIHUGIC SMILE!!

SPIKE (looking like Zeus after getting his first lightning bolt): WOW! This is excellent son. With these plans we can run the mountain at full capacity or more, on a third of the power we are on now! You are a God send buddy boy. You can oversee this so it's all up to spec?

ME (knowin' my shit): Absofricknlutely my man! No doubt in my mind we can be in and out in 39, 45mn tops. Just need some good welders, your best guys, some skilled escorts, and we will nail it for sure. The mountain will never have blackouts again. As long as you maintain the integrity of the connections and ventilate the heat it will generate. Keeping things cool will be as easy as opening a window if you know what I mean.

SMOKE (making his way over with purpose): With Max's permission, and an ok from Spike. I would be honored to lead this mission, and make sure we all come back alive. I know just the crew to take this on, and this group doesn't even have fail as a word in their vocabulary. You copy?

With that, it was set. I shook the hands of some brave men and women, and then we parted to have one day of livin' it up! In about 48 hours, maybe less, we might not be around to live at all. So, for the small platoon of 50 people, give or take a few, it was time to say things that were never said, and do the things that had yet to be done. It was a tradition in this place to let those who were about to risk it all have a day to live it up. This way they won't have any regrets if it was to be their last days on this planet. For the rest of the mountain it was a busy bee hive of activity, with one goal in mind. To save the future of the mountain, and ensure victory for Team HOPE. Team Rock Eaters began to clear out some major stone, enough stone to make sure the opening would be large enough for our crew and its vehicles to fit through. Each team set out to reach a goal, helping in any way they could to aid the ones who were ready to risk it all for their sakes. Team Eats set out to hydrate and feed the crews properly for the task at hand. Team Farm was harvesting what they could, while securing goods for storage just in case the people had to leave the mountain. Team Ammo secured what limited ammo the mountain had, cleaned weapons, and took care of properly arming the people. A platoon like group of skilled workers, with post-apocalyptic soldiers by their side, filled will courage and character, embarking on the mission of our lifetimes. There will be an offensive on the undead that are camping out at the front gates. Accomplishing the diversion that would mislead the hoard of Z-Bots in a big way. This distraction would give our group the chance needed so we could truck into the warehouse, and protect Team Electric at the same time. The ironic thing about the warehouse itself... Well, Spike let me in on a secret that only a few members of the council knew about. The hidden building has sentry guns controlled by cameras with the capability of keeping the building undead free and intruder free. The guns do this by identifying the enemy from the ally in a fully automated way. Once the guns are activated, the people of the mountain can fight while being safe from the gunfire of these weapons. Unfortunately, the building itself only had enough power to run the security key pads that lock up the entrances, along with the computers that regulated the facility. The mountain's turbines run off the underground river that flows under the fortress itself. Accompanied by some windmill aid to help with power gaps that caused unscheduled blackouts in years past. Now I know what you're thinking! "Why not just use the power to kill undead and be done with the upgrades and what not?" Normally I would agree. But if we do! The hoard will hear the action, and then there would be no way to secure the warehouse and the turbines inside. It would be overrun with the undead bastards, and the fight would take place where damage to the turbines could leave the mountain powerless and vulnerable. This plan gives us the best chance to succeed, and with minimal casualties, hopefully. Once Spike and his crew were done with the upgrades, the mission would go into phase two. It would then come down to Smoke and I, with the Raiders in tow, to join the fight at the front gate. Using vehicles, the Raider's guns, and Smoke's combat experience to flank the army of flesh eaters. Relieving the fighters at the front gate, and finishing off any leftover undead that happened to still be moving. I mean no pressure or anything, just the fate of five thousand plus human beings, not to mention a platoon of brave men. All of them depending on a plan that I had planted in their heads so they would think it was their own. I was pretty much responsible for everything that was about to go down. I remember looking up at the mile high ceiling of the huge fortress and thinking to myself, "It feels good to unite these people in their time of need. I just hope that this was the right way to go about it. If not I will have a lot of explaining to do."

> KAMI (feeling my pain): Don't worry Zacky. You've got this, no doubt in my mind that you and the team will succeed.

> ME (with a smidge of "HOLY HELL WHAT HAVE I DONE?" written on my face): I hope so, Kami. A lot of the success of this hinges on them buying into my plan. Never mind, that I care what happens to this mountain in a big way. I mean where did this storm come from? A small part of me feels that there is more to this than meets the eye.

> KAMI (looking at me like there is something going on): Do you mean like something behind it? Driving it on purpose?

> ME: I know it sounds stupid and unbelievable, but I can feel those undead focusing on the front door. Hunger is the last thing on their minds! They want to destroy this place! I have nev...

KAMI (looking pale as she realized I was right): No stop it!

ME (with real concern): You feel it too, don't you? What is it Kam?

KAMI (giving in to my obvious concern): It... it is nothing like that, but I do feel their focus. It scares me to death... I need you Zack! NOW!

ME (feeling her need as if it was my own): I'm coming to you!!

KAMI: YES, ZEE!! Come 'n' find meeeeee...

A beautiful image of flowing water and a rock waterfall hidden deep in a cave stopped me in my tracks as it flashed into my mind. The smell of fresh water soaked in aged minerals from the rocks that it flowed through. Healthy green moss covering the dew drop walls, glistening from the small amount of illumination, shining through softball sized skylights a thousand years young. She wanted to show me just how alive this mountain really is. Coming to me in an instant, and leaving just as fast. Staining the memory into my mind forever. My feet followed her tantalizing, teasing flashes, showing her twirling around as her hair flowed with her like heavenly ribbons of color. Her eyes were green and big... struggling to focus I followed without care. Knowing this could be the last days of my life, I no longer struggled with the question of IF! She was pulling me to the kiss I never knew I needed, and I was driven to want nothing else. It was like walking in slow motion, ever so slowly getting closer to the moment! Huge steroid fed butterflies filled my chest to the point of no return. I was hers. She knew it, and I wanted it that way. It made me feel freaking unstoppable. Strong and confident! You know, looking back, it was like gravity had a direct pull on my soul. All the people that had comments hidden behind their kind smiles didn't even matter. The things people will say to themselves to comfort the fears and doubt in their hearts is comical:

NOT SO NICE OLD LADY: I bet his private parts are all decayed, and disgusting.

A VERY LARGE SKEPTIC: Do you think he has ever eaten someone's butt before?

A MAN WHO SMELLED WORSE THAN THE UNDEAD: He probably smells real bad, don't get too close. You might end up smelling like he does!

OLD MAN WHO REEKED LIKE MOTHBALLS: How is that rotting flesh eater gonna save us? Eat all the other walking corpses before they eat us?

BLONDIE LOOKIN' HATER: He looks hungry, what does he eat? Not us right?

JERK FACED BUTT SCRATCHER: I say shoot him and take care of the undead scum ourselves. He is nothing but a smelly walking disease, just waiting to infect us all!!!!

This would usually devastate me, but this was a memory I will cherish and protect with all my power. Not even the "private parts" comment bothered me! For nothing could kill the feeling that filled my chest with anticipation. The moment that every experience, and chance I took led me to was steps away.

I passed by shops and eateries that immediately made me think of home, but not even home had the internal, uncontrollable draw on me that she did. I walked for a minute 'til Kami gave me a ping to let me know that her scent was strong. It drew me right to her, there was no resisting the attraction. Like I wanted to resist, ha! I ran through passages blindly following her lead. I totally trusted her, and we had the whole night to spend together. With everybody prepping for the battle, certain mind readers and half undead guests are just a distraction. So Eldermum told us to go "talk", you know... So that's what we did. 'Mum was no fool, and although she wasn't giving us her approval, she understood.

It finally was here, the moment I have been waiting for, and so has she! The stone gave way to a scene that was as beautiful as it was breathtaking. Imagine a well deep inside the mountain, where a sky light etched away by time and water was positioned perfectly by evolution, allowing just the sun's light to reach the pond of spring water that was fed by a waterfall deep within its heart! Hidden at the center of it all, standing in front of a waterfall just loud enough to drown out the noise of the buzzing above, the center of my world! The angel of inspiration and love. KAMI... I noticed the moss covered rocks, so bright and soaked with color that if you touched them, the green stained your fingertips as if you had just touched wet paint. The smell of fresh cold mineral water, and the cool breeze it created gave us the perfect excuse to get close. Her luscious, firm, plump lips ever so slightly puckered, as if to suggest that a kiss was expected, and it made my heart stop... Then I slowly grabbed her shoulders, and slid my hands down her arms 'til our skin touched just after her sexy short sleeves. A kiss had begun to take shape. A long kiss that made our world collapse into a hidden waterfall in the center of a mountain. Nothing else existed at that moment in time but us. Her breath tasted like sweet life itself, the tender soft feel of this woman's lips melted the world away. They slid over mine like liquid cotton candy was her lip gloss. It was the sweetest taste that existence had to offer, and it was given to me. We were making out, and it was the only thing that mattered. Despite the impending uncertainty of the days to come, we kissed like there was no tomorrow. She moaned ever so softly, and so did I. The instincts of passion took over, and my tongue slid firmly over her cotton candy lips as she let me in. Our minds and bodies connected in a way no two beings could. It was, and will forever be, the single most life changing event of my ever evolving existence. She pulled away for a second to look into my eyes and then smiled. No words were necessary, our hearts and minds were one. The goose bumps of pleasure were doing the wave across my skin wherever she touched, and I knew it was the same for her. This powerful young intelligent woman wanted me, and let me tell you with no hesitation... The feelings were mutual, and nothing could break the bond we now had. Despite my physical appearance, she wanted me and no one else. In fact she never wanted this with anyone, and neither did I. Not until the moment we met, did either of us even care about this love thing. Almost suggesting we imprinted on each other like werewolves or something. We kissed and hugged each other for a good long time, other things too, but that is just for me and Kami. This Zumie doesn't kiss and tell... Well not every detail anyway.

Keeping track of the time was the last thing on our minds. We sat together against some of the dry rocks, just soaking up the atmosphere loving the feel of it all. Kami quietly fell asleep in my arms, and I knew she belonged there, forever! Unfortunately, the growling of my stomach woke her from her sleep, and since she could read my thoughts like her own...

> KAMI (with a stretch): You sound hungry Zee man, let's get you some good eats from The Pit.

> ME (with a question hanging on my words): The Pit?

> KAMI (laughing in her cute way): Calm down Zack, it is going to be a dining experience you will never forget.

She then put some facts into my head about how they keep the smell of food and its preparation from attracting undead to the mountain. The Pit is a fully enclosed place where food is prepped, cooked, and eaten so the smells are hidden. Big vents suck the smell out of The Pit, and blow the smoke out of the mountain into the air. Via huge ventilation shafts that have a series of filters, this weakens the smell as it exits out of the mountain near the very top of its peak. This is how all of the smells that attract the undead are expelled from the mountain compound. By the time it enters the air, the smell is dissipated to almost nothing, and the mountain stays hidden to the undead, and humans alike. Pretty smart if you consider the amount of food prepared in this buffet style pot luck called The Pit. You have to be close to smell the fortress, I remember being impressed from my own experience with stumbling onto the gates just a day ago!

> KAMI: So, you ready to have one of the best meals of your life time?

> ME (as my stomach spoke caveman): RRRRUMMBLE RAAAABBLE ROBBLBLBBLBLE... Yup, my stomach just said, "Hell Yeah!"

> KAMI (with a smirk on her face because my thoughts betray me): Are you sure that's all you're hungry for Zack?

Not only did my face turn red from blushing, but so did my thoughts, because I was caught looking at her butt. (My bad, but not really! She has a really nice gluteus maximus.) We got up and held each other for one more long, long, long moment. No words, just holding onto a moment we might never get again. Remember it's the post apocalypse, and tomorrow is a gift you only hope to receive. Being here with all of these people, their lives so fragile compared to a Zumie's, I got it. Totally understood through Kami how they felt and lived. Every memory important and precious, because it could be the last memory before... well you know. When she slowly looked up at me and into my eyes I knew she meant it, and not a word needed to be spoken, mental nor verbal.

She smacked my butt and took off running, with the biggest smile I had ever seen on her face. I ran after her with a smile that I can only describe as well, pathetic at best, just know it was the happiest I had ever been. The happiest moment I can remember to this date, not even my Zumie world could rival the happiness her smile brought to my world. My steps felt slow and melodic like a dream, it made me feel like I could remember every second of this day. We ran by people busy with the promise of battle without a care in the world. The jealousy some felt was killed by the hope we brought to the mountain. Seeing us smile at each other the way we were, sparked something beautiful in the hearts of the people, it was nice to feel love. Love from those whose minds were open to the future Kami and I represented. It made me want to fight for them even more.

In the middle of our little playful chase a little girl came up to me. I looked at Kami and she told me with a smile and a nod, that she was someone who could read minds. The little girl's mind was not open, but she was beaming with curiosity, so I decided to take her outstretched hand. My mind was bombarded with basically, a telepathic hug. Our eyes closed and in a sea of color in our minds she hugged me and said:

> LITTLE STAR (that was her name, Star): Thank you Mr. Zee, for bringing everyone together to save our home. I will forever remember you, and our lovely Kami. Go now and live it up Mr. Zee, you deserve it.

I was in awe of how calm, and poised this little girl happened to be. She gave me a small wild yellow flower, and all I could do... Stare like a kid myself. It was the most precious gesture, and it made me feel like a hero. Like I would never let her down, and I was fighting for something more than just a mountain fortress. It was the dreams, and hope of a future that I was about to risk it all for. Like I said, no turning back now. I was fully invested, and would stop at nothing to save these people. Kami smiled and darted towards The Pit. I ran after her like she was the meal herself! She was quick and I made sure not to lose her, but not to get too close either. All due to her uncontrollable laughter that made me want to chase Kami even more, it was intoxicating!

Finally, we came upon The Pit. It looked like a door that was embedded into the side of an internal rock face of the fortress. She stopped at the double doors, just a little winded from the chase.

> KAMI (with her hands stretched out towards me): Come on slowpoke, your dining experience awaits you just behind these doors.

I must have been so tuned into the voice of Kami in my head, and the vision of her just 25 feet or so away from me. I never saw the jealous 210 pound, 20 year old young man charging towards me like a ram defending its cliffs. He attempted to hit me as I jogged blindly towards my girl, who he thought should be his! Unfortunately for he, but fortunate for me, I was tuned into Kam's head and she happened to see him for a split second! Have I mentioned how fast I might be at this point in my new awareness of said powers? Can we say "NINJA"! Well, I got to see what she was seeing, and in a Mila-whatever of a second my response was epic. He drove at my hip with his head down and his shoulder leading. My step to the side, followed by a grab to the back of his collar, allowed me to stand him upright. He slid into a standing position and looked at me with awe. (Like he was thinking, "how strong is this cat?!") He attempted to say something, and instead of humiliating this young man, I gave him a chance to save face.

> ME (with a smirk on my face that held nothing back): So you slipped, did ya?

> THE YOUNG DOUCHE-BAG: Uh, well I... yes, my bad Mr. Z. I was just, umm won't let it happen again.

> ME (sporting a don't "F" with me again smile on my face): No worries there BIG man. Just remember I might not be there to catch you next time... k?!

With that, I stared him down as he walked away looking back at Kami and I one more time. She looked at me and nodded her head:

> KAMI (with pride in her heart): You know even though I'm in your head, you still surprise me, Zee. Let me tell you for our future together. That shit never gets old, K!

> ME (with a belly laugh before my words): Hahaha... ok Angel, I will remember that. I promise. Hmmmmm... Angel! That's what I will call you from now on. My Angel!

> KAMI (with a spark in her eye): Well, I can accept the tag, even though I am no Angel. BUT! FOR YOU, and you alone.

She then opened the double doors to the elevators that take you to The Pit. I couldn't wait to feast. Humiliating a bully sure works up an appetite to epic proportions. Not to mention the heavy petting between me and Kami, but that is all I am saying, for sure. The feasting was about to begin, the sounds coming from my gut were nothing compared to the loud-ass elevator coming from the depths as we waited for it to arrive. It finally settled in its position, and the heavy doors opened inviting us in. We got inside a very dimly lit elevator, and the ride down was filled with her stimulating kisses. What food? That's what I was thinking when our kiss was interrupted by laughter as the elevator came to a stop.

That is when it hit me! The smell of smoked meats, and the sweet smell of the Mecca of food! I thought the Zumies were a food driven species, well our human ancestors were flavor driven. You could almost taste the air, it was that saturated with spices, and steamy goodness. I almost forgot Kami was there:

KAMI (trying not to burst as she felt my excitement): Yup, told you stupid head. You are about to eat food that has been perfected to mouthwatering proportions. Please try not to hurt yourself, remember you have a mission at 4am tomorrow.

That's when I flashed a fact about the bottomless pit of an eater the Zumies are. Fact... The Zumie digests food at an alarmingly fast rate, and that equals to a lot of mass consumption, if you know what I mean. In short, we are PIGS, and we love to eat a ton of crap. AND! We don't even gain any weight! It totally rocks if you ask me, and nothing ever goes to waste.

ME (with my mouth watering like a hungry Bullmastiff): UUUUUUUUH, where do we start?

KAMI: Follow me piggy boy. This way, and grab more than one plate. It's smoked barbeque pork ribs night, plus all the trimmings! It is simply amazeballs!!

She was not kidding either, it was amazeballs! The buffet style setup was like a display of southern barbeque right from the TV shows that we all learned to cook from in the Zumie Valley. All there, just perfect, with steam and color displayed in all its culinary glory, just waiting to be enjoyed. Like us, food was not just for eating, it was a religious experience! I let Kami tell me in our minds how to hold out my tray and accept the portion of well-prepared ribs no matter how big or small. It would all be based on what they had stocked, and what was going to be harvested in the now, and near future. Very well thought out and organized by Team Food. They really know their way around the whole process of storage and freshness for the best experience. Even the beer they brewed was exceptional, from froth to clarity and flavor. This brew had a hint of citrus due to a really good harvest of lemons and tangerines this year. MMMMMMM... It really was a feast! Roasted corn on the cob, slow baked beans, some slaw, and collard greens with a little garlic to give a great smell and taste. My two plates were generously filled because of the mission and the battled to come. I was truly grateful as I sat down and just soaked in the visual masterpiece of meat and sides like I had never eaten before. We Zumies get close-ish, but never have we accomplish food at this high level of culinary genius. I was truly humbled and awestruck by my plates of food. Along with my two glorious beers sweating condensation from the cold glasses that cradled my elixir of life so enthusiastically. Kami looked at me and said in our minds:

KAMI (with her eyes closed): Do what I'm doing, it's called praying. It can be whatever you wish it to be about, no religion or belief is mocked in these walls.

ME: Can I just listen to yours? Whatever you want I'm gonna want too!

She smiled and said yes, and I cleared my mind and just listened.

KAMI'S PRAYER: To the spirit that binds us all. Please give us the strength to be brave enough to save the ones we love. No-matter how scary it may be, or how desperate the situation. All I ask, is the chance to be the best me I can be. AND! Bless Team Food for the great grub! A-men and A-women!

KAMI (looking me in the eyes, with grit in her voice): EAT UP PIGGY BOY! If you think you can keep up!

It was on like Wonky Kong! (For those of you who do not know human history, Wonky Kong was an extremely popular video game that captured the attention of countless generations of the human race. It was about a gorilla, who had to climb up steel beams that a pissed off donkey was controlling. I don't know why it wasn't called Donkey Kong, I mean it was a big scary donkey. The Gorilla's name was Wonky Kong so I guess that's why. Whateva!)

I watched my angel turn into a bonafide piglet. She grabbed her rack of ribs and went to town. It was apparent that manners would be the insult here. In light of this revelation I commenced with the feasting boyeeeeee!!! It was a plethora of taste and texture! My jaw could barely keep up the pace that my appetite really wanted me consuming at. The effort to not pass my Angel went unnoticed as she devoured her one plate in 7mns flat. I finished the one plate right behind her, then dove into the hot links that snapped with flavor in every single bite. The slaw broke up the meats and baked beans just perfectly. Cleansing my pallet for the collard greens that just cleared the way for the next round of hot links and so on, 'til it was completely gone. I would have licked my plate, but that might have scared some of the locals. Kami laughed at my internal struggle with love in her eyes and corn in her hair, sexy as hell. Now for the BEER! It was still cold, and the froth was barely there but it was still there. The glass mug was slippery with condensation as I lifted it to my mouth and tossed it back like a shot. The room went silent for about three seconds and... YEAHHHH WHOOOO RIGHT ON!!!! The room erupted with cheers and compliments as I raised the second mug. Remember fast metabolism, super regenerative cell capabilities and such. The crowd cheered and I tossed it back with ferocity and the room exploded once again, with cheers and love behind it. People were grabbing more mugs and continued to give me the experience of a life time. Songs were sung, hugs were hugged, and just like that I was part of the fold. Food is awesome because it always seems to bring everyone together. These fine people embraced me, and with word of mouth the whole mountain was brewing with hope. The tale of the man who could drink like no other was born, and the flow of positive thoughts in the mountain filled my chest with powerful confidence and resolve. Still feeling glorious and fortunate, I noticed the young heartbroken man, sulking in the corner of all the celebration. You know the dude who tried to take me down just before the feast. I couldn't help but feel bad, and decided to approach the young man with a kind word. Mind made up, I worked my way over to him and tapped him on his shoulder with a cold bottle of ale. He looked up and looked away quickly, with a tone of weight on his mind, and boy I felt it. He reluctantly accepted my peace offering and smiled with humility in his own way. He then spoke, and to my surprise:

> KOLTEN THE BRAVE: Hello, mister Z. sir. I'm sorry I let my feelings for Kam control my actions earlier. It won't happen again. I hope you still want me on your team tomorrow morning. I will not let you down. I am better than what you saw. Forgive my drunken angst?

I opened my bottle and put my hand on his shoulder. We tapped bottles and I said:

ME (remembering we are almost the same age technically, not to mention I had a few pints by then): You're a brave one, Kolt. Just remember that everything that happens opens a door to another chance to be the best you that you can be. I know you will be on point tomorrow and I'm counting on you to show me that bravery can be used for good instead of in haste. You're a good soul... man, I have a sense about these things you know!

KOLTEN (with burden lifted from his shoulders): Thank you, Mr. Z...

ME (sounding leaderish): Finish that brew and get some sleep, you're gonna need your energy for the mission in the early, early, so frickin' early am. Later, Brave One.

He held up his bottle and turned to walk away. It took longer than usual 22 seconds for him to turn the corner and vanish. That's when I felt Angel coming up behind me and:

ME (jumping out of my boots): Whoa mamma-san! That's my butt cheek you're grabbing!!

ANGEL (looking like she means business): You're coming with me... NOW Zacky Zee! No choice to be made, your turn to impress ME! Let's go Zee man, my man... take my hand and follow me.

Because I was no fool, I did as she commanded, and with great pleasure. She led me back to her place without any worry as to who may see. It was clear that we were together, and to my surprise most of the mountain was cool with it. Not that I was in any state to hear anything but the thoughts of my soulmate! Who could ask me to howl at the moon for one single kiss, but instead... She treats me like a man, and I couldn't wait to treat her like the woman she was. Her little dwelling was off the beaten path, under the roots of a ginormous tree that anchored itself into the side of this mountain. However many years it took for this immortal tree to grow is beyond my scope of intelligence. It was then, the first time we kissed in front of her amazing little home, that everything looked like something out of a fairytale. You know the one that involved an immortal boy from never-never world! It was truly magnificent, and it smelled like winter-green heaven, piney and fresh. Even though we were thousands of feet under a mountain, it felt like the outside world was still around us. Through all of this stimuli I could still smell Kami, she smelled just like jasmine, with a hint of sweet cotton candy!

I couldn't wait to take her into our little world, and loose ourselves in each other! Now I understand! When you have a love like this, fighting for it is instinct, automatic, and welcome, nothing would stop me from saving this love. This feeling that transcends the flesh and makes the world seem livable no matter the conditions around you. In my heart of hearts, I now know! This is what being human is all about!

She turned to me and opened the door. It was a museum of humanity, but that was not why we were here. Despite the many fond reminders of what the world once was, I took her into my arms like it may be our last time, and she knew it too. We stowed that depressing shit, and just erupted into passion. I can't write about what happened without feeling as if I am betraying something cosmic and precious. For now, just know this... if making love is truly a real thing, then that is what we did... mind, body, and soul. No regrets, only love. Timeless and real.

As she lay there, asleep I remember just looking at her. Looking at her without a single thought interrupting the gaze. My Angel was the most beautiful naked piece of artwork that I have ever seen. Her silhouette was curvy, powerful, and angelic. My eyes could only see her in the dark candlelit room. That was just enough for me to record this moment in my mind forever. A piece of our lives, that will drive my lust for her no matter how we age together, or how far apart we may be. I stood up slowly so not to wake my Angel, looked out her window and behold. A city of candles, lit to wish luck to all those whom were about to risk their lives for the sake of the mountain and its people. It was warming, the event solidified my love for the spirit of these brave souls. I had remembered hearing about it during the celebration in The Pit, but never did I think it would look this wonderful. The whole mountain cave smelt of incense and fragrant candles burning in the night. Small streams of smoke rose slowly up into the atmosphere of the ginormous cave that was home to this close knit group of individuals. The flickering lights from the candles sparkled like the night sky was right here in The Mountain of Hope itself! The love that was in the act of those candles touched me in a way I thought only the Zumie world could. I was wrong, and unusually happy to be so. As I gazed out at the sea of flickering lights, and orange little amber glow spots coating the rooftops and windowsills of the people. Kam the angel put her arm around me and pulled me back to the last moments we would have together until it was time...

It was almost time for me to leave. Even though Angel would be mad, I had planned to slip out quietly, and let her sleep. I quietly got dressed, packed my backpack, and started to lace up my boots. I knew she was out, due to the fact that she was dreaming about our future. Wow she has plans for all of us, and I will hopefully be able to fulfill the dreams of my girl! BUT! For now, so I can be the soldier I need to be, I must slip away and not have to go through a tearful goodbye. If it's true love, she will just be happy to see me when it is all over! Then kill my ass for not saying goodbye. Knowing the consequences, I crept my way to the front door, and that's when Angel said:

> KAM THE ANGEL: *Please come back to me Zachariah Zee... no words, just go knowing I will be with you, every step. In my heart and mind, you're stuck with me now, so get used to it My Love!*

I turned my head slightly to the right looking back over my shoulder, and nodded knowing it was all she needed. Opened the door, took a deep breath:

> KAMI: *Oh... Check your front vest pocket. It's so you always have a piece of me with you.*

I closed the door while reaching into my front pocket. Only to be touched in my squishy place by the smell that rose up out of my right chest pocket. It was her scent, all over her soft shiny multi-colored hair, the exclamation point on the mission statement of my heart. I walked down her frequently swept stairs and dared not look back. Only 'cause I might run back to her. She is amazing, a rare, beautiful, and compassionate smart ass. Man, she is HOT... and I love the shitaki mushrooms out of her.

I made my way back down into the heart of the mountain, where Smoke was drinking some coffee with Irish whisky in it waiting to accompany me. Steam rose from his cup as he gave me the heads up on the crew that was part of this operation. He heard someone step onto some loose gravel, and immediately looked up out of the corner of his eye. It was nothing, but you could tell he was ready. Not hiding the fact that his senses, and experiences were what would get us through this event.

SMOKE (with a compassionate grin): Ready for the time of your life, little ninja?

ME (with confidence): Yes Smoke, I will have your back, no worries my captain!

SMOKE: OKAY! I guess 'Mum wasn't kidding when she said you were more than ready.

ME (looking humble and shocked): She said that, really?!

SMOKE: Yeah, she also said to tell you that I am trust worthy, and can be told your secret... sooooo?

I couldn't help myself! I scanned his memory just to find out that he was trying to trick me into telling my secret. He was suspicious and rightfully so. I decided to tell him anyway. There was nothing in his M.O. that suggested he wasn't trustworthy.

ME: Ok Smoke, if you think you can handle it, here it is.

SMOKE (with the look of whatever kid): Listen, there is nothing that could shock me at this point in my life. With that said, lay it on me before I decide that it's not really important, and just tell you to zip it!

ME (ok here we go): Well see what happened was... My race is a result of nature meets experimental serum to reverse the effects of the undead viral phenomenon. In the form of a fierce electrical storm it was distributed to me and my people by pure coincidence, as far as we know. We are all very hard to kill, and have 2 maybe 3 times the strength of a normal humans. Our bodies heal fast and we can change out body parts from the undead, and reanimate them into a healthy body part for ourselves. It's quite rad if you think about it.

SMOKE (looking like he just saw a flying saucer or something): Is that why you knocked down 20 brews last night like it was soda pop?!

ME (with the look of a dog who just saw a bird land ten feet from his grasp): YOU HAVE SODA POP?!

SMOKE: What the!!... NO MAN, FOCUS! Now finish what you were saying before the soda-pop distraction.

ME (shaking off the soda-pop comment): Oh yeah... To make a long story a little less long. I was struck by lightning on my way here. In fact, it was that gihugic storm three or so weeks ago that brought me here. Well, times my Zumie benefits by 10, and that's what I am now. Super strength, quickness, agility, and intelligence. Not to mention I heal like comic book characters did in your people's old story telling days. I can build anything based on the materials around me, and I have studied every form of martial arts, weapons skills that your warriors and story tellers had to offer. In light of what I just said, I promise that no worries are needed. I have your back Smoke.

SMOKE (pokerfaced): You may be a super half-breed, but never scoff at experience. It will always outplay the powerful, if not for the sheer arrogance that power breeds. While jading the mind into getting lazy enough to become predictable, and therefore fallible by taking the opponent for granted. Like having a tell in a poker game, and being unfortunate enough that you are the only one who doesn't know it.

ME (humbled by a hero in his own right): Thank you sir. I needed that... Really, I would like to stay humble. That is why I have not revealed it to the mountain yet, also because I was afraid they would resent me for it. But I was so wrong, and I only want to use this power to help.

SMOKE: I know kid... Your secret is safe with me. Until you need to use it, ok?

ME: Ok, sir. You got it. OH! One more thing, I am not sure, but I think my powers are evolving into the mental kind. Not sure how much, but don't be surprised if I can do more than just fight, OK!

SMOKE (nodding with approval): I understand now. SHE DID IT TO ME AGAIN!

As Smoke put his hand on my shoulder, he revealed what Eldermum had said to him:

ELDERMUM: Okay Smoke, when the time is right you'll know. I need you to tell Zack this: A hero is not born specifically for some great moment in time, sugga. In fact, a hero isn't born at all. Instead, they are forged from these moments in time. Making impossible choices to do what's right, no matter the personal cost! Inspiring all those around them to do the same, and in by doing so making the hope of victory real, even when it may seem impossible! This is alot to as Zack, I know, but something tells me you are already there...now go be a hero!

With that it was over, and the weight of being me was lifted. He looked me over and nodded his head while saying in his mind. (Not bad kid, not bad.) Smoke turned and started walking, I followed close behind. His mind was clear while the heart of a lion beat in his chest, I could feel it. I could only hope to carry this much swag someday. We wasted no time in making our way down to the entrance of tunnels. These are the tunnels that would take us safely to the generator buildings undetected. They are built in conjunction with the mountain face for a camouflaging affect. It is only 3 hundred yards from the steel gates. Unfortunately, even though it is usually in walking distance, going around the mountain is the only way we get to it without losing half of the group. Even if we could penetrate the undead as they poured through the gates themselves, the plan was set in motion and the entire crew was waiting for us in loaded trucks with machine guns mounted on their beds. Manned by brave souls who would be on the lookout for any dead-heads coming our way. The heavily guarded convoy was ready to go, and Smoke looked at me and said:

SMOKE (serious as hell): Just be the best you that you can be soldier. Remember that the man next to you is your responsibility, and the man next to him is his. This is how we have always done things! No one quits. GOT IT BOY!

ME: YES SIR SMOKE SIR!

SMOKE (grinning with an unlit cigar in his mouth): Good, then let's POP THIS CHERRY BOYS!!!!

He yelled out, the response was instant. Watches were synchronized, and the group split up into units of ten. Five soldiers and five engineers into each vehicle, ten vehicles in all with escorts in the lead. I stood ready next to my truck and looked over my gear. One katana, check. Two nine millimeter fully-auto pistols, with oversized clips holding thirty rounds of dead-head shredding capability. Bad ass! Plus, a utility belt full of six way tools and some schematics of electrical wiring I wrote up while Angel was sleeping like an... well you get it. I got on the truck and sat down with a group that only fate would stick together. The gears of the truck were ground into place and we were off. No turning back now, in fact... I want to be here. I belong here!

THE STEEL GATES

SOUTH EXIT

THE GENERATORS

THE MINES

THE MOUNTAIN OF HOPE

MAP

MOUNTAIN ROAD

STORAGE SHED

SMALL MOUNTAIN TOWN

THE C-TURTLE

I HOPE YOU GUYS ARE USED TO THIS CRAP BY NOW! ENTRY# DOCE

6th Chapter

AS LUCK WOULD HAVE IT!!

We pulled away into the dimly lit tunnels, the very tunnels leading to the new exit of the mountain. A timely triumph for this community, even if it had to be coerced out of the Rockeaters to reveal it. The newly acquired tunnel is the very reason we have any kind of chance at this plan working in the first place. Don't tell Rockface that though! 'Cause you would never hear the end of it, like never ever 'til the day he died ever, never!

Anyway, let us get back to the truck and its crew! (That only a God, with a sense of humor matched by Loki himself would put together.) Hmm... let's see? There was the unshakable Smoke. The ever so clever Spike, and his son everyone called Sparki. Then there was (just a little full of himself) Rockface, accompanied by machine operation specialist, Diesel. A man who I was told could drive, fly, or operate any piece of machinery there was on earth. Plus, a rookie soldier who happened to be The Brave One himself, yup it was no other than Kolten. (Looking humble and determined to prove his worth.) Followed by the very large, ass kicking B-Bear, a man that can make anyone feel small. Last but not least, you guessed it! None other than my biggest fan, Pyro himself. Now I know that's only a 9 count, and I said that there was 10 in each truck. BUT, the only reason we have this many, is because B-Bear is a BIG MAN! So, we opted to take one less person, and enough equipment and explosives to level the mountain itself. There were 6 vehicles loaded for the mission, the others were full of Rockface's people. Shadowed by a small group of patrolmen to secure the new access to the mountain, until the engineers could build another gate. Their responsibility was to drive ahead of us to secure the opening with some support beams, and make sure we had a clear path to the dirt roads that led around the mountain's backside. This stretch of dirt roads would get us close enough for a brisk half mile walk through the trees, and to the power grid. Driving the rigs up to the loading docks of the building would just attract too much attention. Walking was the only way to assure a stealth like approach to the plan. They left at a pace that separated us by two hours. The signal was a go last time we spoke to the first 4 vehicles, and we were 10mns from the point of no return. I looked over our crew and felt the anticipation and adrenaline driving the silence in the "room". Their thoughts were vague but the message was clear. Even though these men didn't always see eye to eye, they were locked into each other's plight. A common goal in a great time of need brings out the best in men like this. I could feel their need to succeed, not for themselves but for the people that made this mountain home for everyone.

Diesel

The cab of Diesel's favorite six-wheel military machine was quiet with the silent wishes of the warriors it carried, when!

ENGINEER (sounding desperate): ROCKFACE COME IN MAN, COME IN!! AHHHH NOOO, IT CAN'T BE THEY WERE WAITING FOR US... AHHHH It's a trap... nooooo... (silence)

ROCKFACE (desperate to hear from SAMMY, his right-hand man, and longtime friend): SAMMY! COME ON TALK TO ME! WHO WAS WAITING? WHAT THE HELL IS...

Smoke stopped Rockface in his tracks. He grabbed his shoulder while pointing to the carnage and aftermath of Rockface's people on the path in front of us. It was an ambush that left everyone eaten or dead, and ready to turn. Smoke sent the other five trucks ahead to scout the situation out and report. Meanwhile it was up to us to end the suffering of the ones who would turn in the near future. Rockface had tears rolling down his hard-edged face. He wanted to be the one who plunged the knife that Sammy had given him as a gift into his friend's ear. (Gently as if it hurt his soul to do so, even though it was the right thing to do.) When his friend gave him this knife for his 45th, Rockface never could have imagined that Sammy was giving him the very knife that would free his trapped soul. How could this happen to his hardened crew mate and best friend? We all put our right hand on our chest, and observed a moment of silence as Rockface said goodbye. It took a few minutes for us to clean up, but when we were done we loaded up, and radioed for intel on the whatevers that had been responsible for this great loss to the mountain. It wasn't long, but nothing could have prepared us for what was waiting near the exit. I could feel them. An entire hoard of organized undead, but how? All the men were dead and I was the only one who knew! Whomever or whatever was the driving force controlling them, I couldn't tell, and I tried to read them. Nothing was in their heads that I could hear, except a tone, like the emergency tone you hear on a television for emergency information or something. In my desperation, I called out to Eldermum in my mind, and shot her all my knowledge.

ELDERMUM (replying within seconds): NO... It is as I feared. There is a being even more powerful than I behind this, and he can even block out my gaze. Fortunately for us, I am still powerful enough to keep you and your small crew hidden from this monster. I will transfer my knowledge to the remainder of the team, and I promise Smoke will back you up. I know it scares you Zee, but it is time to reveal your powers to the mountain. BE READY! This is your fate!

ME (gulping down my fears and manning up): I won't let you down 'Mum! And tell Angel... I mean Kami that...

ELDERMUM (with a smile in her heart): She already knows sugga, she already knows.

It was just then that the group's eyes went white, and their heads went back at the same time. I called out, but there was no reply! 5 seconds later, and the group was ready to Rock! It was 'Mum, she did it, clued them in and they looked at me and nodded. Smoke took point, and let us know what time it was. Words were not first on the list, there wasn't enough time because the undead soldiers were mobilizing for the heart of the mountain. This evil one who had no name wanted us all dead, or converted from what 'Mum could make of it. The force powering this army of undead was envious, and hell bent on our destruction.

SMOKE: The time has come ladies! To earn our reputations, save the mountain that we have called home for twenty trying years... And no army of mindless flesh eating shitheads... are gonna kick me out of MY FUCKING HOUSE!!

The team slammed our hearts with our fists and barked like dogs at the man we called captain. We were a team, a unit, a pack, and failure was just unlearned from our vocabulary! Pyro was ordered to set explosives so that the undead would be crushed and the tunnel would be sealed off. While he set the tunnel to blow, the truck had to be camouflaged so the undead would walk by us unnoticed. Rockface and B-Bear took care camouflaging the diesel monstrosity that we were privileged enough to have.

They got Spike and his son to help along with the rookie. Diesel backed her into a dark corner that hid three quarters of the huge vehicle. Giving the team a way to hide, and a chance to then start it quick with the hope of getaway as the tunnel was remotely blown to bits behind us, destroying and trapping the bastards under the weight of the mountain forever. Smoke used a hand mirror while hiding behind the edge of the turn that led out of the tunnel. They were about 30 or 40 seconds from being on us and we scrambled to hide the only chance the mountain had. The team quietly climbed into the back of the two tone truck, and held our collective breath.

The sounds of a thousand undead marching was so loud it gave me chills. With tree limbs, two by fours wrapped in barbed wire, and rocks in their hands clutched as if they were weapons. They walked as though the whip of the master himself was at their backs. I turned to Pyro and asked:

ME (in a bit of distress): DUDE! There is like a thousand undead marching down the tunnel! Will the blast trap or kill them all before we are clear??

PYRO: UUUUH... well let me...

SMOKE: Are you fucking kidding me Pyromaniac?!

PYRO (as his shit eaten grin turned to shit itself): Shit, boss... 'Mum didn't say how many, it's gonna be close.

There was a long pause before Smoke called it!

SMOKE (calmly turning to address Diesel): Well... Then we don't wait until we are clear. We will take off when they are a hundred feet or so past us. I know this beast is super charged and faster than it looks, right Diesel???

DIESEL: You betcha ass sir, I git us out fasta den a bullfrog on a flies' ass!

B-BEAR: COME ON MAN!!! Pyro, you best have yo' shit in check...

PYRO: Listen man, the blast will start at the far end. Then pop a half second at a time in sequence coming towards our asses. WE WILL MAKE IT B... hehehahahohwee!

B-BEAR: LOOK MAN! I'm just saying.

SPIKE (looking pissed the hell off, rubbing his earlobes to calm down): Whooosaaaaaa, whooosaaaaaa... Ok dammit, stop acting like this is your first rodeo and cowboy the hell up! The last flesh eatin' shit head has passed us by... In ten seconds Diesel is gonna get this monstrosity movin' and those flesh eatin' assholes might notice. So, lock and freakin' load ova here! Right Smoke, my man?

SMOKE (with a grin that showed confidence): That's correct Spike, but mother is using the mountain rock, combined with her powers, to block our escape from the gaze of this EVIL ONE, or whatever it is!

ME: This way "The EVIL ONE", that's what we will call him. (As I looked at him, to say credit to you smoke!) This bastard won't even know that we exist. To this jackass we will be invisible, not even the people around her know. We are in her gaze, but basically, we are all alone.

THE BRAVE ONE KOLTEN: Uh, guys...

We turned, it was the undead soldiers...

They were almost past the point where the blast wouldn't stop them. That is when you heard Pyro say with a huge grin, "LETS' GET IT ON!"

The big five ton diesel turned over as Pyro squeezed the trigger that he made out of a radio controller from an old drone. Diesel stepped on the clutch and took off like this truck was a street racer, not a military transport. The charges that Pyro set went off without a hitch as the undead army never knew what hit them. There was just one issue that we weren't counting on. The blasts were collapsing the tunnel faster that the truck was accelerating!

Smoke (yelling out to Diesel): Come on, you big hairy beast! Kick this thing into light-speed or we are all gonna be buried alive down here!!!!

Diesel looked back at the crew as the walls were crumbling around us. Just imagine! It sounded like a thunderstorm, fireworks, and an earthquake rolled into one big concert of destruction. If I wasn't scared shitless, it would have been awesome to witness! BUT, I was about to soil my newly acquired badass soldier outfit with the huge meal that was consumed the night before. (Fast metabolism and all.) No really! It was just then as I looked around at a group, and not one of them was cowering in fear, but instead they were cheering Diesel on like will alone would get us through. The cheers of our team, of these men was almost as loud as the fireworks display that was threatening the very lives this beast of a truck was carrying. Rocks were crashing off of the steel framing above us, trying to rip through the tough ass canvas mesh it was supporting, and that's when the cheering turned to... HOLY TORQUE, AND HOLD ON TO YOUR HUEVOS!!!!!! Diesel turned on a super charger of some kind and we were GONE! It was the fastest the monster of a truck had ever traveled, and man it felt exhilarating to say the least. No real time to enjoy it, but man I remember how cool it felt. Coming in the nick of time too, because the last blast from Pyro's show was to be the biggest one yet. It would be the blast to seal the tunnel enough to keep any Evil One, and his army from flanking our efforts. Most importantly blowing the south entrance will protect the unsuspecting families that were taking refuge in the mountain. It would have been them who had to fight the undead first, because the soldiers and Max were prepping at the front gates for the battle a few hours away. Smoke and I had looked at each other as the rumbling of the blast rocked the ground underneath us. Enough to cause Diesel to make an emergency maneuver around the rocks falling in front of us. Smoke surprised me when he said to me in his thoughts as he stared right at me:

SMOKE (with a calm tone to his voice): Put a shield around the truck with your mind or we won't make it Zee. 'Mum told me all about you and if she believes in you, then you can do nothing but believe in yourself. DO IT ZACK, IT'S THE ONLY WAY NINJA BOY... NOW!!... COME ON MAN, DO IT NOW!!!!!

I let the power take me to that place, and it happened... My eyes began to glow as I knelt to the ground and slammed my hands on the floor. I yelled out YYYYYYYAAAAAAAAAAAHHHHHHHHH!!!!! The sheer energy I was creating shook the monster for a brief moment, and then left my body! Billowing out of me as a bright, translucent, greenish light surrounding the beast in some kind of protective shield. Smoke egged me on and said, "THAT'S IT BOY, YOU JUST HAVE TO... BELIEVE!!!!"

The team was so distracted by my outburst that they almost didn't see that the rocks had overtaken us! But the power within me shielded us! Even Rockface was speechless at the time. The super intense cry I let out, and the event itself shook us all to the core, and then it all went silent. Besides the motor, my shield left it quiet in the cab of our diesel beast, and in this moment of silence B_BEAR said:

B-BEAR (with a look on his face like he figured it out): IT'S LIKE HE HAS THE GLOW OR SOMTHIN'... you know from that old Kung-Fu movie?... With that cat, Bruce Lee-Roy!

The crew looked at each other resulting in a silence that was deafening... until:

ROCKFACE (laughing like an earthquake himself): HUUUHAAAAAAA... OHH... HOHHOH... HAAAAAA... HAUUUUUUH... HAAAA... HUAH... AAAH... HAHA... HAHAAA!!*

His bellowing laugh was deep and uncontrollable, not to mention contagious. It wasn't long before the whole team was laughing and relishing in the miracle they couldn't quite understand. Thankful, but just a little on the laughter before fear angle that men of honor will choose every time. My concentration was killed with me joining in on the laughter as... WE BURST THROUGH THE WALL OF AVALANCHED ROCKS, LIKE WE WERE A FOOTBALL TEAM BREAKING THROUGH A BANNER AT THE OPENING OF THE BIG GAME.

BAAAAAMMMMM!!!!!!!!!!!!!!

The team continued to laugh even harder as we survived an army of armed, organized undead! An avalanche of falling mountain rock, caused by a series of too close for comfort explosive charges! That we set! To save the mountain! Before, really saving the mountain! You know what I'm saying Mannnnnnn?!

The monstrous vehicle was ordered to keep going and not look back. Smoke was focused in his binoculars to make sure that the mountain tunnel was sealed for good. The team wasn't laughing any more, as a moment of silence was being observed for the valuable lives that were lost forever in defense of the mountain. One by one, hats and helmets were taken off and placed over the hearts of every teammate. Smoke put down his binoculars and began to say a few words for the fallen:

SMOKE (with a look of conviction and reckoning in his heart): These lives lost today will be remembered. Remembered in the tales of how they sacrificed to make sure that we could complete THE, most important mission The Mountain of Hope has ever needed to accomplish! We are few, but inside this diesel beast is our peoples best kept secret weapon in this battle! I see a team that will plow through these aggressive sacks of decaying ass-wads to get this mission completed. The mountain needs us! AND WE ARE GONNA SAVE THE GOD DAMN DAY! IT'S A GOOD DAY TO DIE! WHAT SAY YOU MEN? WHAT SAAAY YOUUU?!

In unison, the team smacked their chests and called out in a howl like a wolf pack before the hunt!! OOOWWWW... OOOOUU... OUOUOUOUHHHH!!!! OOOUUUU! OU! OU! OOOUUU... WWWOOOOOOOOOOOHHHH!! I never felt so in tune with a group of individuals before! (Nothing like this anyway.) Rebuilding a community is one thing, but defending it against certain destruction, with a group like this! Never did I think that I would be here screemin' my lungs out, in Diesel's War Machine. I remember looking down at the dash of his truck as we howled like banshees, and there it was! "War Machine", in perfect script, like a tattoo on the forearm of this epic machine, built back up to its former glory just for a moment like this. Just like the team, it was perfect in its very existence. In that slice of time, we were perfect for what was about to ensue. (A thing isn't beautiful if it lasts you know!) Since we were on our way to almost certain death, we were beautiful, even if we weren't meant to last. And flinching, never even crossed any one of the minds in that vehicle! These men knew what they were in for, and they welcomed certain honor in the challenge that was about to present itself! To be the ones who would stand up, and save the people standing with them, fighting for the little world that their hands helped to create! I never got it, until seeing it for myself. I've read, watched, and listened to countless stories humans would tell. About the sacrifices men and woman alike, made for the things they loved... and believed in. It was only then, as I was being totally accepted and welcomed to join in the struggle, I witnessed real bravery, and the meaning of honor. Knowing that some, or all of us were going to die, didn't deter us in any way. These honorable souls were grateful that the responsibility of this task was theirs. Not fear, or resentment for having to sacrifice the lives they lived, but pride in the best of ways. With a great sense of love towards the lives that will carry on because of personal sacrifice at its best. It was then that I felt honored to be amongst this beautiful, perfect moment. The moment humanity, at its best, was finally revealed to me. I was then given the greatest gift I could receive from my own set of morals. The justified purpose, and the permission to unleash my power, in the name of honor! No regrets, no worries! An absolute, resolute justification for destruction in the name of any who threatened this mountain!

My soul began to swell with the freedom that this new moment of clarity had given to me. No matter the outcome, my soul would have no regrets! Because these people had bestowed upon me the gift that unleashed my power. A RIGHTOUS FREAKIN' CAUSE! Not unlike the feeling that I felt while on The C Turtle, unknowingly racing towards this very moment. As Diesel put on a tranquil, but meaningful song from the human band PURPLE FLOYD, I couldn't help but hear the team get quiet, as they all fell into deep thought. Just getting lost in the memories of the lives that they were fighting for. It was overwhelming at first, but I managed to block it out finally when:

> B-BEAR (looking like he just couldn't hold it in): So you got the GLOW, right?

> ME (with a smile): Yeah... you could say that man, I'm learning how to use it so sky's the limit until I discover otherwise Big B.

> B-BEAR (with a nod): Right on little ninja man, right on!

The ride was about to take 2 hours, so some of the guys were closing their eyes to rest, Pyro and B-Bear to be exact. This wasn't the first rodeo for them, and Rockface was quiet after the loss of his second in command, and all of his men. His mind was consumed with the families that he now felt responsible for, this was for all of them. Smoke's mind was zen. He wasn't thinking of the future or the past. He was thinking of the now to stay in the moment for the sake of the team (or what was left of it). Spike and his son were thinking about the people they loved, smiling as they reminisced. The Brave One, was all about proving himself, to me, to Smoke, and apparently to himself. He was the last of his bloodline, and he wanted to honor his family. His thoughts focused on how he had a lot to prove, since his father and brothers died in the battle for this mountain years ago. Smoke took him in as a promise to his father, when they were just soldiers trying to forge a home in this place. Pyro, to my surprise was thinking of his three little ones, Penny, Scrappy, and Tink. His little Chihuahua friends, who he loved and adored. Only B-Bear knew about them, and B-Bear well, he really had no one except his niece since his wife passed several years ago. She got bitten while saving a little girl from being eaten. I remember him telling her in his mind that he would be joining her soon! In his mind, if anyone was going to die it was going to be him if he could at all help it. His heart was bigger than its housing, and this is a husky sized individual. Oh, and last on our bus to glory, there was Diesel. He was amped up on energy drinks and pop rock candy. He was singing the songs and had the pedal to the medal. Right where he wanted to be, smack dab in the middle of the action. I myself, well my Angel was on the back of my mind... her hair, her laugh. Enough to inspire any heterosexual man to fight for a cause. For me it was more, she and I were meant to be, the attraction was undeniable. For this mission though, I told her to stay disconnected so I wouldn't be distracted. I also argued that Eldermum would need her strength to hold the gate. She, not without a fight, agreed reluctantly to honor my wish. I now regret it.

The time was drawing near, and I used my mind to venture into the mountain to see if things were going as planned. To my surprise the people in the mountain were at the gates and ready for the battle. But as luck would have it, the fight was coming to them. I grabbed Smoke's arm and let him in on the dilemma at the fortress gates. The undead army was mounting the assault NOW! Attempting to break in as we were making our way to the generators. Using trees that they cut down from the mountain itself. Like a movie from long ago they were taking turns ramming the door to weaken the gate until they could break through. The gatekeepers went through the vent above the gate, and were setting them on fire or shooting them in their undead heads, but with no progress. As one went down another would take its place without hesitation. Smoke opened his eyes and told Diesel with haste:

SMOKE (with urgency in his voice): NOW Diesel! Use the special fuel! We need to be there an hour ago!!!!!

Diesel nodded to Smoke and opened a special feed that lead right to the engine, like he was gonna pump this juice right into the combustion chamber of the engine itself. While we took off in a whole new gear Smoke laid down the skinny of the situation. You know the "short version", the skinny, for those of you not versed in human slang.

SMOKE (putting on his war face): Ok, boys! Get locked and loaded... IT IS GO TIME!! SPIKE, GET THE GEAR READY FOR TRANSPORT ON THE ATVS! PYRO, B-BEAR, PREP THE GRENADES AND AMMO FOR THE FINAL PUSH AFTER WE SECURE THE GENERATORS! MEN YOU WATCH OUR SIX AND KEEP THE NASTY ROBOT UNDEAD OFF OF OUR ASSES. ROCKFACE YOU'RE WITH ME AND ZEE. WE WILL GO IN FIRST AND CLEAR A PATH. YOU KOSHER BIG MAN?

ROCKFACE: YES SIR! SMOKE, I'M YOUR MAN! JUST POINT AND I WILL MOW DOWN ANY OBSTICLE IN OUR PATH.

The team was ready, and the moment was arriving for us to "COWBOY UP"! Diesel put his monster in neutral while simultaneously turning off the engine, engaging a special setting that kept the power steering and brakes on with no brake lights, keeping stealth as our ally. The undead army, and The Evil One behind them thought we were all dead. And we intended to keep it that way for as long as we could. Hoping the sacrifices being made at the fortress gates, coupled with the sacrifices of most of the platoon, would count for more than we could imagine. A moment of despair losing 9 trucks full of brave men and women. Now turning into the greatest advantage, we could possibly hope for. The element of surprise, but the clock was ticking, and the survival of the mountain was at stake.

We rolled up to an abandoned pathway. Looking as if it hadn't been touched in years. A sort of hidden road leading right up to the loading area of the cleverly hidden building. (Originally meant for supplies and upkeep).

The rag tag group of determined bad asses quietly exited the vehicle. Scanning the area with eagle like precision, making sure we still had the element of surprise. If we were lucky, the upgrades would get done undetected. The team's next goal would be laying the smack-down on the unsuspecting undead army, and saving the day! There were a few moments of silence while the team cleared their heads and put on their war faces! Smoke put his hand up to signal for quiet, clenched his hand into a fist, and we took off running. We then peeled off with Smoke taking lead and me close behind. Rockface strolling behind us with the confidence of someone who is no stranger to danger! Sporting the attitude of someone with whom death, was nothing but an unwelcome acquaintance, that always seemed to tag alongside him. After we accessed the situation, Spike, Diesel, Kolten, and Sparki, would bring up the rear with the ATVs, carrying the equipment needed in toe. We made our way to the building that was built to protect the generators, constructed from materials slowly scavenged from a dam which was once the source of power for the city that used to exist 20 miles east of here. With a painful sacrifice of some brave men and women, the group brought it here piece by piece, and then reassembled it for the triumph it is today. After today, its true potential would finally be realized. Our plan was a good one, even though we had to overcome the south exit situation. It is virtually amazing we have managed to keep close to the time table that could ensure us a victory. Standing in our way this time, two undead guards... that were standing at the doors as if they were ordered to do so. Easy, and an obvious trap of some kind, is what came to mind immediately. Provoking me to volunteer in taking them out, using ninja like stealth. Just in case it was a trap, I can take some damage, and heal in seconds. The team... mmmmmm well, not so much. Smoke nodded in agreement... I was gone before Rockface even made it to where we were hiding. I jumped with no sound from hiding place to hiding place. It felt like I was the wind itself: quiet, powerful, deadly! With every move to creep closer, I could see the dark figures standing there with not a move or so much as a wiggle to their existence. After getting close enough to see the dull grey whites of their eyes, (undetected and invisible to the gaze of you know who.) I then looked at the rocks above the building that led to a place where my ambush would never be seen. Before striking I used my mind to see if anymore undead henchmen were in the building, or anywhere else in the vicinity for that matter. Finding no one but these two... I climbed slowly to the perfect spot, still undetected. Again, I was sure that this was going to trigger another event, I just wasn't skillful enough to see it in the minds of these organic security cameras The Evil One left behind. It was a crappy situation that was an obvious trap, but we had no time to waste due to the fact that the front gates were being accosted!! As I contemplated the magnitude of our actions here at the hidden power plant, a choice had to be made. I began to draw my sword slowly, keeping the noise to a silent action, attached to a graceful drop without a warning or sound.

SWOOOSH, SWIPE! There was no sound but my katana cutting through their skulls and ending their existence in a moment of silent death.

Faster than the last time, resulting in a revelation that I was getting even more powerful, but how much more? How much faster? When will it cap off? All these questions pop into my head, bad timing for 20 questions. Lucky for me, Smoke breaks my train of thought with a shout out for an update through his thoughts.

SMOKE (sounding perturbed): ZEE! What's the damn hold up?

ME (sucking it up with a deep breath in... then out): Nothin' cap! All clear for Team Electric to kill this bitch.

The coast was clear, and Smoke ordered the rest of the team to come up ASAP. Many factors will make this mission live in infamy if it is a success, for us it was something more. A suicide mission that none of us thought was suicide at all. We all seemed to be thinking along the same lines! No way in hell, were we going to fail, it bonded us in a way that felt lifelong. It was then that the wonderful sound of the ATVs broke the uncomfortable silence, speeding up to the loading dock side of the warehouse. What appeared as a mediocre triangular building was built into the base of the mountain. In truth, it was a huge warehouse built into the mountain. With a huge chain driven door, for loading, and unloading of whatever was needed. On the second floor were armor plated security shields, for taking on an assault of some kind. Everything pointed towards a well-kept secret that not even my powers could see in the minds of the people that I have come across. This was no ordinary housing for turbines to create power. BEEP, BOOP, BOP, BEEP... The code was punched in by Spike and we were in. A little too easy though, Smoke was thinking, but held back as we unloaded. Spike began to look around in a panic as he remembered an important detail. It was so obvious to us all that we just stared at him 'til he mumbled:

SPIKE (looking sick to his stomach): The schematics for the new plan to boost the...

ME (taping my head as I spoke to calm our engineer): I have it all up hear brother, photographic memory! It's all good, I got your six man!

(The plans were destroyed when we blew the tunnel. I had given them to Spike, and he dropped them while grabbing some tools he thought would come in handy.)

SPARKI (with a spark up his ass): Whoooooo-eeeee! Let's do this then, I'm getting' hungry ova here!

Spike took one look at me, and smiled bigtime!

SPIKE: Nice work Zee, you're the frickin' man!

The door opened slowly and stopped before opening all the way. Smoke took out his tack light and stuck his head in, with the light leading his eyes. He reached into the room and felt along the wall. It was so quiet that the switching on of the buildings lights sounded like firecrackers in a garage. Our fearless leader went in and activated the bay door so the ATVs could be parked in the facility, ultimately making it easier to get this done quickly. Every second counted as we identified the right control boards and got to work. Separating into small groups doing everything we rehearsed in our heads, and out loud. We started adapting the controls to be ready for the super conductor coils that where fashioned to enhance the flow of electricity without increasing heat or wear on the existing equipment. Just like MY VALLEY!... Cool! I remember thinking how well it was all going... until I felt it, a tick of concern in Smoke, looking through his binoculars he sighed. He looked at me and it made my heart drop inside. He didn't dare show it to the team. A sign of a true leader, he kept it to himself so the team would keep on task. Strategically holding in the info, for if no one is in a panic, there is an overall better chance of the mission's success. Unknowing of the army coming our way, we continued to work the board, and we were killin' it. Making great time, when Spike turned the security system that was on energy save mode, back to full sensors. He took off his goggles and opened his eyes wide:

SPIKE (sounding off to his captain): SMOKE, SIR! BOGIES COMING FROM THE GATE!!!

SMOKE (sounding right back at his engineer): I KNOW SPIKE, NOW HOW MANY?

SPIKE (not wanting to believe his eyes): A LIGHT 1,000 SIR... I mean more...

SMOKE: How long Spike? SPIKE SNAP OUT OF IT!

Smoke knowing his friends limits as he call out one more time, but so loud it backfired:

SMOKE (reaching for his teammate to be strong, but instead): SPIKE, DAMMIT, STAY WITH US!!!!!!!

Spike was frozen in his tracks, as his face began to glow, from the number of blips that were showing on his radar screen.

Smoke ran over to Spike and bumped him out of the way. Falling down to a knelt position, Spike was in shock, meanwhile the massive hoard of hypnotized undead marched slowly this way. Our captain's face was not looking scared, but it was a look of concern:

SMOKE (looking at us with his game face on): IT'S TIME TO EARN OUR PAYCHECKS YOU SLACK JAWED ASS KICKING MACHINES!

Everyone checked their weapons, and put on our gear to give any edge possible. Kevlar, knives, ready clips full of armor piercing bullets, and anything else to help achieve the pure headshot to make them really, for real dead! I yelled out loud:

> ME *(feeling the moment a little too much):* IT IS TIME TO OPEN SOME CANS OF WHOOP-ASS JUICE!!!!!!

The guys looked at each other and laughed a little before putting me straight:

> B-BEAR *(snickering at me with love in his tone):* Boy you somethin' else! That's supposed to sound like, "IT'S TIME TO OPEN A CAN A WHOOP ASS ON DESE BITCHES!!!"... If we might die today, I just thought you should know that ninja Zee.

> ME *(in a silly but serious tone, feeling loved):* Thanks B-Bear, I need to brush up on my slang. I appreciate ya man.

We all BUSTED out into laughter for a few seconds... Then Smoke stopped laughing on a dime, and gave us the signal. It was go time. The windows were armor-plated, with openings for weapons to shoot through, but visibility was limited. And these assholes seemed to know it, they maneuvered to flank us and cut off our sight. So, we opened the armor-plated windows all the way. The sheer mass of the army of armed undead, marching towards us was chilling to the bone. When I killed the two idiots guarding the door, it tipped off The Evil One. I felt so stupid for not expecting more for my actions, whether I had to or not, I could have warned the team. Too late now, the shadows of raised two by fours, pitch forks, baseball bats, and other objects for bashing our heads in covered the walls behinds us, like they were inside the building already!!!

Who knows how many were stomping towards us, ready to cripple the mountain's lifeline and trap the people inside the mountain like a huge tomb. The hearts of the team, already one man down with Spike still in shock, seemed to deflate in the wake of the massive numbers stomping towards us. Smoke saw our despair and turned towards us in slow motion, as if time slowed just to hear his words:

SMOKE (in a moment that will live as the single greatest motivational war speech I might ever hear): MEN LISTEN TO ME... I KNOW THAT FEAR IS GRIPPING THE HEARTS OF YOU AS I SPEAK... BUT THAT FEAR YOU FEEL CAN TURN INTO A GREAT SOURCE OF ENERGY AND POWER... (He points to the army before us.)... REMEMBER WHAT YOU ARE FIGHTING FOR, AND USE THIS FEAR... USE IT TO PROPELL YOU TO GREATNESS IN THIS MOMENT... BECAUSE IF ALL MY YEARS HAVE TAUGHT ME SOMETHING IT IS THIS... EVERYTHING I HAVE BEEN THROUGH IN MY LIFE, WHAT I HAVE SEEN, AND WHAT I HAVE DONE HAS LEAD ME TO THIS MOMENT IN TIME... AND HEROES AREN'T BORN FOR SOME GREAT MOMENT IN TIME!... THEY ARE FORGED FROM THE GREAT MOMENTS IN TIME ITSELF! (Using Eldermum's words to inspire us, he could see the light in our eyes as we came back to life inside.)... SEE ANYONE CAN BE A HERO, AS LONG AS YOU NEVER SURRENDER IN YOUR HEARTS... THAT IS HOW THE FEAR BECOMES STRENGTH... AND FUEL FOR THE FIGHT!!!!!! SO, WHO IS READY TO BE A HERO?!?!?!?!!!

We all raised our weapons and roared so loud, the undead idiots stopped in what seemed to be awe of our defiance. Smoke put his hand up, palm open signaling for us to cowboy up. I looked to my left, and all of our guns were lined up, trigger fingers at the ready... One smiling troll of a dead-beat sounded off, and their assault began.

We were calm and poised, awaiting the command of our captain. You could feel the boots of our enemy stomping on the ground as the building itself began to vibrate...

SMOKE: OPEN FIRE LIKE EACH BULLET IS AN EXTENION OF YOUR HAND!

The team took a deep breath in, and opened fire with everything we had! Heads were popping like party favors.

Imagine that our bullet fire was an invisible wall that was slowly being pushed back, and forth! The sound of our relentless defense thundered out into the air like a choreographed fireworks display. We tossed down spent weapons and picked up freshly reloaded ones that Pyro had readied for us. The bullets were nonstop, since we happened to be highly motivated to hold this building. The team dug in like woodland ticks. Knowing it was all or nothing, we shot for the head only and wasted anything that moved.

Smoke was a sniper in a past life before the apocalypse and took out undead in the distance like his bullets were heat seekers. Not missing a beat or looking slow for his age; it was an honor to witness. The weapon he used was barely able to keep up with his skills and I was geeking out inside. I'm a great shot, and this guy's talent with a rifle made me struggle to keep up! Rockface had a crate of grenades and Diesel was popping the pins so Rockface could toss the rock, so to speak. I mean these guys demolished ten to fifteen dead fighters at a time... impressive. The soldiers, consisting of Kolten and Sparki, were at the back door holding them off as best they could. I heard Kolten's doubt in his mind. The undead were smart by attempting to flood the loading dock, seeing as only two men had it covered at the time. I left the upper level without even wasting a second, jumping down to back them up. (Just in time too!) It's always timing that decides the fate of a soul in situations like this, and it was Sparki who looked like fate was punching his time card. He never flinched knowing his dad had a panic attack of some kind. He wanted to fight for his father and the mountain. Like a son wanting to impress his father, he gunned down undead with reckless abandoned!

> SPARKI (screaming for help as he began to get overrun by the soldiers of the undead): HELP ZEEEEEE, I CAN'T!!!!!

> ME (assuring Sparki I had his back): Spark don't know worries man! I'm on this!

Pyro being the sick individual he was, turned on the PA system and turned on his BOOM BOX while yelling out:

PYRO *(smiling like it was a party): HERE IS SOME INSPIRATIONAL MUSIC, BIG GUNS!!!!! HEHEHAHAHOHWEE!!!!!!*

(WITH MUSIC BLARING!)

I quickly took out my twin auto 9 Millimeters, and proceeded to take out the same number of undead as there were bullets in my oversized clips.

Every bullet counted as my talents began to show themselves effortlessly. It felt like I wasn't even aiming, and there wasn't a bullet that missed. (The music kinda worked, but I will never tell Pyro!) It was enough to keep Sparki from becoming dinner! He pulled the Uzi from his back and began to push the bastards back again from one knee. Waves of undead were charging for the weak spots of the building, but we were holding them until Sparki ran out of ammo. I still had bullets left within the modified clips that Smoke had given me earlier today. (Awesome gift if you ask me!) As the shell casings of the bullets flew by my head, I could see the frustration on the faces of every undead soldier I ended. The Evil One himself was behind their eyes, and you could feel him fighting with Eldermum to break down her shield, clawing at her mind so he could see inside the minds of our team. His power was great, but Eldermum was in the mecca of where her power was greatest. He was quickly weakened by the attempt at breaking 'Mums shield protecting our thoughts. This resulted in him being distracted long enough for me to accidentally see into his dark mind. It may have only been 4 seconds, but it was enough to reveal his entire plan in a terrifying montage. His plan was to kill everyone, just so he could enslave them all! It was the undead that this A-hole ruled, but that was it. And for that, every LIVING thing on the planet had to die! Animals, people, bugs, you name it. If he sees a threat, it will be dealt with in an expeditious manner. It sent chills down my spine, until Sparki screaming for help snapped me back into the now. Kolten shouted Sparki's name as I cleared The Evil One's ass-hats from the legs of our teammate. No time to check for wounds, because even more of these hypnotized undead fighting machines lined up and let out a battle moan as Kolten and I braced for their arrival:

SMOKE (sounding a little disappointed that we didn't think of this ourselves): SHUT THE FUCKING DOOR! I MEAN COMMON MEN! IT IS 12 INCHES OF SOLID STEAL ALLOY! NO ONE IS GETTING THROUGH!!!!!

ME (feeling dumb): OK! Dammit why didn't we think of that?

Kolten shrugged his shoulders as I jabbered on. Kolten smacked the button that closes the doors, but not before six or so of the Evil undead got in. SLAMM!!! The big loading dock doors closed! I stared down six undead intruders that were already shredded, but just didn't know it yet.

I wasted no time in lunging for the closest skull I could slice in half, instantly killing it before the dumb bastard could even make a move. Then I quickly moved on to the second undead, starting an inside move. The slow biter lunged at me with a telegraphed swing of his baseball bat. A pivot and turn of my hips, seemed to be enough to evade the attacker. I swung the katana like it was weightless in my hands, leaving a lifeless body of the freed soul behind me. The rest on the other hand, well they took a defensive stance like someone was directly behind their eyes. Defeating us was so important that The Evil One himself was guiding any undead that were close enough to give him a card to play in this wicked game of survival. I wasted no time in ending his view of our equipment and gear that could give him any hint as to our tactical advantage in this battle. HIIIIIYAAAAAAAAA! It was a scene out of a Kung–Fu flick as Kolten shot one! BANG! to the head and it was over. Meanwhile I blocked a hatchet swinging for my head, and cut off the arm of the one who tried to swing a two by four with a nail sticking out of it into my skull. I then thrusted the katana into the chest of the one with no arm and swung in an upwards motion completely slicing his head in half as Kolten shot the second idiot, but missed the head shot! Fortunately, he stunned the beast of burden long enough for me to do a spinning move, and swing with almost no sound. I used so much speed and technique that his head stayed together for a second and a half before sliding apart. It slowly fell to the ground sounding like a wet fish smacking against the deck of a boat after being caught! The last one standing dropped his weapon and shocked us both as it began to speak in a raspy and dry struggling voice!:

UNDEAD ASS-HAT: *You will not survive the day young ones. Fight if you must! I have seen enough to know that you do not have the ammunition to stop my army. It is only a matter of ti...*

Smoke shot him through the head! Nodded for us to get going, and rejoin the fight. Kolten looked rattled a bit:

ME (reading his mood): *Don't give up now Brave-One! We still have some tricks up our sleeves that he doesn't know about. IT'S NOT OVER YET!!! OK!*

KOLTEN (looking like faith restored): *Fuck yeah! I'm good Zee! Don't worry about me, I'm in it until the very end! No retreat!*

ME: *NO surrender!*

SPARKS (that was his name from now on): *Don't fuhget about me dammit!! I'm not bit, but can you help me get this two by four and its nails out of my frickin' leg ova here!!!!*

KOLTEN (happy to see his friend wasn't bitten): *You really kicked ass out there half pint! Don't ever fuckin' do it again!!!*

SPARKS (with a look of holy shit, can't believe I made it on his face): *That was enough to convince me to leave that hero crap to bad asses like you!!!*

We then barricaded the big door with a couple of forklifts, before rejoining the fight a level above us. Smoke was almost out of ammo and the Grenade Bros. were down to their last crate of rocks to toss. Kolten patched up Sparks and one thing was on the minds of us all. "Where were all of the undead coming from?" No way was anyone gonna be the first to show despair or weakness in this group. Then, with no warning The Evil One's soldiers retreated back over the hill, causing a sort of break in the action while blanketing the moment in an uncomfortable silence. You could still see them, but they were just swaying in their boots and didn't move at all. This confused the team for a second, causing us to look at each other and scratch our heads. It was a cerebral attack that was meant to rattle us. Like some wicked tactic from a master chess player or football coach. He made the army regroup, just to see what we would do; to see if we would relax. Letting us fester in our minds as to what was coming next. For us it was a chance to check our ammo and reassure each other that we had this shit under control. That whatever was coming, no matter what they threw at us, we would be victorious. I think that this Evil mind gave us no credit as we kept on working together. Upgrading the facility while he played possum. It gave us the precious time that we desperately needed; we thought that we would have a couple of hours before being noticed. That was destroyed instantly by us just showing up period. Like true professional ass kickers, instead of sulking and wondering what was coming next, we kept working. Getting closer and closer to our goal and not letting the undead puppet master's tactic get to us. A full 26 minutes went by, and any second they weren't attacking we used to finish the mission at hand. Digging in even deeper, we prepared for phase two as the moaning army of undead began rumbling with activity. Sparks was doing his family proud, coaching Kolten as they both worked the computers to program and time everything just as I instructed for maximum output! Just a few more minutes and we will be ready to install the super cooling coils to complete the upgrade, enabling the mountain to self-sustain for generations to come. Smoke and I went through the ammo and loaded as many clips that the ammo would allow. Unfortunately, it didn't take long to realize that the words of The Evil One might come true.

Just then the activity of the undead army turned into a march, and the Evil hoard began to crest over the hill once again. Slowly approaching it was hard to see, but this march came with even more numbers than before. Now these two BIG personalities have been just blasting fools with automatic weapons and lending support, but that's not their specialty. B-BEAR and PYRO stood up with conviction as if to say ass kicking wasn't just a hobby, no it was their passion!!:

> B-BEAR (with a sigh): Time to light up the night Pyro, you game?

> PYRO (with a shit eating grin that only a man who loves to blow things up could pull off): I thought you would never freakin' ask! Hahahahahahaheehehe!!!!

> SMOKE (putting his hand up and sounding off with great concern): NO, NOT YET! An explosion could draw the undead that aren't being controlled into this area, too. Then this Evil One will have more soldiers for his army.

> B-BEAR (looking disappointed and confused): But boss what else do we have? I don't see another

way. Spike is down, and we're almost out of ammo. If we don't push now, we'll be overrun!

I recall mulling over the sad fact that we were in a situation where we most likely were going to run out of bullets before The Evil One ran out of soldiers. Just like that Evil bastard predicted. In that moment of doubt, as luck would have it Spike snapped out of his stupor! At the hand of someone nobody expected to have such a big set! (If you know what I mean!) The young Sparks smacked his much older dad across the face: SMAAACK!! Echo... echo... echo...

SPARKS (sounding off in his east coast Irish-Italian mafia way): DAD SNAP OUT OF IT AND GROW A SET! YOU GOT TO SNAP OUTTA THIS. I CAN'T UNLOCK THE SECRET YOU'VE KEPT ALL THIS TIME!!!! ONLY YOU CAN DO IT, NOW COME ONN! YOU'RE SPIKE FOR FUCK'S SAKE!!!

SPIKE (grabbing his sons face and looking him in the eyes with pride): Yes!!! My BOY! I am Spike, and you! You my son, are a better man than I could ever hope to be. The best thing that ever happened to me! This is for you son!

He then started to pluck away at the command board of the facility like it was second nature. Miraculously Spike snapped out of his trance, and in seconds. You might never have guessed that this man had just been through a mental breakdown. His efforts began a chain reaction that you could hear, the reawakening of a secondary system. It sounded like turbines winding up to power something old, ancient in some way. This was the secret of the mountain, a secret only few knew about. The ground began to shake as rocks danced on the ground like they were coming to life. The undead stopped advancing as double barreled pulse gun turrets revealed their places of slumber.

THAT'S RIGHT! I SAID PULSE GUN TURRETS FOR FUTURISTIC AWSOMENESS SAKE!!!!

At that moment Eldermum's voice was faintly coming through in Spike's subconscious   s; she was helping him. Saving the day once again, with just a nudge in the right direction. What a clever, wise sexy old spark plug of a woman! In this moment when I faintly picked up her presence, she began to speak to me as well:

> ELDERMUM (in a calm way that put me at ease): It is time my young ward. Time for you to let the power within become a part of your consciousness. It will still do all the things that you think make you special Zack! Except now, it will not take over! Now, instead of losing control, the control will be yours. Let it

happen, it is time you fully understood your power. It is not just a part of you anymore. It is you, you are it! Oh, and one more thing my special boy. Understand that the topic you are to about to be privy to... this is the reason for all the sacrifice, all the secrets. Read Spike's mind, look for the key words 'experimental weapons'... good luck, and believe my boy... BELIEVE!

At 'Mum's request, that is what I did! During Spike's programming genius moment, formatting the ancient new tech from the human military to save the day. I used 15 seconds to dive into his subconscious memory, all the while remembering that a huge army was slowly marching towards us. Spike's mind was more complicated than he let on. Since he was alive before the virus spread, he has a past, a life, a job, and it involved experimental weapons. Don't get me wrong, he was an electrical engineer. "FOR THE COMPANY THAT HAD THE CONFIDENTIAL, TOP SECRET, EXPERIMENTAL FACILITY GOVERNMENT FUNDED CONTRACT"! It took a second to wade through his brain, but there it all was, clear as day. During the construction of the mountain facility, he befriended the men who are now the Pack, including a young sniper named Smoke in his prime. When the virus spread and the world went to shit, this place was three quarters of the way done. All the people working on Project Mountain Pass took refuge inside the incomplete facility. Using what supplies that were left, they pushed forward to complete the gates as best they could. It had housing, and the makings of a military base, all hidden within this mountain. Scavenging what was needed over time, it took years to get where they were today. For these people this was the last step to a good night's sleep, because keeping its secret 'til this very moment had to be a great weight on the few who knew. Just waiting for a way to power it up and make The Mountain of Hope what it was meant to be. This explains the joy that was shown when my upgrades were explained to Spike. The waiting for an answer to the biggest piece of the puzzle he ever had to solve. Activating the secret weapons that would render the mountain unstoppable and help defend from all invaders would finally come to fruition!!! My new long lasting, hyper cooled coil system would power batteries and the whole mountain without breaking a sweat. Including ancient futuristic pulse weapons that can take out intruders, and identify the allies during a fire fight. This mountain actually has the potential to restart the resurrection of mankind itself. That's what 'Mum was getting at. I'm here to help mankind start over, a second chance to flourish and get it right this time. With the Zumies by their side...

CHUUUUUUAAAAARRGG... KIILLLL!!!!! The undead started the assault, not knowing what was lying in wait for them.

> SPIKE (with the devil in his eyes): I have it! EAT THIS YOU UNDEAD SCUMBAGS!!!

The pulse cannons popped up to an attack position, and a glow shined from gill like vents that cooled the magnificent cannons. Dust filled the air, you could see it through the iridescent bright blue-white light that lit up the faces of the undead that were about to be blown apart. Their assault on us was about to be over before it ever could begin! Storm clouds hid the sun, but using motion sensors along with tracking tech the pulse guns began to even the odds and lit up the hypnotized army like it was a special light show at a Purple Floyd concert, just for us! The undead became cannon fodder as the momentum of the day started to shift in our direction. Heads of the evil undead soldiers were rolling, not an undead would be missed by the extremely accurate turrets that rang out like music to our desperate ears. The turrets were so accurate, they shot the hapless undead soldiers at the base of their necks in the perfect spot to also kill the brainstem! Not one undead was being spared. Spike started laughing out loud like he did when we were all bursting out of the mountain earlier today, and sure as shit, we started laughing too! Heads were popping up into the air in slow motion, like a high school graduation scene with caps being thrown into the air. We looked at each other as tears rolled down our faces from laughter, even though the battle was not over by a long shot! Sparks put us back into mission mode by colorfully reminding us:

> SPARKS (slamming down his fist to grab our attention): COME ONN! IT'S NOT FREAKIN' OVA YET!!! WE STILL HAVE TO WELD THE THINGIES TO THE... THE... RELAYS YOU ASSMUNCHERS!!!! SO, STOP GIGGLING LIKE WE'RE LITTLE GIRLS, AND CLOSE THE DEAL FOR FUCK'S SAKE!!!

I looked at Smoke and he was not laughing. In fact he had become more serious than I have ever seen him before!

> SMOKE (leaning in loud, but not too loud, seriously laying down the gospel of our mission): The super cooling coils that will activate this security system, and boost the power to the mountain for years to come is going to be finished! Because, while this display was impressive, imagine if the rest of the mountain was set up this way. The people we have fought so hard to protect will finally be safe for generations to come. Let's finish this shit once and for all!

(The men looked at Smoke with confusion in their stares, so he told them the secret of the mountain... it was time!)

SMOKE (finally letting the cat out of the bag): You see, a small nameless few, including ME and Spike here. Well, we knew about this long before some of you were even born. This mountain is surrounded by a turret security system that can pinpoint enemies and allies while live combat is taking place. In other words these guns shoot with such accuracy, that while our people fight, the guns are shooting alongside of them, next to them, and around them during battle while not hitting any friendlies with fire! This mountain would be untouchable for years to come... (He looked around and saw the hope in their eyes come to life!) That is right boys, we are fighting for so much more than just today. Now I know this really isn't fair to put on you few. But this is the way it is, and we are the only ones who can pull this off. I believe in you men! Believe in yourselves and this will be the single greatest accomplishment of our lives! For ourselves... AND HELL, FOR MANKIND ITSELF!!!!

ME: HELL YEAH!!

B-BEAR: LET'S GET CRACK-A-LACKIN, MUTHAFUCKAS!!!

ROCKFACE: YES! LET'S GET THIS SHIT OVER WITH!

SPIKE AND SPARKS (with a two thumbs up): WE'RE WITCHA ALL DA WAY SMOKE!

SPIKE (adding to Smokes words): Well, if my memory serves me right, according to the original architects, the weapons were the first things that were installed into the mountain. Unfortunately, our energy setup wasn't enough to run the secondary system to power the load. Pulse cannons with computer/man guided tracking systems would be a significant problem for this patched together system.

As PYRO was about to educated us, an automated alarm interrupted him mid-sentence.

PYRO (with his index finger pointed to the sky): WELL... AS MY PAPPY USED TO SAY! THERE IS NO... (some sort of warning alarm sounds off)...

BEEEEYUUUUU... BEEEEEYUUUUU... BEE...

ROBOTIC ASSMUNCH VOICE: Backup power... to main security is depleted... 15 minutes 'til shutdown of AutoTrack Pulse 1000 Security Systems... Have a nice dayeee.

We all looked at each other for about three seconds... B-Bear sprang into action! Grabbing the heavy coiled units two at a time, we had six in total that had to be replaced. There were four in this building alone that B-Bear, Pyro, and Sparks had under control, those would be a piece of pie! Spike and Diesel had the control board, and they were doing all they could to keep power to the pulse cannons. Unfortunately for the rest of us, the remaining super cooling coils had to be replaced on a relay tower that fed the mountain its main supply of power. It looked like a huge ski transport put on top of an elevator tower, that was shoved into a mountainside, with major relays that would get extremely hot without my cooled coil system. I knew that it was up to me, Rockface, and Kolten. Smoke would be covering us when the backup power ran out, alongside Diesel who was rocking the stationary machine gun. (It was his baby!) Our only hope was that the others could get the four coils fitted and operational by the time we were done with the upgrades ourselves. This way the power to the gun turrets would be reactivated and then re-engaged, aiding us in surviving the relay coil upgrades all together. These critical upgrades would give much needed power to the rest of the mountain, in which we already installed the cooling systems required to complete the huge series of circuits throughout the fortress. That's right, we kept it secret, at the request of Eldermum the awesome, with no questions asked. Now I understand her wise ingenious way of faking out this powerful enemy. All because if The Evil One had infiltrated the thoughts of one soul in the mountain. All he would need is one, unsuspecting soul, and all would be lost. Having crews sworn to secrecy while installing the upgrades was essential to the mission inside the mountain. Now, everything hinged on the install of the cooling system. The ones that belong to a tower surrounded by an unending sea of organized, hungry for flesh, Evil One hypnotized, soul trapped, rotting A-Holes! So, not the way I thought this day was going to go!

ROCKFACE (without a doubt that we were going to succeed): OK MEN! It's time to earn our honor with blood, bravery, and brotherhood. Join me as we tempt fate, and laugh in the face of death's concubine! Join me as we save the goddamn day!

ME (with a little smile on my lips): It's a great day to die you old Viking! I'm with you all the way!

KOLTEN (stickin' his chin out, while he cocks the assault shotgun that was once his father's): I was waiting on you two! Enough talking, time to express ourselves with automatic weapons 'n' shit!

Smoke looked at the young man he watched grow up, and no words were necessary. They loved each other, but men like them... They never can say it... it is just known!

SMOKE (looking to Rockface and me): You watch that one, he might leave the two of you in the dust. So, keep up ok!

We nodded to Smoke because we understood, this was man talk for, "Bring my son back alive... if at all possible!" Even though we all knew this was a mission some of us might not come back from. Rockface went down one level and packed the ATV as fast as he could. Diesel jumped down to help his old friend get ready for what could be the last time they'd speak in this world.

DIESEL (with a smile that looked different than Rockface was used to, while still being familiar): Time to say nutin', and evrytin' at once, you ol' stubborn mule.

ROCKFACE (with a look of respect, and gratitude): You know it was really you... without you I would just be some other loud wannabe with a chip on his shoulder. I never said thank you... SO... I WON'T NOW YOU PRICK... HAHAHAHAHHA!

DIESEL (hugging his old friend like men do): HAHAH HOHOHOHAHHA... YOU SOM' BITCH, WE'LL T'ROW BACK SICK AMOUNTS OF VODKA WHEN DIS IS OVA!

ROCKFACE (looking like he had to fake it just a little): YEAH... KEEP THAT SHIT ON ICE FOR ME!

Time was not on our side, and we had to at least make it there before the backup power was fully depleted. I looked at Kolten and said:

ME: So, did you think it would be so exciting, Brave One?

KOLTEN (looking confused): Why do you call me that anyway?

ME (with a smile of approval): Because anyone who tries to kick my ass?... Has, to be one brave son of bitch!

Just then the big chain driven door began to open, we both smiled and bumped fists knowing we had respect for each other. I know he needed it, and hell, the kid deserved it in every aspect of the word! RESPECT!

ROCKFACE (looking like he was going to ralph on his steel toed boots): Ok, love birds! Kiss already so we can get on with this crap! I have some ice-cold vodka waiting for me!

The door opened... It was like world war eight was going on out there! Undead trying to get close were obliterated by pulse cannons as we ran behind Rockface, who was not going slow for anyone! Some of the undead soldiers were using each other like shields, sacrificing themselves in an effort to get one of us before we could get to wherever we needed to be going. I mean did they know, it seemed like The Evil One himself was popping from soldier to undead soldier, but the cannons would cut him down before he could grab one of us. Rockface got to the small building first, and began punching in the code, opening the electric fence surrounding the small building that had the fate of the mountain inside of it. It was then that the douchey voice announced our doom:

BUTTHEAD, ROBOTIC BAG OF ASS, VOICE: SIXTY SECONDS TILL TOTAL SECURITY SHUT DOWN. IN T-MINUS 60... 59... 58...

ME (turning to Kolten): RUNNNNNNN!!!!

He did as I said, put his gun on his back and began to run for the fence that needed to be closed before power was lost. We were a good fifty or so yards behind the big Russian! Having some ground to cover I made sure the boy would definitely make it. Because if it came down to it, Rockface would have no choice! If I couldn't make it back in time, he would have to shut the electrical fence locking me out to save the mountain. He knew it, and so, did I! 45... 44... 43... 42... The clock was ticking, and it was time to turn on the Kung-Fu action grip, so I dug my feet into the ground, with a little twist. WHOOSHH! I ran with my katana in hand, positioned behind me like a ninja as I dodged, ducked, and dove with cat like speed. SWOOSH, SLASH, SLICE!

My technique was flawless as I cut down the evil dead soldiers like I was cutting brush with a machete in the Congo.

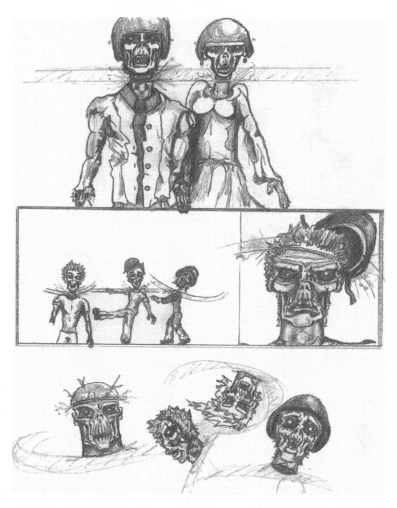

It was aided by the final efforts of the backup power that fueled the amazing pulse weapons. In seconds they will be forced into slumber once again... 28... 27... 26... 25... The annoying robotic tool of a voice rang in my ears as Smoke pointed towards the tower. I turned and started to run as undead were dying, again, right in front of me as I ran full speed towards a shutting gate. All sound faded away as the gate shut with a thud. THUD!

The pulse guns hacked at the dead soldiers as they charged for the trapped me, standing in front of Rockface and Kolten who had no choice. I nodded to them to look up at the relay. We all knew, nothing needed to be said. They turned, and started to unload the ATV as the douchebag robotic voice counted down the last ten seconds of cover I had left. Kolten started to turn around. Rockface grabbed him tight, as he was right in his face:

ROCKFACE (with a sad but strong look to his brow): If we don't do this, he will be dead for sure. Besides... If he dies it won't be for nothing. Those electric fences will only hold for a few minutes. He still has to hold them off long enough for us to save the mountain. You know he won't go down without the fight of his life... YOU KNOW I'M RIGHT KOLT... LOOK AT ME! He *understands YOU HAVE TO LEAVE HIM!... come on young man. We have important work to do! Come on, KOLT!*

I shook my head up and down to let him know it was ok, and the elevator door Rockface could hold open no longer closed. They went up the tower to finish the job. I had about five seconds to figure a course of action, because this wasn't over by a long shot. A final group of undead soldiers started to crest over the hill. I mean... THEY HAD LADDERS, THAT'S WHAT I SAID... F'ING LADDERS!!!!! This Evil One had definitely won this poker hand! BUT! As luck would have it, I still had some chips left, and there was one more hand to be played!

Inside my mind and body, something was about to happen!!! My fear of the power taking over and changing me forever, was no longer a good excuse for denying its existence, not to mention what good I might be able to do with it! 5... 4... 3... 2... 1. Douche-bot announced the end, and the beginning, the beginning of the rest of my life without even knowing it! The amazing shield of cannon fire stopped! The slow march of this army was over, it was time for the full out sprint, with the whip at their backs... I could feel their master snapping it with pure joy. Joy in the thought of our deaths! OF MY DEATH! He was afraid of me, and I could feel it in his relief, thinking the day was his! WELL THAT IS ALL I FRICKN NEEDED, A NUDGE IN THE RIGHT DIRECTION!

My power and my consciousness merged as the very ground under my feet shifted. BOOOOM... A wave of power rippled out of me and hit the ground. Disturbing the sand and dirt around me as if it was liquid under my feet... not solid ground! I felt the world melt away, and a voice that I have never heard before warmed my body as it uttered these words:

MYSTERIOUS WISE VOICE: Now you will realize your fate... The fate of every powerful being the universe has ever known, Zee. A choice. The choice between using the power for selfish mongering reasons, or to use it for protecting what good you find in a universe full of suffering. Suffering at the hands of those who wish to challenge the power you now possess!... Choose young ZEE... and rise anew. A soul who has the power to change the world!

In that very moment, my eyes opened! I could hear Smoke, yelling in slow motion for me to run towards him, so he could lay down a clear a path with some cover fire. But there was to be no more running for me, not now!

The world slowed down for me in that instant, and I knew, I just knew. If I didn't make a stand now, Rockface and Kolten never get the chance to finish the mission. Nothing is more important than not letting my team down, and the people! ANGEL!!!!! Right then I began to open the well of power inside me. The rush was intoxicating as everything around me became mine to toy with. Even the very air we breathe felt pliable, as I absorbed it into my lungs, and felt the power in every molecule that surrounded me. The eyes of the army before me revealed the mind of The Evil One, who hid behind them as I took a deep breath, and made it happen! I reached into the minds of his slaves, and there he was. Powerful enough to beat me in a mental battle under normal circumstances! You know, if we were actually, face to face, but he didn't realize that I cracked his big secret! A secret that even 'Mum wasn't aware of. That he was thousands of miles from here. Even though he was still powerful enough to keep me from seeing his true form. His power couldn't stop me from meeting him on a separate plane of mental existence all together, to wage a mental war. A war that I could win!!! His use of power to hide his true form was my way in, and I concentrated with all my power to shut him down. He wasn't going to go peacefully though, as undead soldiers were dropping left and right from the sheer power that was surrounding me. I braced for it!!! Even though we has thousands of miles away, the first hit from his telepathic power was shockingly hot, with weight and pressure attempting to rip me apart, it put me on one knee! I stopped it from pinning me down, and pushed back with a powerful blow that got me back on my feet! I found strength in mimicking the powerful moves of the fighting monks who were able to channel their chi into physical power.

EVIL ONE (wincing, and then laughing out of pure pride): HEHAAHHA... OOOOH! Is that all you've got little man. I think you are in over your head this time, boy!

ME (not having that shit): NOPE ASSMUNCH! I HAVE PLENTY MORE WHERE THAT CAME FROM! YOU KNOW, VITAMINS AND ALL!

EVIL ONE *(pleasantly surprised): Goooood, verrrry good!!! Nice to see you can think through the pain, and still have a lucid conversation.*

ME *(with a wtf): WHAT PAIN... AAAAAAAAAHHHHHSHSHHIIIIIIT!!! RRRAAAAAAAAAAAAAAAAAAAAA!!!*

In our minds, it was a no holds barred, all-out match, using will alone to match each other's tug of war with our powers. Whomever could rip the other apart first would be the victor, and I could feel him trying to tug at the very molecules that were holding me together on this plane of existence!

Meanwhile, Smoke and Diesel were knocking down undead with desperation as they were intent on saving me. The Evil One's soldiers were pressing the fight and I had to make a move, find his weakness. With the help of those two I knew in my gut, it was up to me to finish this harbinger of death's vessel. This is the way he has connected himself to rest of the slaves he controls. If I can find his vessel and concentrate my power on it, he will be harmed himself. It takes all of him to control the undead while fighting me. It is the only way to win this battle for the mountain, and stop him from ending mankind. That's when it revealed itself, a hitch that he forgot about! The undead soul he was possessing, holding his essence, was falling apart as he channeled his power through it, to counter mine. I could feel him hiding his pain! IT WAS ON!!!!! More soldiers were dropping like sacks, as the blood dripping out of their skulls, were steaming from the power melting their brains as we fought for control of his army. It was in that revelation that I knew! The flood gates had to be opened! Every ounce of energy and power I could muster in my being, had to be exhausted to win this day. Destroying the vessel that houses his power, would send a chain reaction. Melting every undead brain he was connected to for miles! One drawback though, I could also fry mine, because the only way to hurt this ass was to bait him into firing back with all he had to destroy his vessel. Overloading it with power, as his ego has already distracted him from the warning signs that his vessel was giving him.

In the meantime, my teammates were working their butts off to complete their task at hand. Smoke was a machine, cutting off the heads of any undead within forty feet of my position. His skill with firearms still amazes me to this day! Even though Smoke was unstoppable, it was Diesel and his efforts that made the difference. Using everything he had to steady that .50 cal., he was a machine himself. His arms shaking with the rhythm of the ferocious beast of a weapon, as it devoured undead like they were potato chips! Making sure I had a chance, as I struggled and yelled out in what must have sounded like agony to everyone around me. My eyes were glowing from the sheer amount of power being exhausted from my being. (The glow was lightsaber green like that series of movies called... Star Battles or something, Darth Hater was AMAZING! He was like a confused, futuristic Samurai, or something! Great movies!) I was going to win no matter the consequences, preparing myself mentally to die in the effort. A short run for a young powerful entity, a wonderful peace took over my soul and left me with a confidence I had to hide from my enemy. (Poker-face is the expression I am looking for.) See to defeat this ass-hat, I would have to be clever, and give him nothing to use against me. He looked up as my power started to shred the undead prisoner he was wearing to fight me in this plane. Piece by piece drifted away from his skin as it became ash from the magnitude of my power, and I knew this day was mine. Unknowingly taking my final onslaught of power, my senses felt him get hurt when it reached him. From this great distance, even I was shocked at how much it affected The Evil One, who was shocked as well, and weirdly pleased by it at the same time. His smile was one that resembled a man who was sure he was about to win. It was time in his eyes to make one last crushing blow, in an effort to stop me, and take back what was left of the army that was decimated by our powerful exhibition. Playing possum, I pretended to be utterly exhausted by my move to take him down. In fact, I did such a great job of acting, the sleeping giant of our unit awoke!

B-BEAR (bellowing out his battle cry coming to my aid): IIIII'M COMMINN' ZEEEE, HOOOLD OOONN! RRRRAAAAAHHHHHH!

Bear jumped down from the open windows of the second floor like he himself was a super hero! Standing up in what seemed like slow motion he reached behind him, and from his back came "THE HAMMER"!

B-BEAR (looking like this is what he was made for, stompin' undead into the ground): YOU CAN'T TOUCH THIS, BUT I CAN REACH OUT AND TOUCH YOUR ASS!!!!!!

One swing of his ginormous hammer mowed down undead with great malice and angry force! He was a gentle giant, but when it was time, the beast inside would take over. His strength was unmatched, and he risked everything to even the score with the army still trying to take the building. Biters were all over him, big mistake! B-Bear ripped their heads clean off their bodies with his Bear hands! (Pun intended!!) The Evil One smelt blood in the water, and was about to show his hand in this poker game of death. I braced myself, realizing that I was going to win, even though I was about to die.

Just knowing that Kami was going to live, and that humanity would have a chance was enough to give me the strength for one last shot to finish him off. If I timed it right, this laser beam of a telepathic burst, draining me to a point of no return, should meet his own move as it reaches his beat-up vessel! Resulting in the sheer destruction of it, and ripping into every one of his undead soldiers as his vessel is destroyed. I screamed out with one last shout!!!! EEEEYYYYAAAAAA !!!!...

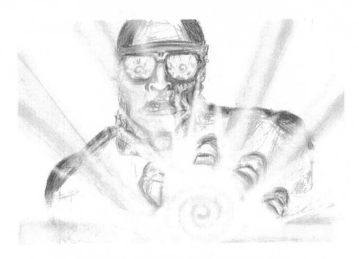

I felt my body fall like a ton of limp bricks!

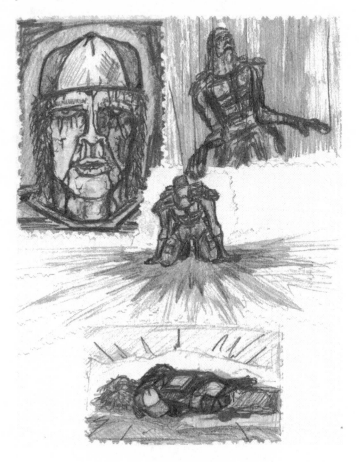

I had given it all away for the mountain so hope would still be its name, and the people I have grown to care about would live on! A choice that made it feel good to be me. As my body fell to the ground lifeless, the me in the battle zone of the mind was standing with a huge smile on my face, as the power left my entity and crashed into his. (Just to let him know he was played, and that he had met his match.) His reaction was classic:

EVIL LOSER: NOOOOOOOOOOOO! YOU LITTLE WEASEL! THIS IS NOT OVER, AND WHEN WE MEET AGAIN! (He calmed his voice, knowing this was only the beginning. Then looking up at me as he clutched his stomach in pain!) You are going to need a lot more than a good poker face to defeat me in the future BOY!! This is not over Zachariah! AAAHSSHHHIII!!!!!

He then winced in pain one last time as the ripple of power reached his true form and his vessel was destroyed. ZZZZWWWHOOOOOSSSSCH... BOOOOOOOOOOMM!!!!

A HUGE WAVE KNOCKS EVERY UNDEAD BACK A FEW STEPS. Then one by one they fell. Lifeless, as boiling hot black blood seeped from their eyes and ears. Completely brain dead, and free from their captor forever! It was done... And so was I...

SMOKE *(running over to me, then kneeling over me): ZEE... ZEEEE!! Stay with me ninja boy! Is he?*

DIESEL: I dunno... pick'm up, hurry, double time... He gotta be ok... he jus' gotta be!

PYRO: He saved us all...

B-BEAR (looking hurt): BUT... but he had the glow! HE HAD THE GLOW! You all saw it, I know you did... He was da masta! Sword swinging, karate kicking, bad ass... HE CAN'T DIE!!!

JOURNAL ENTRY# TRECE
<u>Chapter #1</u>

FEELING LOVED!
SAYING GOODBYE TO MY NEW FAMILY...
SO, I CAN SAVE THE OLD ONE.

W ell, it has taken some time, but as you have guessed by now, I survived the battle with The Evil One. Although my scars aren't visible, they are buried deep within. Someday I will deal with them. But for now this is war, and not just for the Mountain of Hope, but for the freedom of the world, and life itself! For he is healing too, and the world is still on the edge! The edge of being lost forever, or becoming something even better than it was intended to be in the first place. I've made my choice, and I choose to fight for the good that is left in this wounded world. For about two weeks now I was out of commission, and experiencing a kind of coma. Even though for me it felt like a nap, timewise. In the beginning, I scared the heck out of my Angel. It seems, that a few times it looked like I might not make it. Disappointingly enough I cannot remember one single event, or have a single memory, smell, anything for that matter when it comes to my injuries. The whole event of how I ended up in this recovery room, and who was there, escapes me. Only a feeling... A feeling that I was never alone, and for good reason. Due to the love of my team, Eldermum, and Angel. There wasn't a moment that one of them wasn't by my side, waiting patiently. I heard that even Pyro did 8 hours, helping Angel out when she was in need. So, I was truly never alone... and that is why these people will always be family. Something that I never thought would be a part of my life. Zumies are my people, a bond that will always be sacred to me. But these wonderful people! They helped me save my life, their lives, and gave me the path to fulfilling my true purpose. Because deep in my heart, there is nothing that my chicken-fried ass wouldn't do for any one of them, and it comes as a great comfort to know that they would do the same.

A chance, a long shot, just a matter of time! All of it based on how awful I appeared when my extra-crispy butt had been carried into the secret military emergency infirmary. Which was now operational inside the installation that was not just a housing for the mountains energy source. It was once the beginning of the secret entrance that all unexplained cargo would have been brought to, then checked over before entering the facility that the people left in this world now call their home. My recovery was anything but slow, which was fine with me, not into being seen that way if you know what I mean. It was bad enough Angel had to see it, let alone anyone else that wasn't there to see my battle. My skin was charred from the wave of pure energy that occurred when our powers met on the cerebral plane, where the battle took place. In three days, my skin was healing so rapidly that it looked like I was a brand new shiny me. The internal damage was severe, but my heart was still beating, and a fully functional brain was completely intact. The internal damage healed nicely over another period of just a day and I was looking like the old me, but my mind was still on hiatus. Maybe my body, or my powers shielded the brain during impact. This way I could defeat the Evil One, while being allowed to survive the ordeal itself. See I think my brain went into some form of protective hibernation. When I was brought into the emergency room, it was the only thing that was untouched. I protected it somehow, knowing my relentless regenerative powers would eventually give me back my awesome, ninja ready physical form. What took the longest, was switching back on the brain after it was in protective mode. As long as it survives, I survive! So, when my body was fully healed, my consciousness started to boot up once again. A miracle, and if you ask me, it was my natural Zumie gifts that saved me! With a huge dose of love and loyalty to grease the wheels, so to speak. Being told details regarding how I looked, and how worried everyone felt, it was an awesome feeling knowing how many cared. Even though I couldn't remember any of it, realizing my feelings for them were the same, made me feel justified in my sacrifice. There is one thing that I can't seem to shake though... the only thing I remember right before I awoke. You know the one who welcomed me in a strange way, to the fate of all powerful beings in the universe. Letting me know I had to make a choice, it was that voice! Whomever he was, he had more to say:

WISE VOICE FROM THE BATTLE: Zee... Soon you will awake, but before you do! I would like to share with you my thoughts about the choice you have made. It pleases me greatly you have chosen to join the fight for life on this planet. It was clever, and impressive how you defeated an enemy that was more powerful than you were. Using his overconfident nature against him was wise, and you have rattled him. No one has had the ability to challenge him yet, and for the first time he feels fear, pain... defeat. It intrigues him, and his ego will not allow it to scare him. He will crave it like a drug now. The mere temptations of the challenge to destroy you will drive him to avenge this loss. Beware young Zee! He will not stay down for long, and if he knows of your people. Well, that could be the first place he decides to hurt you, through them! Remember, great power puts pressure to make the right decisions on the backs of those whom chose to care about anything in this struggle! For not caring is easy, and therefore, the temptation not to care is great as well. That is why power usually chooses to be cruel, and not care. This is where the justification of caring makes you weak comes from. When the true fact is, caring requires more strength than any other emotion you have. See, as the colors on a color spectrum all come from the existence of light, so does the emotional spectrum of the mind from caring, or the denial of caring. Without light, without love, there is only darkness, and despair. You must return to your home, and prepare your people for the war they will someday be a part of. They will need your strength, and love to defeat this new foe. For it is already started, and the front... is everywhere... anywhere!...

Long story made to look short but isn't, it took about two weeks total for me to wake up. Part of the reason these people are my family has something to do with their sick sense of humor. I learned while I was in my coma, the compassion I thought they were showing was partly for a prize. Liquor, hard liquor! Something that was very hard to come by these days (pun intended), for whomever was there when I awoke. The mountain contains an underground cellar that houses all the liquor still intact from the pre-apocalypse that was brought back from the gatherer's excursions! Years of scavenging all assembled in this musty awesome naturally cooled museum of spirits from all over the world. Whoever it was, multiple people, or just one, that witnessed me coming to would get to pick two bottles of whatever they wanted from the legendary stockade of Good Times! The good money was on Angel, due to our connection and all. Good thing for me, Kami isn't the jealous type, because it was not her that I awoke to. Surprisingly enough, it was a guilt-ridden Kolten... sleeping in the corner of my room when my toes started to wiggle. I remember breathing in real deep, and sitting up faster than a man in a two week long coma should have! I opened my eyes, and there the snoring beauty was, with his arms folded over in a slumping, slouching sleep. Having been so exhausted, that an otherwise uncomfortable chair felt like a king-sized mattress to the sleeping hero. Being fully recovered and ready for anything, I yelled out in a crazy voice to scare him awake!:

ME (feeling on top of the world, and up for a good laugh): WAKE UUUUUUUUP!!!

KOLTEN JUMPS OUT OF HIS CHAIR, AND LANDS FLAT ON HIS KEISTER!!!!!!

ME (not able to contain a laugh well deserved): ppppssss... OOHHHHNO I CAN'T... AHA... OOO AHAHH... AHOOOO... HAAHAHAHAHAHHAH... YES... yes that was classic!

KOLTEN (with a huge smile, looking like a thousand pounds had been lifted off his back): ZEEE... (With his hands on his head in disbelief!) I CAN'T BELIEVE

IT! THANK THE FATES YOU MADE IT!... I missed you...
you damn show off. Welcome back!

I asked Kolten to get me some clothes, hoping some of them survived the powerful display they had fell victim to. He was quick to act so I could reunite with my Angel! (Man, I am smitten! I mean, I should write that "I was smitten", naaah, 'cause both are the truth! Oh well, must move on.) There was a moment where I had to accept I might never get to see her again. Now all that stood in my way was some clothes and a few hallways, because she was on her way, and the teasing in my mind was unbearable. She was taunting me with her sexy voice, describing what she was going to do to me when she got here. I can't repeat what she said, because then I would be a douche, but man she is amazing when she turns it on. Kolten wasn't back with my clothes yet when the door busted open! It was my girl, looking like the Angel she was! Beautiful multi-colored hair with pink dominating the scheme. A slender, but strong silhouette, and round ample cheeks that take your breath away. She locked the door, clutching my clothes as if they were hers to toy with. She turned slowly with a smile that almost put fear into my heart, and I loved it! Her look was one that resembled a tigress, that was about to pounce as she slinked over to me standing in the barely covering my ass hospital gown. Pounce gives her no credit, as another coma was needed to recover from her appetite. She was not slow to remind me that it had been two weeks of torture for her, and it was my job to make up for lost time. And make up for lost time we did! Over, and over again! She was a stick of dynamite... with a long... slow... fuse... and I was just the spark she needed to light her up...

(MANY HOURS GO BY...)

We laid there just holding each other, sweat rolling down our backs, but we didn't care. It all just felt goooooood, her smell, her just a little bit cooler than mine skin. If perfection is in the eye of the beholder? A picture of us holding each other, in a made up recovery room, huddled on a single person mattress, would be next to the word in the dictionary, PERFECT! The room was ours for as long as we wanted, we made sure every moment counted. It was funny because we both knew the moment was coming upon us. We both dreaded it, but never did we say a thing to ruin our perfect moment.

> ANGEL (looking at me with her big blue eyes): I will cherish this moment in time forever. It will fuel my undying love for you, and keep me warm at night while you are gone...

> ME (realizing she was ready to say it): Not yet... please, I just found you!

> ANGEL (with tears in her eyes): I don't want you to go... but you must, or your people could be next. Who knows how far this Evil bozo's gaze can reach? If we are lucky... he is still recovering from your battle, and you will have a head start to warn your Zumies. Someday soon they too will have to join the fight! It is up to you Zack, to make sure that it happens, or all could be lost!... Again...

> ME (knowing she was right, but man it hurt): I will ache for you while I am gone.

> ANGEL K. (kisses me and says): Now make love to me one more time... then you must leave as soon as possible. Your Zumies survival depends on it! Besides, if you stayed with me, and something happened to

them. I would feel responsible, and you would feel it, and so on and so on! It would tear us apart! Now go and save your peeps, stupid head!

I honored the wishes of my smart ass Angel, and selfishly took one more memory to hold onto. Being apart would be less awful, as these memories of my Angel K. and I fill my dreams when I sleep. This could be the last time I see my girl for a long, long time; I miss her already.

JOURNAL ENTRY# TRECE
<u>Chapter #2</u>

IT'S HARD TO SAY GOODBYE...
SO I GOT THE HELL OUT OF THERE!!

Well this will be my last entry for a while, so I better explain how I left the Mountain of Hope. WELL, SEE WHAT HAD HAPPENED WAZZ!! Under the circumstances of how I came into the medical observation center, everyone had been under the assumption that I had bit the big one. Screwed the pooch! Rode the bus to the end of the line! Cooked too long on HIGH HEAT! Was more human than undead! So, I died!!!!! There was a lot of speculation pertaining to who The Evil One could read if they traveled outside of the protection of 'Mum's power. To keep the people safe, it was the decision of a small few who are in the know, to fake my death. Only the ones who fought by my side, Eldermum, and of course my Kami would be privy to the knowledge of my fake passing. The small few that harbored the secret of me, would always be under her protection, no matter where their travels would lead them. This was done to make sure their minds could never be gazed upon by anyone, and I mean anyone. To everyone else, I was dead, and that was that. This just might keep the target off their backs long enough for him to look the other way, giving me a window of opportunity that I might escape without him noticing. If the Evil nuisance thinks I'm dead, then maybe! Maybe I could get back to Z. Valley with enough time to convince the council to evacuate the city and prepare for his coming. The battle will be fierce, and I must be ready to give even more of myself if there is any chance of surviving this war, let alone the long shot, of winning in the end!

As we lay there in our last moments, I realized how long it could be before we saw each other again. She read my mind and began to joke:

ANGEL (hugging me with all her might): WELLLL!... mmmmmm... It won't be hard for me to cry at your fake funeral tomorrow!

ME (smiling, almost like I was grateful): WHY!

KAMI (looking at me like I'm a D-bag): Because stupid head! Who knows when I am going to see you again? I could cry right now just thinking about it!

ME (feeling bad now): Aww crap babe, I'm sorry, I was trying not to think about it, and the result was blocking more than just the sadness. It was blocking your feelings as well, my bad Angel... for reals!

KAMI (with a soft little touch of cute): It's ok Zacky-Boy! I still love ya, like fat kids love cake! Forevz!

I remember that kiss most of all in that day, 'cause it was the last one! We had fallen asleep, and when I woke... a note was left, with her treasured lips imprinted pink on the fold of the paper. Under her lips, a few sentences read:

To my hero!

If I tried this in person, I could never let you go! So, MY LOVE! Please come back to me as soon as you can! I already weep for you, and long to be in your arms. Until then, this letter protesting my love is here for you! Only open it when you feel lost, and I will be there to help you find you. For now, this kiss will have to be enough. All my love Zacky Z, come back to me...

I honored her wishes, put on the clothes that she left for me, and listened for Smoke to mentally give me the ok. It was up to him to make sure the coast would be clear, this way I could come out the back door for a secret escort out of the mountain. It was hard to leave. Even harder to say goodbye. Although I wanted to shake the hand of every soldier I fought the hoard with, and tell them I felt honored to have fought by their sides, I knew I couldn't. This was just the beginning, and only we knew it, so I got the hell out of there! Only Smoke could get me out with nobody noticing. (Hence the name SMOKE!) I strapped on my katana and custom semi-automatic 9mm pistols, with the 40-round clips for maximum carnage. Wow I looked like a bad ass! I picked up my letter from Angel, and tucked it into my inside vest pocket, for safe keeping. We were at war! The mission wasn't over by a long shot for our small group of rebels. Looking back, this was really the best, and only way for me to leave. Fake my death, become a ghost for a small time. Hopefully by the time he figures it out, and he eventually will figure it out! I will be at full strength, whatever that is, and even more ready to finish what we started.

I felt his presence. It was time, and I took another long look at the door Kami burst through hours earlier, remembering her vision... I was gone, dead to the Mountain of Hope. For Now! Carefully snuck out the back door of the building they were hiding me in, and there my mentor was. Smoke looked me in the eyes, and smiled. He used no words that need to be spoken, there would be a time to say goodbye, and now was not it. We had to sneak out in the late hours of the night. Nobody could see us, and unfortunately, even though the Evil One can't read our thoughts, if we happened on some wandering undead out there, the possibility that he is looking still exists. This is why Smoke told me to follow his every mental command, without question, and that is exactly what I did...

We cautiously went through the service tunnels recently opened for access to the new and improved power facility. Spike made sure nobody but Sparks would be monitoring the cameras, and gave us a 10mn window to sneak out of the mountain through the very area that I almost died in. We ninjaed through the area without so much as a peep. Proceeding down the mountain, making sure nothing, or no one could see us coming or going. I didn't think about my sadness or the fight ahead, just focused on Smoke, and absorbed his techniques like a sponge. We made our way down the mountain in an expeditious manner. All the way down to the shore, where The C Turtle was waiting for me, like an old friend. Smoke signaled to stop, and took a long hard look out over the horizon with his gihugic binoculars:

SMOKE (with the look of a proud master, letting his student go): Well, I can't go any further son! This shit is very time sensitive, and I have to get back unnoticed... It has been an honor to fight the good fight *with you Zee. Don't forget who you are, power often corrupts the soul. Only once in a great while does someone come along that can handle the weight, and the responsibility it comes with. I believe the time is now, and that person is you! I will be ready to join you when the time is right young friend. I owe you for making sure my boy stayed alive in the battle. I will never forget what you did for me, and him. The people of the mountain are your people, too. When you need us, we will be there! I will be there...*

ME (feeling the words): Smoke, you have taught me more than you know. I will fight with honor and compassion, always, the way you do!

SMOKE (with a small grin as he turns to walk away): I know you will, Zeeman... I know you will... (Silence!)

He then disappeared into the night, without a sound. Just the way I imagined it would be... Kick ass!

I strolled over to my vessel... and I couldn't believe my eyes! While I was passed out, they improved my Turtle into a twin engine streamlined machine. She never looked so cool and ready for anything! I ran over and jumped into my newly improved ship. It even had a solar rechargeable battery system, with a refrigerator inside! Guess what was inside the frickin' fridge! SODA POP... SODA POP... AND BEER!!!! WOOOOOHOOO! That is right. All kinds of flavors, and brands! Cold, too! AWESOOOOOME! I closed the fridge, and put my pack down. It was time to go. With a heavy heart, and a lump in my throat, I pushed the start buttons on my huge twin engines, reversed off the shore, and into the sea. The smell of the air was cold and refreshing. As I throttled forward, pulling away from the place of my true rebirth, the shoreline slowly faded away. I will never be the same again, and I don't regret a single action, or choice that had a hand in forging me into the man I have become.

JOURNAL ENTRY# TRECE
Chapter #3

MY NAME IS ZEE!

The C Turtle and I traveled down the coast with haste, 'til the sun went down over the mountains I once strived to get to. Taking the helm of my vessel, dreaming of the events that could unfold as I pushed on. Ironically doing the same thing I did when I first set out to contact the new family I just left. It seems a lifetime ago I risked it all, to bridge the gap between humans and my kind. As the twin engines with a sick amount of horse power hummed in the background, I couldn't help wondering if I am enough to accomplish all that is set before me. Except now... it is my own kind I fear for instead of humanity. Unfortunately, I feel closer to the mountain people than I do my own. Will they accept me, believe me?... All I can do is be myself and show them the way, as I have always done quietly behind the council. THE COUNCIL!! I will show them the truth! This will WORK! Through the few, I will move the many, and it will be their choice... their idea! YES! Familiar it does sound, but the truth is.

Zumies are just the awkward, goofy, distant cousins, of the human condition! It should work! I hope!

Even though bitter sweet was the taste, it was nice to once again be out on the open sea. The freedom it represented still feels new, and I welcome the challenge of the currents as they attempt to pull me out to sea. The weather was on my side, even the distant horizon was smiling upon me as south was my heading. The comfort that the heated cabin of my newly upgraded Turtle provided me, made this ship feel even more like a home away from home. As soon as a spot revealed itself, I would settle for the night. (One full day from my love Kami, I miss her already, it hurts!) Make a fire, and warm up the ribs Kami packed for me in the fridge, stocked with soda pop! It's the little things in life that make you happy. So cherish them when you can! They get you through the hard times that are in-between. It wasn't long after my revelation the spot revealed itself. A familiar spot, the same little cove that offered me rest before the storm changed my existence forever. I throttled back heading for the small cove, and the familiar little shoreline that once hid me so well finally revealed itself. I ran her ashore and tied her down to the ground for the night.

As I lay here on the shore of this hidden cove, I wonder if the world knows the war that is about to be waged on its lands. In fact, going home is not as relaxing as I hoped it would be months ago. Knowing the things I now know, about The Evil One, and his intent to kill all life on this planet. Killing until all that is left is undead for him to control. For reasons unknown, we do not understand why this is what he wants from our world. Even though this makes it very hard to sleep, I am comforted to know the mountain and its people are on my side in this fight for our planet's survival. Good thing I slept for a few weeks, huh? Besides, I had to record this in the journals at some time, this was the time. I mean he is the opposite of me in every way, except our powers. The fuel for his power is death and hate, my power is fueled by life and love. With this power by my side, I hope I am enough to convince my people to save their own existence on this planet? They can be hard headed at times, but when motivated correctly, the Zumie are a force to be reckoned with. When and if the undead soldiers of the Evil One come to our valley, my people will give them the fight of their lives. I just hope we have enough time to prepare for his coming. No matter, we will make due and win the day, or days, weeks, months, whatever it may take to push him back once again. Until we find the real Evil One in the flesh, and someday take the fight to his ass!

It is time for me to sign off on this book of journals. I will write again soon! I never wanted this power. That is what I said when I first started this book of journals, but the lesson I learned is this: I now know that those who want power at any cost are going to abuse it, and do not deserve it. But those who are given power through respect, humility, and compassion, usually never wanted it in the first place. For some reason, this quality makes great leaders possible. Maybe it's because they respect who gave them the power in the first place. My examples of powerful people helped me to end up this way. It is the love and compassion of these respected people that will guide me on my journeys, always! And for those who wish to use their power to hurt the ones I love?! I feel sorry for them, because they will have to deal with me!

My name...... is ZEE!

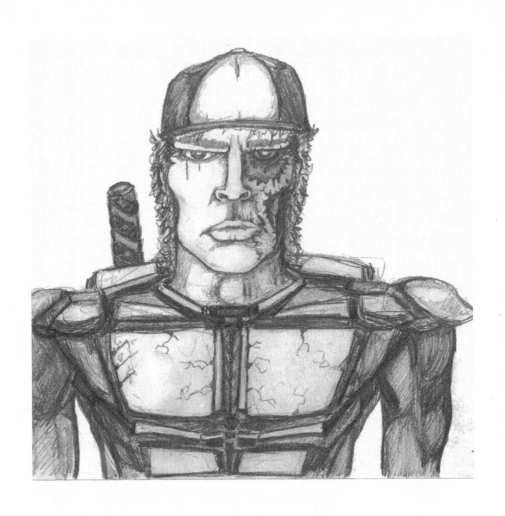

Made in the USA
San Bernardino, CA
20 April 2019